Popcorn

FOR ANDIE MERRY XMAS
WHEREVER YOU SPEND IT
CUZCO - PARACAS? ENJOY
THE BOOK, COMPANY + TIME
OFF
                LOADS OF LOVE
        YOUR MATE JOE
                        XOXO.

Popcorn

BEN ELTON

SIMON & SCHUSTER
A VIACOM COMPANY

First published in Great Britain by Simon & Schuster
Ltd, 1996
A Viacom Company

Simon & Schuster Ltd
West Garden Place
Kendal Street
London W2 2AQ

Simon & Schuster of Australia Pty Ltd
Sydney

A CIP catalogue record for this book is available
from the British Library

ISBN 0-684-81612-1

This book is a work of fiction. Names, characters, places and
incidents are either products of the author's imagination or
are used fictitiously.

Typeset in Meridien 11/14pt by
Palimpsest Book Production Limited, Polmont, Stirlingshire
Printed and bound in Great Britain by
Butler & Tanner Ltd, Frome & London

Chapter One

O n the morning after the night it happened, Bruce
Delamitri was sitting in a police interview room.

'Name?' said the interrogating officer.

It wasn't really a question. The officer knew Bruce's
name, of course, but there was a procedure and he was
required to follow it.

On the morning before, Bruce had been sitting in a television studio. Opposite him, across the sweeping curve of
the presentation console, were two Ken-and-Barbie-style
presenters of indeterminate age.

'His name' (pause) 'is Bruce Delamitri,' said Ken,
employing the sincere, plonking tone he reserved for
really big guests.

'Occupation?' said the policeman on the morning after,
as if he didn't know.

'He is probably the most celebrated artist working in the

motion-picture industry today. A great writer, a great director. Hollywood's golden boy.'

'I heard he makes a great pasta sauce too,' interjected Barbie, by way of adding a little human interest.

It was the morning before, and the last day on which Bruce would hear himself described in such terms.

'Marital status?' the cop enquired.

'But career excellence takes its toll, and Hollywood was recently saddened by the news that Bruce's marriage to actress, model and rock singer Farrah Delamitri was in big trouble. We'll be talking about that also.'

The red light on top of the camera facing Bruce lit up. He adopted a suitably sardonic 'shit happens' expression. The next twenty-four hours would prove him right about that.

Bruce tried to look the policeman in the eye. Marital status? What a question. The whole world knew his marital status.

'My wife is dead.'

'Tell me about last night.'

'Tonight is Oscars night,' Ken beamed. 'The big one. Numero Uno. Nights don't get any bigger than this. The night of nights. The nightiest night of them all. The night which, according to all the forecasts, promises to be the greatest night of Bruce Delamitri's life.'

'Last night?' said Bruce, who had given up trying to make contact with the cop and now spoke almost to himself.

'Last night was more terrible than I could have imagined possible.'

'You're watching *Coffee Time USA*. We'll be back after these messages,' said the male presenter, whose name was not Ken but Oliver Martin. The studio lights dimmed and the *Coffee Time* logo came up while Oliver and his female colleague, Dale, stacked their papers in an important manner. There was of course nothing on their papers, but maintaining the fiction that TV presenters are proper journalists, as opposed to people who read whatever comes up on the autocue, is one of the principal duties of current-affairs broadcasting.

Bruce watched on the monitor in front of him as Oliver and Dale disappeared and were replaced on the screen by four bikini-clad babes clutching soda bottles and tumbling ecstatically out of an old VW Beetle.

'A girl, a beach, it's happening, it's real.
It's a boost, it's a buzz, it's the way you should feel!'

The studio controller killed the volume, and the bikini babes were left sucking on their bottles in muted delight.

'One and a half minutes on the break,' said the floor manager.

This was the signal for the make-up girls to rush in and pat gently away at all available faces. Oliver turned to Bruce, addressing him through a flurry of powder and pads.

'I think what we need to concentrate on here is the fact that our industry is not a dream factory any more. We deal in gritty realism. We show it like it is.'

The make-up lady applied another layer of slap to

Oliver's already heavily caked features. The gritty reality
was that anyone who had acquired such a deep and
lustrous tan would long since have died of skin cancer.
But Oliver was of the old school of TV presenting: he
believed that sporting a thermo-nuclear tan was a mark
of respect to the viewer, like wearing a nice shirt and tie.
You had to show you'd made the effort.

'One minute to the break,' said the floor manager.

Across the vast pastel-coloured desk, Dale's voice could
be heard from the midst of a cloud of hair-spray. 'I mean,
surely the big issue, Bruce, has got to be this whole
copycat killing thing, hasn't it? I mean, that's what
America is concerned about. As an American woman,
it sure is what I'm concerned about. Are you concerned
about that, Bruce? As an American man?'

'America's population is not as young as it was, and
soon the number-one issue concerning the majority of
Americans will be adult incontinence.'

This was not Bruce. It was the TV. The studio controller
had pumped the volume back up preparatory to going
back on air. It was after nine, and the network advertisers
were beginning to switch their focus from workers and
schoolkids to a 'coffee time' audience, which meant
young mums and old lonelys. Soda-sucking babes were
giving way to nipple pads, denture fixative and nappies
both infant and adult.

'No, I am not concerned about copy-cat killings,' said
Bruce, speaking with difficulty because a young woman
was painting some kind of menthol-flavoured grease on
to his lips. 'I don't believe that people get up from the
movie theatre or the TV and do what they just saw.
Otherwise the people who watch this show would all

have their hair set in concrete and their brains sucked out along with their cellulite.'

It was scarcely a comment calculated to endear him to his media colleagues, but that was Bruce. Tough, sarcastic and a bit of a stirrer. If you wore a leather jacket and shades on TV at nine in the morning, you were almost duty-bound to be abrasive. In fact, Bruce had guessed that Dale would not hear his answer anyway. He could see she was the type of interviewer who used her guests' answers as quiet time in which to consider her next question.

'Good, good, you should make that point on air,' said Dale absently, checking her eye-liner.

'Fifteen seconds on the break,' said the floor manager. Four, three, two, one . . .

Oliver's face lit up. 'We're talking to Bruce Delamitri, the hot tip for tonight's "Best Director" Oscar. But amidst all the glory and the adulation there lurks very real controversy.'

Dale picked up the ball. 'Bruce Delamitri's movies are hard, tough, witty, sassy street-wise thrillers, where the life is low and the body count is high. Remind you of something?'

'You tell me, Dale,' said Ollie, deploying his serious and thoughtful face.

'How about America's streets?' said Dale, looking equally portentous. 'That's right, the streets of America, hard, tough and dangerous, where the kids grow up fast and dying is a way of life.'

'You're saying that the movies of Bruce Delamitri reflect the streets of America?'

'Some say reflect, some say influence. America, it's your call. We'll be back after these messages.'

The studio lights dimmed again. Oliver and Dale went dark and shuffled their papers.

'Do you have sensitive teeth? Does ice-cream make you go *ow!* when you should be going *mmmmm*?'

Chapter Two

On the morning after it all happened, a young woman, hardly more than a girl, stared across a bare formica-topped table at an interrogating police officer. She was being interviewed in the next-door room to the one in which Bruce was being questioned. Unlike Bruce, however, the young woman was considered highly dangerous and was therefore in chains, her thin wrists manacled to her almost equally thin ankles. In fact, so petite was she that it looked as if she could have slipped off the steel bracelets if she had wished and just floated away on the next breeze. She was indifferent to whether they chained her or not. She had nowhere to go anyway.

'Name?' said the policewoman.

On the previous morning, this same skinny creature had been asked the same question in the diner of a truck-stop motel just off the Pacific Highway, about a hundred miles north of Los Angeles.

'I been called a lotta things,' she had replied.

The short-order chef with whom she was conversing gave her a knowing wink. 'I'll bet one of them things wuz beautiful.'

The Chef was right. She was beautiful, with her big eyes and thin face. If ever Disney decided to do a stage version of *Bambi* they would be looking for a girl like her.

The young woman accepted the chef's compliment with a giggle. 'Are you flirting with me?' she asked, twisting her purse in her hands like a nervous girl.

'Ain't nuthin wrong with talking to a pretty thing, is there?' said the chef.

'I guess not. 'Cepting you're lucky my boyfriend cain't hear ya. On accounta he's real mean when it comes to flirty guys. Specially Californian guys, who he reckons is just a bunch of no-good faggots.' The young woman picked up her change, which was lying on the counter.

'His name' (pause) 'is Bruce Delamitri.'

It was Oliver Martin's voice. A TV hung from a bracket in the corner of the room, and the waitress had turned up the volume. She liked *Coffee Time USA*.

'He is probably the most celebrated artist working in the motion-picture industry today. A great writer, a great director. Hollywood's golden boy.'

'I heard he makes a great pasta sauce too.'

Oliver and Dale were working their morning magic. Their guest, Bruce Delamitri, smiled sardonically out of the TV set. The girl at the counter turned to look. For a moment she and Bruce stared into each other's eyes. Much later, the girl would wonder whether she had felt something at this point.

The chef was not interested in *Coffee Time USA*. 'You say your fuckin' boyfriend says I'm a faggot?'

'He don't mean nuthin by it,' the scrawny girl said apologetically as she gathered up her Cokes and burgers and fries and headed for the door. 'It's just he's so tough and hard 'n' all that I guess pretty much everybody looks like a faggot to him.'

'You come back soon, little girl. I'll show you who's a faggot,' said the chef. 'Bring your boyfriend.'

'He'd kill ya,' the girl remarked casually over her shoulder as the screen door slammed behind her.

'Tonight is Oscars night,' said the television set.

'So tell us about last night,' said the policewoman on the following morning.

'Well, I guess he kinda got the idea when we was having breakfast and Bruce Delamitri was on *Coffee Time* with Oliver and Dale. We wuz in a motel, see. I like motels. They're so clean and nice, and they give you soap and stuff. If I got the chance, that's where I'd live all the time, motels.'

The girl walked across the parking lot from the diner to where the line of chalets stood. There had been a summer rain storm and she was barefoot. She sought out the puddles. Warm water on warm tarmac was a lovely sensation. She had very sensitive feet. Sometimes, if they were touched just right, it could make her entire body shiver. She was always trying to get her big tough boyfriend to give her feet a massage. She might as well have asked him to crochet a toilet-roll cover.

'I don't believe in no New Age, faggot, hippy bullshit,' he would say, 'which in my opinion is eating away at the soul of this great nation and turning us all into old fuckin' women. Now get me a beer.'

There were certain subjects on which he was entirely intractable, but that didn't mean that he couldn't be tender and gentle when he wanted to be, and when he was, oh how she loved him.

She entered their little cabin with the food. He was lying on the bed where she had left him, a gun resting on his chest and another at his waist.

'Here's the food, honey. Seeing as how it's breakfast, I got you a bacon burger. I told him to be sure to grill that bacon good. I know you don't like eating no raw pig.'

'Quiet now, honey. I'm watching TV here.'

On the television Bruce Delamitri was working on his indulgent smile. 'Copycat killing? Pur-lease!' he said. 'I mean, *come on*! The whole thing's a media beat-up, the story *du jour*. Four networks in search of a controversy.'

Bruce could be his own worst enemy at times. You didn't sneer at the presenters of *Coffee Time*. Not if you wanted to win the hearts and minds of Middle America, which was the purpose of Bruce's appearance. Many of *Coffee Time*'s viewers saw Oliver and Dale as their closest and most loyal friends, and did not take kindly to clever-clever, sneery film-school grads acting like these friends were dumb.

Oliver sensed the atmosphere of the interview souring. He knew that 'atmospheres' of any kind were not good morning TV, and he always desperately sought common ground with his guests.

'C'mon, Bruce, cut us some slack here,' he appealed. 'This is a very serious situation. There are two genuine psychos out there, shooting up malls and killing just about everybody they meet, right? Now, in your Oscar-nominated movie *Ordinary Americans* there's a very similar young couple who do exactly the same stuff. These two genuine lunatics have blazed a trail across three states massacring innocent strangers.'

'And every time these crimes are reported in the media,' Bruce interrupted, 'the story gets illustrated with a still from my movie. Now who's making the association? The psychos themselves? Or is it the news editors of America, desperate to get an original angle on yet another boring news bulletin about murder and mayhem?'

'Copycat murders, for God's sake! Human beings aren't Pavlov's dogs. You can't just ring a bell and make them salivate. They don't simply do what they see. If it were that easy to manipulate people, no product would ever fail and no government would ever fall.'

In the motel chalet the scrawny girl was getting bored with watching Bruce on the TV.

'Baby?' she said.

'Quiet, honey. I'm thinking 'bout something.'

There was a knock at the door.

In an instant the man was off the bed and across the room. He clamped himself against the wall beside the door, naked save for his tattoos and the guns he held in either hand. He put one finger to his lips, instructing the girl to say nothing.

They waited. Inside the TV Bruce continued to pontificate: 'Our industry's in danger. It's under attack. We're the scapegoats, the whipping-boys. Every time some kid lets loose with a gun, who do they blame? They blame Hollywood. They blame me. They don't like my movies – they say they're wicked. Well, they're entitled to their opinion. What they're *not* entitled to do is foist their craven and reactionary opinions on to everybody else. Censorship is censorship and it sucks!'

'Provocative? Thought-provoking?' From inside the TV Oliver addressed the room where the two fugitives waited. 'You betcha sweet grandma it is. You're watching *Coffee Time USA*. We'll be back after these messages.'

'Now you can eat what you want *and* stay trim.'

There was another knock at the door of the motel room. Still the young man and woman did not answer.

Then they heard the rattle of keys. The man nodded to the girl. She was still lying on the bed, although she too now held a gun, which she had produced from under her pillow.

'Who is it?' she called out.

'Please, you want I make up your room now?' a small Latin American voice asked.

'No, that's OK. It's fine,' said the girl.

'OK,' said the maid. 'I just give you fresh towels.'

'We don't want no towels.'

'OK.' There was a pause. 'You want soap?'

'No.'

'OK.' Again a pause. 'How about some sachet coffee and milks? Or maybe you got plenty.'

'Yeah, we got plenty. We don't want nuthin.'

'OK, that's fine. Thank you.'

The man, whose every muscle had been taut and every vein pumped full, relaxed a little.

But then the small voice came again. 'So I just check mini-bar, please.'

Suddenly the door of the chalet burst open and the maid found herself confronted by a furious and stark-naked man. She would scarcely have been more taken aback if she had known that behind the cover of the door-frame he was holding two automatic weapons.

'No fuckin' disturbo, comprende? We fuckin' honey-moono. We make amoro like Speedy fuckin' Gonzalez, OK?'

He slammed the door and returned to the bed. His girlfriend was not pleased. 'There was no call to—'

'*I am trying to watch TV here!*'

She knew she must not cross him further, and slumped into a sulk instead.

Bruce was still holding forth on the television. 'You can't ban a movie because you don't like it. Today it's sex and violence that get banned, tomorrow who knows? Homosexuality? Blacks? Jews?'

Oliver and Dale shifted uneasily in their seats. Words like 'blacks' and 'Jews' were not really *Coffee Time* words.

'I've heard a lot said these past weeks about the Mall Murderers,' Bruce continued, 'so let's talk about them. I made a move about two sick maniacs, and lo and behold we got two real sick maniacs out there. Hey, what d'you know? Put two and two together and it's *my fault*! I am responsible. Oh *yeah*! Weren't there any maniacs before I made my movie? Weren't there any sickos and psychos around before movies were even *invented*? Did Bluebeard and Jack the Ripper get in a time machine and come forward in time to see my picture? Did they think, "Hey, great idea! When I get back to my own era I'll start murdering people"?'

'But you can't deny—' Dale began in a brave attempt to stop the flow. It was useless: this was a subject on which Bruce felt strongly.

'We are scapegoats! This nation is facing a law-and-order crisis of cataclysmic proportions and someone must be blamed. The politicians don't want to take the heat, so who gets it? Us, the entertainers, the artists. Well, I've got news for you. Artists don't create society, they reflect it. And it you don't like that, don't change us, change society.'

Oliver threw to another ad break, and in the motel room the naked man got himself another beer.

'Well, you gotta accept,' he said, knocking the top off a Budweiser with the butt of his Smith & Wesson, 'the guy has a point.'

'I think he sounds like a jerk,' his girlfriend replied grumpily.

'Hey, everybody's a jerk, baby, one way or another. Cain't hold that against a man. One thing's for damn sure. Bruce Delamitri makes the best fuckin' movies in the world, and if they don't give him that Oscar I for one will be extremely pissed.'

There was another knock at the door.

'Please,' the maid said, 'I must just check the mini-bar. Sorry.'

The man got up off the bed. 'I'll handle this, honey.'

'Tell me about him,' the policewoman said.

'I just used to sit there looking at him,' the young girl said, 'just thinking he is the coolest, most beautiful guy that ever was. Better than everything. You could take Elvis and Clint Eastwood and James Dean . . . and I don't know . . . all those other cool guys, and mix 'em up, and you wouldn't get no one half as cool as him.'

In the other interview room, Bruce was responding to a similar enquiry. 'You have to understand that he was a psychotic monster,' he told his interrogator. 'Do you hear me? A monster, the devil . . . a monster.'

Chapter Three

'I stand here on legs of fire.'

It was after eleven on the morning after the Oscars, and the police had left Bruce alone for almost two hours. They had given him some breakfast, which he had surprised himself by eating, and since then he had been sitting drinking cold coffee (institutional blend) and watching himself on the various morning news shows. He did not watch *Coffee Time*: that would have been too much to bear. He could just imagine how happy Oliver and Dale would be to see him brought so low after the mugging he had given them the day before. What crocodile tears they would shed over his bloodied remains. No, that he could not watch, although he found no better comfort on any of the numerous other channels that were covering his story.

Over and over again he accepted his Oscar. On ABC and CBS and NBC. On Fox and CNN and about a million other cable channels, there he was, grinning like the idiot he had proved himself to be.

'I stand here on legs of fire.'

Legs of fire? Horrible. Ugly, mawkish, inept, mean-
ingless.

They loved it.

'I want to thank you.' Of course he did. 'Each and
every person in this room. Each and every person in this
industry. You nourished me and helped me to touch the
stars. Helped me be better than I had any right to be.
Better than the best – which is what you all are. What
can I say?'

Here Bruce's voice began to crack slightly, and over
a billion people had wondered whether he was going
to cry. He didn't. Even though he had turned into the
creature of the mob, he was not so far possessed by
them as actually to blub on cue.

'I am humble,' he lied, 'humble and small . . . but
also proud and big, big in heart, big in love, big in
head' (for one eerie moment it had seemed as if an
unheard-of moment of veracity was about to intrude
on the proceedings. 'Did he just say "big in head"?'
the glittering throng were about to ask themselves.
But Bruce had merely stopped mid-word in order
to gulp down his emotions) 'big in headstrong dedication to being the best artist I know how,' he continued, 'the best American human being I can be,
and to improving my one-on-one relationship with
God. Thank you, America. Thank you for giving me
the opportunity to be a part of this great industry.
Because this is a great industry, a great American industry full of wonderful people. People whose extraordinary, awesome, monumental, towering, Heaven-sent
talent has made me the artist I am. You are the wind
beneath my wings and I flap for you. God bless you

all. God bless America. God bless the world as well.
Thank you.'

Bruce watched himself on the television screen and
felt ill. He actually gagged at the horror of it. A tide of
nausea welled up inside him, as if an air-bag had gone
off and was pushing the contents of his stomach up his
neck. He swallowed hard, and his throat burnt with
gastric acids. How sick could a man feel? Very. He'd been
awake for such a long time, and his police-issue breakfast
sat uneasily on top of the fifteen-hour-old soup of party
canapés and booze he'd consumed in his previous life.

How *could* he have made such a dreadful speech? No
wonder bitter gall was surging up his gullet. It was the
acrid taste of shame. After all, the man on the screen
holding the golden statuette represented Bruce at his
zenith: this was how he would be remembered in his
moment of glory.

I stand here on legs of fire!

The sound of sirens jerked Bruce out of his reverie.
There were police cars on the TV now. The same footage
of his home being surrounded by the forces of justice that
had been playing endlessly all morning. There again was
his garden, full of cops. His drive, full of cops. His roof,
covered in cops. How many cops could swarm round one
house? All the cops in Los Angeles, it seemed to Bruce.
And TV people. TV people everywhere. In his flower
beds, outside his four garages, milling round his pool.

Bruce wished they hadn't put him in a room with
a TV. He could switch it off, of course, but somehow
he didn't.

The news story arrived once more at the limousine
jam. Slowly the stars and big shots got out of their
enormous cars. Bruce had watched the same footage

so often that he knew the order by heart. There they
were again. The long, slow stream of tuxedos, polished
chins, magnificent bosoms and ridiculous gowns. Absurd
gowns. Ludicrous gowns. Every one of those women was
like a drowning swimmer desperate to attract attention.
I'm over here! Look at me!

There was the purple one now, slashed up to the
armpits. Such thighs! Hollywood thighs. And nipples.
Nipples like thimbles. 'She's just iced those in the car,'
Bruce had thought approvingly at the time. He always
appreciated professionalism, an actress's dedication to
her craft.

Now it was the turn of Bruce himself; he always came
after the purple one with the thighs and nipples. The
cameras of the waiting paparazzi began to flash before
his car had even stopped. He was the star of the show,
the hot tip for 'Best Director' and 'Best Picture'. What
a night! What a moment! The star of the show.

Now it was the morning after and he was still the
star, though of a rather different show. Whoever said
all publicity was good publicity was an idiot.

The old Bruce stepped out of his limo and on to the
red carpet, just as he had done twenty times already
on every channel that morning. Turn, smile and wave.
Check the bow-tie. Tug at the ear-lobe. Nervous, humble
body language. Tiny little moves that screamed, 'Love
me, you bastards! Look! Look! This is my night. I am the
greatest director in the world, and yet I have the grace
to pretend I'm just an ordinary guy.' Bruce knew every
ingratiating little twitch by heart. How they cheered. How
they loved him.

Except that they didn't really love him, any more than
he believed he was a regular, ordinary guy. Everyone was

just acting in the manner expected of them at such an event. Television has taught the whole world how to behave. Except, of course, for the protestors: prophets as they now appeared to be, illuminated by the deceptive light of hindsight.

The pickets. Mothers Against Death. Wouldn't *they* be pleased this morning. 'Mr Delamitri,' shouted the anonymous woman who had now become a TV star, 'my son was murdered. An innocent boy, gunned down on the streets. In your last picture there were seventeen murders.'

Bruce sat in the small, bare police interview room and watched his past self, thinking, 'Yeah, and there was plenty of sex in my movie too, but I bet *you* haven't had any for a while.'

That was what he had been thinking. Why hadn't he said it? He couldn't suppress the uneasy feeling that things would have been different if he had told the truth. It was completely irrational, of course, but ever since the police had left him alone he had been tortured by the thought that somehow honesty might have saved him from the terrible fate that had overtaken him.

'I stand here on legs of fire.' Jesus! Legs of fire? Just for that, he almost deserved what had happened to him.

He couldn't have been honest, of course, particularly not to that picket line. Not in his old life. He'd had different priorities then. It was one thing haranguing Oliver and Dale about the absurdity of blaming a film-maker for some murder that had happened in a place he'd never been to, and quite another to do it to the anguished relatives. It would have been the most terrible thing he could have done. Imagine the headlines: 'Bruce Delamitri Insults Bereaved Mothers'. It would have been the number-one story from the ceremony, a terrible, terrible scandal. Bruce found himself actually laughing at the thought. As if he'd care now. Funny how one's sense of proportion changes when the cops have been swarming all over your lawn and a SWAT team has smashed its way through your roof.

Bruce muted the TV. He knew by heart what the anchors were saying. What else could they say? This had to be the most spectacular reversal of fortunes they had ever had the ghoulish pleasure of reporting. The catastrophe that had overtaken Bruce had (in his opinion, anyway) the stature of a Greek tragedy – with, he was forced to reflect, all its attendant ironies.

Hubris, pride, comes before a fall. When a person is so big, so bold, so beautiful, that they come to believe that the rules that govern others no longer apply to them, that's when fate sticks the boot in, and you can't get any bigger, bolder or more beautiful than winning the 'Best Director' Oscar.

Bruce's house was back on the screen. No cops now: it was the 'before' shot, serene, tranquil, to make it absolutely clear to morning America just what Bruce had lost. A gorgeous piece of footage from a video guide to the homes of Hollywood's élite. He remembered the helicopter coming over taking the shots and what an outrageous invasion of privacy he had thought it. Again, proportion. He was a man for whom the notion of privacy no longer existed. He was public property. His lawn was on the TV and there were cops all over it. Every news agency in the world owned him. They could fly a helicopter up his backside and say it was in the public interest. Bruce stared at the beautiful home where his life used to be. He glanced around the bare room where he now sat.

What a journey he had made.
In twenty-four hours.

For the manacled young woman in the adjoining interview room her current surroundings were something
of a step up. There were no cockroaches in the room,
no flea-bitten dogs poking around trying to get at the
food. There were no abandoned cars and no burst-open
plastic sack of garbage with rats fossicking about in them.
This young woman did not hail from a mansion in the
Hollywood hills. Her home was a beat-up RV in a trailer
park in Texas. She, too, had come a long way.

But her surroundings left her completely unmoved.
She didn't care. She didn't care about the cops and she
didn't care about Bruce. She didn't care where she came
from or where she had ended up. Wherever it was, she'd
rather be dead. He was gone and she was alone. She'd
known him such a short time and now it was all over
and she was alone.

Chapter Four

'All I said was that it's like trying to find a needle in a haystack.'

If it hadn't been so serious, a casual observer might have laughed: the almost Gothic nature of the scene was in such stark contrast to the banal conversation that accompanied it.

It was early afternoon on the day of the Oscars, and the captives were being held in a dark and dingy cellar. Toni, a woman in her early twenties, lay on her back across a table, her ankles and wrists chained to its legs. Her boyfriend, Bob, hung from a chain on the wall. His clothes had been cut away, and he looked rather sad dangling there in the tatters of what had once been an Italian suit.

The man who had made the remark about haystacks was called Errol. He and his companion, who answered only to the title of Mr Snuff, were gangsters. They carried enormous pistols wedged under their arms, which must have been very uncomfortable, and their conversation was continually punctuated with the word 'motherfucker'. Errol and Mr Snuff were of the opinion that Bob was holding out on them in the matter of some missing drugs. Bob denied the suggestion, of course, and a search had been conducted, unsuccessfully, prompting Errol to draw the age-old comparison with the needle in the haystack.

A comparison which irritated Mr Snuff not a little. 'And I'm saying it's a dumb thing to say,' he snapped unkindly. 'There ain't no haystacks any more. Leastways, not in the experience of the average individual.'

'That's just being pedantic,' said Errol.

'Listen, man, if the stone-cold truth is pedantic, then I guess that's what I'm being, because I'll bet if you was to ask every person within one hundred miles of where we're standing if they'd ever *seen* a haystack, let alone left their works in one, they'd say, "Get the fuck outa here, motherfucker."'

Errol spotted the point of confusion. 'It don't mean no works,' he said.

'Say what?'

'The needle which is referred to in the expression "a needle in a haystack" does not mean no drug paraphernalia. It means a needle for sewing.'

Mr Snuff seized upon the point like the practised debater he was. 'It don't matter what kind of needle we're talking about here, you dumb motherfucker,' he explained. 'The point is that no one is going to lose it in no haystack. You need to bring your metaphors into the twentieth century, man.'

Bob, still hanging from the chain, groaned a little. The two gangsters ignored him.

'How about if you was to say it's like trying to find

a line of coke in a snowdrift? Now there's an image a person can understand.'

Now it was Errol's turn to be contrary. 'No, man, that's bullshit,' he said angrily. 'The whole point about a needle and a haystack is that they are very different things, and although it would be difficult to locate the former within the latter, it would not be impossible. Cocaine and snow are basically identical. You could never tell one from the other. One concept is improbable, the other is impossible – which is an entirely different thing.'

'Less you snorted up the entire motherfucker. You could sure tell them apart if you was to stick them up your nose.'

Errol laughed. It was a relief for both men. The discussion had been in danger of turning acrimonious, but now the tension was broken. For the two gangsters, that is; for Toni and Bob things remained stressful.

'That's right,' Errol conceded with a grin. 'If you snorted up the entire snowdrift, when you got to the stuff that made you talk bullshit at three o'clock in the morning, that would be the cocaine.'

Mr Snuff, having scored such an effective point, was in the mood to be generous. 'I don't want to make no Federal case out of this,' he said kindly. 'I just think that language ought to reflect the lives of the people who are speaking it. Not some rural bullshit like needles and haystacks or . . . or . . . the early bird catches the worm. I don't want no fucking worm, man. What is more, if I had a horse, which I don't, I wouldn't waste no time taking the motherfucker to water when it wasn't thirsty in the first place.'

Bob groaned again. 'Let me go. I didn't rip nothing off, man.'

He might as well have appealed to a couple of concrete gangsters for all the good this was going to do him.

'Don't insult me, Bob. You think I can't count? You think me and Mr Snuff here are so dumb that we can't count?'

Bob quickly assured Errol that he had intended no such slur.

'In which case, how come I ain't supposed to know the difference between one hundred kilos and ninety-nine kilos, you sewer-rat? A one-hundredth part is a substantial differential. Suppose I was to cut off a one-hundredth part of you? Do you think you wouldn't notice?'

It would have taken a more stupid man than Bob to have misunderstood the meaning of Errol's question, but nevertheless Errol rubbed that meaning in by grabbing at Bob's crutch. It is said that men who practise the ancient Chinese art of kung fu are capable of retracting their testicles at the first sign of danger. They probably couldn't do it if the testicles in question were held in the vice-like grip of a large gangster.

'I gave you what Speedy gave me,' Bob protested. 'I didn't steal nothing. I'm not a thief.'

Errol released Bob's hundredth part and turned his attention to Toni. So far she had made no contribution to the conversation, and perhaps Errol felt some social pressure to include her. He and Mr Snuff were, after all, in a way the hosts.

'Toni?' he enquired. 'Is your boyfriend a thief?'

'Listen, Errol,' Toni said, attempting to sound calm and considering – no easy task when one is lying prostrate and securely bound across a table – 'we ain't getting nowhere here.'

'I know that.'

'If Bob tells you what you want to hear, you'll kill him.'

'I'm going to kill him anyway.'

'But you can't kill him till he's told you where your damn hundredth part is. So he won't tell you. We'll be here till Christmas.'

It was a valiant effort. That she could think at all, considering the horror of her situation, was a miracle, but to have put Errol's problem so clearly was impressive indeed.

'OK, Bob,' Errol said, levelling his gun at Toni. 'If you don't tell me right now, I'll shoot her.'

This was a hopeless ploy. Bob was, after all, a heartless drug dealer. The chances of his being moved by appeals to his chivalry were small. Toni knew this too, but before she had time to request that she be left out of it Errol shot her.

It was a powerful gesture: the smell of gun-smoke, the echoing report in such a confined space, the scream, the blood. All this might have moved a lesser – or indeed more honourable – man than Bob to speak up and save Toni further discomfort. But Bob was, of course, not a lesser man; nor was he a more honourable one. Nobody ever is.

'I didn't steal your drugs,' Bob said.

Errol sat down at the table, oblivious of the dying woman who lay across it. He was at his wits' end. He and Mr Snuff had searched Bob's apartment, his car, his clothes. Where on earth could the missing drugs be?

'Could a person get a kilo of heroin up their ass?' he asked.

'Maybe,' said Mr Snuff. 'People get all sorts of things up their asses.'

A pair of plastic gloves lay on the table next to a set of scales. Errol had been wearing them earlier on when weighing out the heroin. He picked up one glove, shook Toni's blood from it and put it on.

'I don't have no heroin up my ass, man' said Bob, hoping, perhaps, to save Errol the trouble of further investigation.

'Well, I wish I could trust you, Bob,' said Errol. 'To tell you the truth, I am not relishing the prospect of probing your butt with my finger any more than I imagine you relish the prospect of having your butt probed. But I cannot trust you, Bob, which is what all of this unpleasantness is about.'

Errol stuck his hand down the back of Bob's jockey shorts and executed his investigation. 'No drugs up here,' he said.

'Maybe she's got them,' said Mr Snuff, peering up between Toni's legs. 'No drugs here, I think,' he said from beneath her skirt, 'but a very nice—'

Then suddenly a voice from nowhere said, 'Thank you. Stop right there.'

And they stopped.

Errol froze. Mr Snuff froze. They all froze. There was not the slightest movement. Mr Snuff's head remained under Toni's skirt, Errol's expression remained one of bored indifference, Bob's grimace of pain seemed to have been painted on. Everything had stopped – not just stopped but *really* stopped. Nobody was doing *anything*. Toni was not bleeding any more. Nobody was even breathing.

Chapter Five

The voice spoke again. 'Go back, but slowly, nice and slowly.'

Mr Snuff removed his head from under Toni's skirt and Errol put his finger back up Bob's backside.

Toni's body began to suck back into itself the blood it had lost. The red stain shrank across the table. She even appeared to revive slightly.

Errol removed his finger from Bob again and returned to sit by the table. He seemed to be in pain: he made sad, guttural noises. He took off the glove, got up again and, backing away from the table, addressed Bob in the same strange, incomprehensible sounds. He drew his gun and pointed it at Toni.

A miracle was affecting Toni. Her wound was healing. Almost all the blood she had lost was back in her body, and all that was left of the gaping blast was the bullet.

Then Toni shot Errol.

Or at least shot *at* him. A bullet emerged from her body and hurtled towards the gangster. Fortunately for

Errol his gun was in the way, and the bullet Toni's body hurled at him disappeared straight up the barrel.

The disembodied voice spoke again.

'All right. Thank you. Let's leave it there for a moment.'

And suddenly there was darkness. Bob, Toni, Errol and Mr Snuff all disappeared. It was if they had never been there at all. For the moment at least, they had ceased to exist.

'I just wanted you to see that last sequence backwards,' said Bruce Delamitri, 'because I think it's easier to deconstruct the shots when you're not being distracted by the narrative flow. Remember that trick when you're checking your edits.'

What a sentence! Calm, commanding, all-knowing. Bruce could feel the sap rising – deep within his Calvin Kleins. The good feeling he had got earlier that morning from obliterating Oliver and Dale on *Coffee Time USA* was as nothing to the buzz that now surged through him as two hundred fresh-faced, puppy-like college kids hung on his every word. They were sitting there, awestruck, scarcely able to believe that the main man, the *mainest* man, the mainest, mainiest, most main *mongous* man of them all was really there, talking to them!

Bruce loved showing off in front of students. Especially the girls. Punky ones with great big Doc Marten boots on the end of slim, delicate legs. Preppy ones in smart little jumpers and cute John Lennon glasses. Goth types swathed in black, with pale skin and purple nail varnish. Tough, vampy ones with pierced belly-buttons and who knew what else. It wasn't that Bruce was a dirty old director. In fact women liked working with him: he was a recognized non-predator. But this was different. This was a treat. When Bruce had attended college he had been something of a dork and had had to work extremely hard to get anywhere at all with girls. Oh, they certainly *liked* him. They all found him funny, with his perfect impression of the sound effects in *The Texas Chainsaw Massacre,* and his plastic space-gun, stolen when he was an extra on *Star Wars*. His contagious enthusiasm for absolutely anything and everything to do with movies had always been attractive. But being funny and enthusiastic does not get you laid. Nor does it get you respected by the other guys – who had all been into Kurosawa while he was into James Bond.

'Of course *The Magnificent Seven* is a better movie than *The Seven Samurai*,' he used to say. 'For one thing it doesn't have subtitles.'

Bruce had been popular at college but no kid had ever stared at him the way these kids were staring at him now.

He was home. The film studies course of the University of Southern California where he had spent three happy but sexually frustrated years. He had returned at last to the one place in the world where he *really* wanted to show off. This was why he had agreed, on Oscars day of all days, to drive clear across LA from the *Coffee Time* studios to address his Alma Mater. To spend three precious hours viewing and discussing clips from his movies. To show off. What other reason would anyone have for going back and addressing their old college? When the heads of student committees write and ask famous old boys or girls to return and speak, they imagine they are asking an enormous favour. They themselves think the place is crap and can't wait to get out of it. But for the old boy or girl, that invitation represents acceptance at last, an opportunity to finally come to terms with the gawky nerdiness of their late adolescence. A rare chance to reach back across the years and – in thought at least – consummate all those glorious student flings that had never been.

So there Bruce sat, a king on his podium, puffed up with pride and eagerly anticipating a splendid hour or so humbly making it clear to these fine young people exactly how brilliant he was.

Opposite Bruce sat Professor Chambers, a sad-looking, dusty old Mr Chips whom the students had asked to chair the occasion. A teacher in the chair! In Bruce's day it would have been an ace king of teenage cool doing the job, but times had changed. The two-decade sixties hangover, when youth still seemed full of infinite promise, had finally evaporated. A colder wind blew now, and students had become much more timid, more conservative. Hence their decision to invite a professor to chair this major event: they felt safer with an authority figure around.

'So,' said Bruce, 'any questions or observations about the clip we just saw? Let's hear what the future's got to say.'

This was, of course, greeted by silence. Fear of looking stupid or uncool is a powerful censor, particularly if you've just been referred to as the future.

'I would like to ask something if I may,' said Professor Chambers.

Bruce cursed inwardly. Surely this old turd was not going to have so little style as to try and grab some reflected glory for himself? Bruce had not given up three hours of Oscars day to discuss the finer points of postmodern *film noir* bullshit with an anal academic. He had done it in order to strut about in front of nymphs.

'Go right ahead, professor,' he said, throwing a half-smile at the kids in the audience as if to say, 'Let's humour the sad old goat.'

'Do you feel that the same effect could perhaps have been achieved in your scene without delving into the female protagonist's private parts?'

Bruce was somewhat taken aback. Was this guy *criticizing* him? Surely not. Bruce was Oscar-nominated, for Christ's sake.

'Say *what*?' Bruce demanded.

'Ahem.' Professor Chambers cleared his throat, uncomfortably aware that all eyes were most definitely upon him. 'I was just wondering whether you feel that the same effect could perhaps have been achieved in your scene without delving into the female protagonist's private parts.'

There was a pregnant pause while Bruce debated whether to crush the professor like a small, bearded insect beneath his super-cool pointy-toed boots. A moment's reflection convinced him that this would look uncool. He didn't want to imbue the man with more significance than he deserved, which was none. Instead Bruce opted to wither him with a look of hip bemusement.

'The girl's private parts are not shown,' Bruce said. 'Didn't you watch the piece, *professor*?'

'I realize that the girl's private parts are not actually shown,' said Professor Chambers rather nervously. 'Nevertheless, they seem to play a disproportionately central role in the proceedings.'

The guy *was* criticizing him. As if he was the subject of some essay. Bruce decided that this had already gone on too long. He wanted to talk to cool kids not old jerks.

'I do not make exploitative pictures,' he said with an air of finality, and turned away from the professor to feast his eyes again on the sea of adoring and expectant young faces before him.

Professor Chambers sighed. He looked older than his years, with his lined face and grey beard. He felt like a schoolmaster forced to confront a brilliant but wayward pupil. A genius boy physicist who spent his time making stink-bombs, or a gifted young writer who insisted on putting swear-words into all his creative-writing assignments. He did not consider himself old-fashioned or a bore; he had once written an appreciation of Jim Morrison's poetry for the *Boston Literary Review*. There was however, in his opinion, a limit. Eroticism was one thing, pornography another. He felt that the place for delving into people's private parts was a doctor's surgery or in the context of a loving relationship. Not while searching for cocaine.

'Nevertheless,' he said to the back of Bruce's leather jacket, 'the character Mr Snuff does stare up the girl's private parts. That is the case, is it not?'

'Ironically,' Bruce replied without turning round.

'Ironically?'

'Yes.'

'I don't understand.'

Bruce drew upon all his reserves of patience, which was almost no patience at all. 'The character Mr Snuff,' he said, as if addressing a man who had donated his brain to an organ bank, 'stares up the character Toni's private parts in a manner that will imply an ironic juxtaposition to the audience. Didn't you get that, *professor*?'

'No, I'm afraid I missed that. Any ironic juxtaposition entirely passed me by. Am I being terribly dense?'

Bruce threw a look of tolerant exasperation at the audience, but the sympathetic response he anticipated was not forthcoming. The students were a bit lost: most of them thought that ironic juxtaposition was something dirty you did in bed. Some of them giggled nervously.

'With respect,' the professor added quietly, 'I thought it was just rather rude.'

Things had suddenly become a little tense. Bruce, like most people, hated tension. His whole pose was one of laid-back street cool. He was the grown-up teenager in the Ray-Bans who just didn't *give* a fuck. The naughty thirty-something genius who broke all the rules. It was his job to needle authority figures like college professors, not the other way round. And on this day of all days, Oscars day, when he should have been luxuriating in the sweet ecstasy of fame, basking in a hormone-packed wave of adolescent admiration, this dusty old fossil was pissing on his parade.

Bruce struggled to stay cool. He reminded himself just how far above the old turd he was. Only that morning the *New York Times* had published an adulatory two-thousand-word profile of him, using phrases such as 'cultural icon', '*Zeitgeist*' and 'defining images of the last decade'. Cultural icons did not let bearded gnomes with pens in their breast-pockets wind them up.

'You remember that the next shot is the POV of the girl's snatch, right?'

This got an easy laugh, as Bruce had calculated it would. Using rude words in lecture halls showed just how much of a fuck he did not give.

'POV?' asked the professor.

'Jesus! I thought you ran a film course here. POV. Point of view, for Christ's sake, point of view.'

'I know what POV means. I just don't—'

'We see Mr Snuff's face from the point of view of Toni's vagina.'

'The vagina's point of view?'

'Yes, the vagina's point of view.'

This was an entirely new concept for the professor. He wondered how a vagina could have a point of view and, if it could, what its attitude would be.

'I'm sorry, but I don't—'

'Mr Snuff stares at the vagina,' Bruce snapped, 'and in a subliminal way the vagina stares back at Mr Snuff.'

'And that's ironic, is it?'

'The irony is in what we take away from the image, professor. I want to show that this is all in a day's work for Mr Snuff. I need to see his face in these extraordinary circumstances, so that I can show his expression of casual indifference. He's almost bored. This is just a job, an American job.'

This bland assertion was too much for Professor Chambers. A faint note of irritation crept into his voice; you would have needed a sharp ear to spot it, but it was there. The students, who knew their tutor, shifted nervously in their seats.

'Is shooting women in the stomach and then rummaging about in their vaginas for drugs a common occupation in your experience?' the professor enquired.

'Killing is, pal. Being a killer is a career option in America, like teaching or dentistry.'

'Perhaps not quite as common.'

'Ha! You wish.'

'Statistically, I think you'll find I'm right.' Professor

Chambers decided to drop the point and move on. 'Mr Snuff's next line is perhaps one of my least favourite moments in your motion picture, Mr Delamitri.'

'I'm heartbroken.' Bruce smiled wearily at the students and they rewarded him with a laugh.

'Hmm, yes, well, I understand that taste is subjective and that you are indifferent to mine. Nevertheless, Mr Snuff's observation "nice pussy" seems to be beyond the bounds of taste altogether.'

Bruce groaned audibly. He was genuinely offended now. He no longer cared what the pretty young things thought. It was between him and this pathetic man who seemed to be going deliberately out of his way to apply an attitude of archaic prurience to Bruce's brilliant, startling and challenging images.

' "Nice pussy" is an important line, a pivotal line – the keystone line of the movie! I put it there so that even dummies wouldn't miss the point I'm making.'

The audience was becoming genuinely uncomfortable. Confrontational debate like this was a rarity on campus these days: the consequences of giving offence to one special-interest group or another were too severe. Bruce sensed the nervousness and attempted to moderate his anger.

'Look, Mr Chambers, I am not insensitive to the fact that some people might find this sequence unsettling. I am also not blind to the possibility that other people might be titillated by the images I present. The woman has been brutalized and violated, tied down, shot, had her clothing removed, and as she breathes her last she finds herself being intimately inspected by a strange man. I do not offer up these images lightly.'

'I am delighted to hear it.'

'I am aware of my reponsibility to place all this in a suitable editorial context. That is why I took the vagina's POV of Mr Snuff's reaction.'

'Which was to smile and observe that the character Toni has a nice pussy.'

'Exactly!' Bruce exploded. 'Listen to how he says it for Christ's sake! He doesn't say, "Wow, get this! I am searching a dying girl's private parts. Is that amazing or *what*! Am I going totally *insane* here?" He shrugs and he says it's "a very nice pussy". It's a throwaway. He is relaxed, he is indifferent. He's at work. Like I say, to him, it's just a job, an American job. That's what I want people to take away from this scene.'

The professor sighed. He was sick of studying film. Drugs, bullets, vaginas, this never-ending use of the term 'motherfucker' – it was all so very depressing.

'Perhaps we should take the next clip,' he said, nodding at the student technician.

The film rolled and the scene began. It was set in a low-life roadside bar and grill. A near-naked woman was dancing seductively to slow country music playing on a jukebox. Two aggressive and unpleasant truckers were leering at her from the bar.

'Now,' Bruce thought, 'the old swine can't possibly object to this one.'

Chapter Six

The young man and the scrawny girl were still lying on the bed in the motel chalet. *Coffee Time* had long since concluded and now they were watching videos.

There was a woman on the screen, dancing to the juke-box in a roadside bar and grill.

'I'm sick of watching the tube, honey,' the girl said.

'Quiet now, baby,' the man replied. 'This is important. What I'm doing here right now, hon, is researching.'

'Researching what? You ain't doing no researching. You're just watching dumb movies which you seen a hundred times already. I want to go out.'

'What I am researching, sugar,' the man said, his tone hardening slightly, 'is our salvation. Y'hear me now? Because what I have here is a plan to get us saved. You want to be saved, don't you, precious?'

'Sure I want to be saved. Everybody wants to be saved.'

'In that case, honey pie, shut the fuck up.'

He fixed his eyes on the TV and cranked up the volume. Slow, sugary country music filled the room, music recorded thirty years ago, which had been utterly and terminally uncool for every one of the intervening years. Music that had become briefly hip. Everything gets credible if you wait long enough; one generation's cringe is another's kitsch cult classic.

The woman kept on dancing. And such a woman. A truck driver's dream. A cowboy's fantasy. Poor white trash, but what poor white trash would look like had it just descended from Mount Olympus. Tanned, shapely legs stretching up for ever from the glossy painted toes on her bare feet to the jeans cut down to a tiny pair of shorts that inadequately covered her buttocks. A naked, undulating stomach, writhing to the rhythm. A perfect naval, like a cup, a bronzed abdomen contrasting beautifully with the white cotton of perhaps the smallest vest a woman might wear and still hope to keep her breasts from public view. Breasts which knew nothing of Sir Isaac Newton or his absurd gravitational theories. Above it all a cloud – no, a mane – of impossibly blonde hair crowning sleepy eyes and a fat mouth. A fat, wet mouth that never closed but hung lazily ajar, lips slightly parted, ready, one might easily imagine, for anything.

There is a children's movement exercise in which the kids are told to dance 'in the manner of' an abstract concept, like hunger or the wind. The girl in the bar was dancing in the manner of an orgasm. Her hips, her behind, her shoulders, her bare feet sliding on the floor, all seemed to suggest that dancing on her own to a juke-box in the middle of the day in a shit-house bar was to her the ultimate in sexual excitement. As she danced her hands even stole occasionally to between her legs, brushing at the little concertina of denim that disappeared below the zip of her jeans.

If this woman wasn't masturbating to music in a public bar she was by way of doing a very good impression of it. An impression that was not lost on the two large good ol' boy cowboy trucker types who were leaning against the bar resting their beer bottles on their beer bellies. They were, of course staring at the dancing woman, leering in fact. Dribbling would perhaps not be too strong a word. Their jaws were dropping, their erections were rising. Had it not been for the vast expanse of gut between the two, jaw and erection might well eventually have met.

'Hurrr hurrrr,' said one good ol' boy.

'Hurrrr,' replied the other and despite the poverty of their language it was clear that they were discussing the young woman's charms. Perhaps she was flattered by their obvious attentions, because she seemed to be directing her dancing towards them. A rough translation of her body language might have read, 'Should either of you two gentlemen feel in any way inclined to screw me rigid, you would not find me an unwilling collaborator.' That, at least, was how the bigger and uglier of the two good ol' boys interpreted her look, for he released the bar stool that he had clamped between his vast buttocks and, pausing only to spit some tobacco on to the floor, grunted his way towards the near-naked siren dancing before him.

What a contrast they made. One so beautiful it was almost unbearable, a walking, talking, living doll, a sex puppet, achingly seductive. The other a repulsive slob, beer bottle in hand, so many chins it looked as if he had rested his face on a stack of crumpets, his belly so vast that one side of it was in a different time zone from the other. The woman's chest might defy Newton's laws, but this colossal gut seemed to exercise it's own gravitational pull. At least, the woman certainly appeared to be drawn towards him, and it was hard to imagine that this had come about through any sort of desire.

And yet everything about her demeanour suggested that it had. It really seemed as if she was attracted to this man. She pouted at him, wiggled at him. His lumpy movements and phlegmy grunts seemed to excite her and spur her on to greater displays of lithe sexuality. She took his beer bottle from him and, even though there was only an inch or so left in it, took a pull. The man had clearly been nursing that bottle for some time and one could only guess how much of the beery dregs was made up of his spit, yet the woman sucked greedily at it, her fleshy lips pouting round the bottle neck as if to say, 'Normally, of course, I prefer to do this to a fat, ugly truck-driver's penis.'

The woman emptied the bottle but instead of putting it down she rolled it around on her tummy, apparently so hot that she needed to take any opportunity to cool down. Having rolled the bottle around for a while she turned it upside down so that a small dribble of the remaining foam ran down over her belly-button and into the top of her tiny shorts, drawing attention (as if this were required) to the fact that the waist button was undone and it was only the zip that was holding the shorts closed.

'Hurrr,' said the good ol' boy, as well he might.

The woman put the bottle down on top of the juke-box and closed the gap between herself and her new companion. Now her body was against his, her hips grinding back and forth. The trucker, clearly feeling that some gesture was required on his part, put his arms round her and in lieu of a formal introduction gripped her buttocks.

'My name's Angel,' she whispered at two or three of his many chins.

'Who cares what your name is, honey?' the trucker said. 'Pussy is pussy.'

He had struck the wrong note. Whatever Angel had hoped to hear from this disgusting man, it was not that. Her mood changed even as he gripped her more tightly.

'Loosen your grip, buddy,' she said. 'I like to keep my tits on the outside of my rib-cage'.

Her appeal fell on deaf ears. Digging his huge, fat banana fingers into her behind, he dragged her body harder against his.

'Honey, if you dance like a whore you're going to get treated like a whore,' he growled. 'Now, how about you pucker up for daddy?'

'I'd rather kiss the stuff I cut off my dog's ass,' Angel remarked in a forthright tone. With that she reached out an arm, grabbed the beer bottle from the top of the juke-box and brought it down on top of her dancing partner's head, shattering the base of the bottle. This gesture was understandably enough to make the man do as he was asked and disengage himself, but he did it with no good grace and indeed seemed ready to draw back his big pudgy fist and punch the woman. She was, however, ahead of him. There was a heavy glass beer jug on the counter. Somehow or other it got into Angel's hand and she swung it against the side of the big man's head. Down he went, semi-stunned, to the filthy bar-room floor, where he lay prostrate in the mud and the blood and the beer. At the bar his pal began to release his stool from the buttock-clamp in which his ass held it. Angel dropped the jug and, reaching into her tiny shorts, produced – by some kind of miracle, for it certainly could not have been there before – a little snub-nosed pistol.

'Sit the fuck down and shut the fuck up,' this woman of strange emotional contrasts shouted, levelling her weapon at the second trucker. You could almost hear the fear as the terrified fellow reinserted the stool into his enormous lardy backside and shut up.

Meanwhile Angel turned her attention back to her ex-dancing-partner, who still lay semi-stunned upon the floor.

'Cocksucking son of a bitch!' she screamed in wild, uncontrollable, unbalanced fury, kicking the stricken man in the head and face. 'Still want me? Still looking for pussy, you goddam faggot bastard? Well, you've had your last piece, you rat turd!'

The broken bottle with which she had begun her assault was still in her hand. Dropping to her knees, she rammed its jagged edge into the stunned man's loins. Blood geysered out of his fly.

The man touched the video remote control and the image froze, the blood stopping in mid-air as it hurtled towards Angel's face.

'I wuz just starting to enjoy that, honey,' said the girl.

'Got to take a leak,' said the man. 'Don't you mess with that control, now, girl. 'Cos' I'm working here. What I got is a plan.

Chapter Seven

A hundred miles south, in the university lecture hall
Bruce and Professor Chambers sat beneath the
same frozen image of blood geysering from the fat
trucker's loins. There was applause from the students,
which Bruce graciously acknowledged. He felt back on
safe ground. Surely the senile, bearded old back issue
sitting opposite him could not object to such a vigorous
and empowering piece of film-making. It transpired,
however, that he could.

'Don't you think that's rather a clichéd scene?' Professor Chambers enquired.

Bruce could scarcely believe the effrontery of the
odious little gnome. Who did he think he was? In fact,
and more to the point, who *was* he? A teacher. What
did he do that was so great?

'Have you any idea how much I *earn*?' Bruce wanted
to shout. 'Are you aware that the Académie Française
has given me a dinner?'

He didn't say that but he might as well have done.

He hit the tweedy old jerk with everything he had.

'Cliché? *Cliché?*' he said, jumping to his feet. 'Well excuuuuuse me if I opine that the meanest, most derivative cliché I ever produced is more original than everything you have ever said plus everything you have ever done.'

It was a mistake. It was meant to be a joke, sort of, but it didn't come out that way at all. Bruce had hoped to look sarky and disrespectful, the street punk in a leather jacket and pointy-toed boots thumbing his nose at authority. He forgot that he was not a punk but an impossibly rich, Oscar-nominated director, whereas Professor Chambers was a public servant on forty grand a year. Bruce was Goliath and the professor was David, not the other way round. The kids in the hall began to whisper to each other. Sweat trickled down Bruce's back and into the the top of his black 501s. He had let himself get angry; getting angry was uncool and he knew it. He was supposed to be the guy who didn't care. He realized that he must get a grip, bite the bullet, chew the carpet, go home later and kick the dog.

'Just kidding,' he said, with a little-boy smile. 'You don't "dis" the prof, right?'

The students relaxed a little. Bruce had concentrated all his considerable personal charm into this jokey semi-apology and it worked – for the students. Not, though, for the professor, who was looking at the screen again and shaking his head sadly. The woman in hot pants was still astride the trucker, the broken bottle was still embedded in his loins, the geyser of blood still hung in mid-air like a cruel red spike.

'I'm supposed to feel all right about this piece of violent soft porn because the woman triumphs, am I?'

'Well of course,' said Bruce. 'It's immensely important that the female protagonist is shown in a befittingly empowering light.'

This provoked a smattering of applause from some of the young women in the audience. Bruce was even gratified to hear a couple of whoops.

'Right on!' shouted a girl with a ring through her nose.

'Hmmm.' Professor Chambers sucked on his pen as if it was a pipe. 'You can have no idea how tired I am of film-makers like you cynically cloaking their salacious, smutty entertainments in some laughably two-dimensional anti-sexist agenda.'

This was getting silly. Bruce was a *guest* for Christ's sake! When was this nasty old man going to give him a break? Bruce took further refuge in self-righteous feminism, the modern equivalent of hiding behind a woman's petticoats. 'Maybe you find images of strong women threatening?'

'Right on!' shouted the girl with the nose-ring. Bruce wanted to kiss her. Fortunately he didn't; had he done so she would have brought a civil action against him for rape. Professor Chambers did not seem even to have heard her.

'I do not consider a woman who deliberately titillates some ignorant and unpleasant oaf merely to bury a broken bottle in his private parts, strong, I consider her psychotic.'

'Listen, pal, a woman can dress and dance any way she wants.'

'Any way *you* want. This is your fantasy, Mr Delamitri. The whole scenario is a fiction created by you, and the actress playing the role dressed as you wanted her to and did what you told her to do.'

The young woman with the nose-ring kept quiet. They all did. The debate was getting out of their league. They liked things simple, and an uncomfortable suspicion was dawning on them that what their professor and their hero were discussing was not simple at all.

'Yes, I created it,' Bruce admitted, 'but what did I create it from? These things are going on out there.' He was no longer concerned with looking cool. He had a point to make, a position to defend. He wanted to get through to the professor in the same way the professor had got through to him. 'The connection between sex and violence is for real. It's out there and it's happening, USA-wide. That isn't my fault. I didn't start it and I didn't kill anyone. I just hold up the mirror.'

'Rather a flattering mirror, isn't it?'

'Excuse me?'

The professor let him have it. 'Why do your murderers and psychopaths have to be so attractive, Mr Delamitri? So cool? It seems to me that if the scene we have just watched had involved the near-rape of a plain woman, a fat, boring woman, then you would probably have let her get raped. Except there never would have been such a scene because the whole purpose of the entire grubby business was to show us a beautiful woman in a state of provocative near-undress—'

Bruce did not let him finish. Chambers had walked into a trap. Bruce had heard this ancient, purile argument many times before, and he was in a position to crush it with the utter contempt it deserved.

'You ever see a Greek statue of an ugly chick? You ever see a painting of a battle when the guys didn't look cool and noble? Where the blood didn't look exciting and seductive? Artists make pictures and stories. That's what we do. Dull, ugly people leading boring lives devoid of sex and adventure do not make good stories. I'm not a journalist. It is no part of my duty to report life. I am an artist. My duty is to my own muse, my creative self. I take what I want in order to create what I like.'

'Really? I thought you said you were a mirror.'

'I'm . . . I'm . . .' Bruce knew when to throw in the towel. 'Actually, I'm running kind of late here.'

In the motel cabin the tough-looking guy had returned from the bathroom, grabbed a beer from the mini-bar and lain down again beside the girl.

'That sure was a fine motion picture,' he said. 'I may just have to watch it one more time.'

'Oh, honey,' said the girl, 'can't we go out now? *Do* something?'

'You want to go to prison, sugar pie?'

'No, of course not.'

'You want to burn in the chair? You want to feel your eyeballs melting before you're even *dead*?'

'Don't go saying stuff like that!' Suddenly there were tears on her pale cheeks.

'Then just you go get me another burger and let me watch my movie. Cos what I am working on here is our salvation.'

Chapter Eight

D usk had fallen.
   The searchlights that explored the sky above the theatre could be seen from miles away. The crowd was getting thicker and Bruce's limo slowed down. It's a funny thing about stretch limos: you can usually hire them for no more than twice or three times what an ordinary cab would cost and yet they remain a potent symbol of colossal wealth and celebrity. It crossed Bruce's mind that he ought to be able to extrapolate some great truth from this observation, but he couldn't think what it was.

The great car crawled forwards a few yards, clinging to the number plate in front, a pink number plate which read STAR. Bruce smiled. If there was one thing he knew about stardom, it was that if you had to stick it on your fender you hadn't got it.

A limousine jam. Only in Hollywood could you have a genuine limousine jam. An entire traffic snarl made up exclusively of stretch limos. Here was another observation from which a pithy and illuminating irony could surely be gleaned. No matter how long your car is, in traffic they're all the same length: they stretch from the one stuck in front of you to the one stuck behind. Not bad, Bruce mused. He might trot it out to the press tonight to show that he still had his feet on the ground despite being so very special.

The car stopped altogether.

Bruce leant back in the baby-soft black leather, his wrap-round Rays between him and the world, a drink in his hand and an Oscar very nearly in his pocket.

His mind began to dwell on a particularly gruesome and pointless murder that he was planning. He had it in his head pretty clearly now. A run-down Korean drug store in the Valley. Two white kids enter the store. White trash kids. Better still, middle-class white kids pretending to be trash. Talking dudespeak, of course, or whatever other hellish dialect the generation with no brain affected these days. ('Generation X? Generation X-tremely fucking stupid,' Bruce would say at parties.) The two kids approach the counter and ask for a quarter of Jack plus some Pepsi Max to mix. But the old Korean lady knows the law and doesn't want to lose her liquor licence, so she asks for some ID.

'Here's my ID, bitch,' says one of the boys and hauls out a machete. Not some stupid little knife, but a *machete*. Obviously the old lady tells the kids to forget about the ID, in fact she reaches down a whole pint of bourbon and offers it to them on the house. But it's too late. She has crossed the line with these kids. She has 'dissed' them. They have been pushed too far and they ain't gonna take it any more because, quite frankly, they are sick of the bullshit. So the boy swings his weapon towards the terrified woman in a huge arc and cuts her head off. Blood starts spurting out of the dead woman's neck, which so excites the two kids that they hop over the counter and hack her up into a million pieces.

Bruce would do the whole thing to music, heavy-duty rock 'n' roll perhaps, or maybe something witty and ironic like 'Happy Days are Here Again' or 'All You Need is Love'. He would make it look like a pop video. Maybe he could have a TV on in the background, with a Tom and Jerry cartoon showing. That way, while the two kids were slicing up the old Korean woman, Jerry could be ironing Tom with a steam iron, or dicing him in the lawn-mower.

'What were you trying to tell us by juxtaposing your brutal murder with cartoon mayhem?' assholes like Professor Chambers would ask.

'I was telling you that the Korean woman had Tom and Jerry showing on her TV,' he would reply enigmatically, and hundreds of film students would write essays about irony.

'Bruce Delamitri is trying to tell us that America is now starring in its own animation,' they would write. 'We are all Tom, we are all Jerry, locked in a perpetual cycle of almost surreal violence.'

The limo driver barged in on Bruce's thoughts. 'There's a hell of a queue to drop, Mr Delamitri. We're going to be stalled for a while here.'

A limo jam. A jam of stretch limousines. It was faintly embarrassing.

Outside there were thousands of people, all staring. Faces everywhere, a wall of them. Bruce peered through the darkness of his shades and tried to focus on a pretty one but was disappointed. Despite their excitement, they all seemed drab and sad. Trash. Poor white, black, brown and yellow trash.

He glanced at the locks on the car doors. It was not that he thought he was in any danger – the crowd was well ordered and the cops were keeping it firmly behind barriers – but you could not help but feel a little exposed. All those people wanting something they would never get.

Maybe one day they would just grab it anyway. It crossed Bruce's mind that the princes of old Russia must have stared out of their carriages at faces much like these just before their world got torn to bits in 1917.

But what did they want, craning their necks by the side of the street like that? It certainly wasn't peace, bread and freedom. So what? They couldn't see anything: all the limos had mirrored windows, so all they could see was themselves. Another irony; Bruce was full of them today. The harder those people tried to look into his world the more intensely they saw their own images staring back at them. That was it! The whole truth in one startling image. Why were Bruce's movies so successful? Because people saw themselves reflected in them. Maybe better-looking and a little cooler but none the less themselves, with their fears, their lusts, their most secret desires and fantasies. That damned professor had been wrong and he, Bruce, had been right. He *was* a mirror. He did not create a world for people to watch; they created a world for him to film.

They were his muse, these *lumpen* gawpers, staring at his car, trying to guess who might be inside it. Pointing, pointing their fingers and yet all they could see was their own images, pointing right back at them.

'That's right, point,' Bruce said aloud. 'Point the finger, accuse yourselves, because you and you alone are responsible for what you see. For what you are. For what you do.'

Up ahead the starlet in the purple dress had done her twirls, making the most of her thighs and her nipples.

Then it was his turn on the red carpet.

He stepped out of his limo intending scarcely to acknowledge the crowd, merely to stroll languidly into the theatre as if he was entering a bar. Perhaps he would allow a brief, cool nod towards the throng, but certainly no more than that. The sort of stroll and nod that said, 'Am I the *only* person here who realizes that this is all bullshit?' That was what he had intended, but instead Doctor Showbiz appeared as if from nowhere and gave him a shot in the arm. The crowd cheered and he couldn't resist a stolen moment luxuriating in their attention. He turned, he waved, he checked his bow-tie, he tugged charmingly at his ear-lobe.

'Love me you bastards,' he thought. 'Look! Look! This is my night. I am the greatest director in the world and yet I have the grace to pretend I'm just an ordinary guy.'

'Why, he's just an ordinary guy,' thought the crowd and the cheering redoubled. Except, of course, for the pickets. They did not cheer – well, why would they? As far as they were concerned, Bruce had murdered their children.

Their banners said, 'MAD (Mothers Against Death)'. It was extraordinary the lengths people would go to to come up with a suitable acronym, the tortuous linguistic paths they were prepared to navigate in order to arrive at something they imagined sounded neat. These mothers weren't against death, they were against violence and murder. But that would have spelt MAVAM which was not neat, so they had had to become Mothers Against Death (by violence and murder), or MAD. Bruce knew some of them by sight. They had been with him for months, these mothers whose sons and daughters he was supposed to have killed.

'Hollywood glorifies murder', said their placards. 'Bring back family entertainment'.

'Like incest,' Bruce thought, but fortunately he did not say it. Even cool mavericks in pointy-toed boots had to recognize the limits.

'Mr Delamitri,' shouted one of the MAD mothers, 'my son was murdered. An innocent boy, gunned down on the streets. In your last picture there were seventeen murders.'

'Yeah, and there was plenty of sex in my movie too, but I bet *you* haven't had any for a while.' Again he thought it but didn't say it.

These people were beyond rational argument. Bruce turned away from them and waved at the rest of the crowd.

'Where's the old lady?' one tasteless wag shouted.

Funny how some people seem to think it's perfectly all right to be rude to the rich and famous, as if having a lot of money meant that breaking up with your wife was not a painful experience. Bruce had not got married in public, and he certainly wasn't getting divorced in public, but the whole messy business was none the less public property.

'Where are your manners, you pathetic little no-life?' was what Bruce wanted to reply, but he didn't, of course. He merely smiled a 'what can I tell ya?' sort of smile and for this small capitulation he was rewarded with a thumbs up from his interrogator and another ragged cheer.

The mirror Bruce held up was a two-way thing. Occasionally he caught his own reflection in it. He wanted that crowd to love him, to appreciate him. So he smiled and waved and in their faces were reflected his weakness and his dishonesty.

It began to rain. A summer storm was coming in. Bruce hurried up the red carpet and into the theatre. He was wearing the genuine original tux that had been worn by Bogart in *Casablanca*, but it was only borrowed and he didn't want it to get wet.

North of LA the storm had already broken. The highway shone like black patent leather, the lights of the traffic shimmering on its surface.

Inside the 1957 Chevrolet the young man and the even younger woman peered out at the road as the ancient wiper blades struggled with the downpour.

'Ya gotta sacrifice comfort for style,' the man had said, explaining his choice of which car to steal. 'Even broke down and with its engine up on blocks, this car is a better car than every heap of foreign tin between here and Los Angeles.'

'Leastways the radio works,' the girl said, and found a hard-rock station. Personally, she liked her music a little softer and sweeter, but she knew his tastes. Besides, what she liked to hear was the news. She liked being famous.

'Latter day desperados . . . Bonnie and Clyde for the millennium . . . a Mexican chambermaid found dead in a chalet room, clutching clean towels and soap . . .' The girl thought how strange it had been, watching movies all that time with the dead maid lying there in front of the TV.

'. . . motel short-order cook shot fourteen times . . .'

She should never have told him about that guy flirting. She'd known what would happen and it had.

The radio moved on to showbiz news.

'. . . live from outside the Oscars . . . I see Bruce Delamitri acknowledging the crowd.'

'Way to go,' murmured the man as he peered into the rain. 'You make sure you win, now, Bruce. Just you make damn sure you win.'

Chapter Nine

'**B**ruce Delamitri! Yeah, way to go! All *right!*' the
impossibly cute blonde model-turned-actress almost
shouted, making the most of her last syllable in the spotlight.

On the whole the people brought on to do the presenting at awards ceremonies are divided into two groups,
the big names and the small. The big names are those
who have been nominated for an award themselves and
have been persuaded to muck in elsewhere during the
evening to help things swing. They do not want to do
this of course, since it considerably lessens a star's impact
when they finally appear themselves as a recipient if they
have only recently been welcomed on stage to give some
nobody or other the gong for 'Best Foreign-Language
Lyric'. Nevertheless, big stars often agree to do the
required chore because they are unable to avoid the
tiny, unworthy suspicion that a refusal might somehow
affect their own chances. Traditionally, big names who
have not been nominated refuse requests to present.
They are happy to turn up, of course, and sit in the

stalls observing proceedings with a bemused tolerance, but they are not prepared to play John the Baptist to some hated rival's Messiah. Which means that the organizers of these events are forced to fall back on the second group: small names, people who have been around for either a very short time or a very long time. The former are not yet famous enough to cause much excitement, and the latter are destined to provoke excitement only once more in their lives and that, paradoxically, will be when they die. It is these people who fill the gaps between the genuinely important names.

Bruce scored a not-yet-famous-enough.

It should not have been that way, of course. 'Best Director' is one of the jewels in the Academy's crown, and under normal circumstances one of the press-ganged biggies would have presented Bruce with his statuette. But Hollywood is a scared town. Nobody wants to be connected with any controversy, and with his placard-waving band of MAD camp followers Bruce was highly controversial. His presence on the list of nominees had been enough to cause all the glittering superstars originally approached to get headaches.

'Bruce Delamitri! Yeah, way to go! All *right!'*

Bruce leapt out his seat like an eager puppy at the sound of his name. He had intended to arch his eyebrows in surprise and then rise slowly and rather reluctantly. Instead it looked as if his backside was spring-loaded. Recovering slightly, but still grinning like a lunatic, he set off towards the podium. Behind him a tuxedoed extra slipped into his place; the Oscars ceremony is, when all is said and done, a television programme, and no seating gaps are allowed to mar the perfect picture.

The cute starlet beamed at Bruce as he approached

her. Held firmly in her grip and pressed hard against her impossibly, absurdly perfect body was the twelve-inch golden icon. If Bruce's mouth hadn't been so dry he would probably have dribbled. This felt *good*. All through the interminable earlier part of the proceedings his mind had been a jumble of possible things to say. He would speak out against the New Right and its creeping censorship, condemn the way hysterical outrage had replaced reasoned debate, call for freedom of speech, proclaim the sacred individuality of the artist in a democracy. Basically, just be a complete and utter hero.

In front of a billion people.

That was what he had been told: a billion people were watching. A *billion*. On the long walk up the aisle towards the beaming starlet, he tried to conjure up some kind of image of what that meant. He thought of all the faces outside the theatre, the ones staring into his limousine; he imagined the whole sky filled with those faces, a big sky, a desert sky, filled with gawping faces from one horizon to the other, all staring at him. He couldn't do it. It didn't mean anything. A hundred people, a billion people – either way it was a lot of people if they were all staring at you.

Now Bruce was on the stage, standing alone in a single spotlight, the Oscar in his hand.

Now was his chance. To tell it like it was. To rise above the sanctimonious emotional manipulation that had characterized the evening thus far. Like the 'Best Actor', who had won his award for playing a person with brain damage and who had actually carried a brain-damaged child on to the stage and presented her with his award. Or the 'Best Actress', who had won so many hearts by accepting her award dressed in a gown designed in

the shape of an enormous Aids-awareness ribbon. Like
the 'Best Supporting Actor', who had pointed out that
Hollywood's duty was the 'inspirationalization' of the
world; and the 'Best Supporting Actress', who had
made an emotional appeal from the podium for more
understanding of everything. The endless list of thanks to
Mom, Dad, 'my creative team', 'the many, many people
whose dedicated work goes into enabling me to be me',
God and America.

Now it was Bruce's turn. To tell it like it really
was.

'I stand here on legs of fire.'

Legs of fire?

It just came out. Despite his best noble intentions
to say what he really felt, the awesome scale of the
event possessed him. The billion people in the mirror
possessed him. Suddenly he was no longer his own man.
He had become an automaton, an unwilling conduit for
mawkish, sentimental drivel.

'I want to thank you. Each and every person in this
room. Each and every person in this industry. You
nourished me and helped me to touch the stars . . .'

What could he do? He could not rain on the parade.
Nobody loves a griper, particularly if that griper is holding
in his firm, manly grasp the one thing that everybody in
the whole room covets the most. Look at Brando. He
wasn't the only person who was sorry for the Indians
or Native Americans or whatever they were called.
Everybody felt bad about them, but bringing them up
at the Oscars? It just looked smug and rude. Besides, the
people who were outside protesting had lost loved ones.
Nothing to do with him, of course, but nevertheless it ill
behoved a man of his splendid achievement to piss on

the bereaved from the Olympian heights of the Oscars ceremony.

'. . . You are the wind beneath my wings and I flap for you. God bless you all. God bless America. God bless the world as well. Thank you.'

The room erupted into rapturous applause. It was an ovation of relief. Bruce Delamitri had acted like a grown-up. When his name was announced, many people had wondered whether he would seize the opportunity to be rude and controversial. Bruce did, after all, represent the young, thrusting, cool, cynical Hollywood which simply did not *give* a fuck. It had been eminently possible – indeed probable – that he would seek unworthy notoriety by being unpleasant and abrasive. A few of the more timid souls feared he might even mention those dreadful pickets outside the theatre who were trying to spoil everybody's big night. But what a pleasant surprise. Bruce's speech had been a model of Oscars-night grace and good manners. Textbook stuff: sincere, self-effacing, patriotic and very, very moving.

Hollywood welcomed one of its own into the fold. Bruce walked from the podium and into the welcoming arms of the upper echelons of the entertainment establishment.

Back up the coastal highway, they were finally clearing away the bodies of the Mexican maid and the short-order chef, two people who had come into contact with a moral vacuum and who had paid the price. The State Troopers shook their heads. The detectives shook their heads.

'Jerry made me a steak only this morning,' said one Trooper as the trolley upon which Jerry's corpse lay was

wheeled out into the parking lot. From the front Jerry
had still looked like Jerry. He had taken any number of
bullets, but modern high-velocity weapons make very
neat entry wounds. Not so the exit wounds. Each bullet
pushes an expanding cone of flesh in front of it on its
journey through the body, and when it blasts its way
out the damage is horrific. From the front Jerry was
merely slightly perforated; from the back he was just
so much pulp.

The maid had been strangled.

'Why'd they do that?' the Trooper wondered. 'I mean,
why the fuck did those bastards have to do that?
Weren't no call. No money nor nothing. So why'd
they do that?'

Contrary to popular mythology, American police officers do not spend all day every day scraping corpses off
walls and floors. Perhaps the Washington DC Homicide
Department do, but not the average cop. Death is not
uncommon in their job but it is not the norm either, and
the two State Troopers weren't so familiar with murder
as to be indifferent to it.

'Ain't no reason why,' one of the detectives answered.
'These kids are just doing it for kicks. Maybe they
was high on drugs, listening to some damn Satanic
heavy-metal music, or else maybe they just watched
another movie.'

There were still a few news reporters left on the
scene.

'So you definitely think this is another copycat killing,
chief?' one said eagerly. 'It's got to be the Mall Murderers, hasn't it?'

'Well, this ain't no mall, is it? Although, hell, those
psychotic bastards ain't particularly choosy where they

perpetrate their mayhem. I don't know, you tell me. Maybe they was copying something they saw, maybe it was two other fuck-ups copying them.'

'A copycat copycat?' asked the reporter, scribbling furiously.

'I don't know. Maybe it's a copycat, copycat, copycat. All I know is that two innocent, ordinary Americans are dead.'

'And that's the point isn't it?' said the reporter, seizing on the detective's words like a dog with a bone. 'That's what this is, just one more ordinary story of *Ordinary Americans*.'

'Well, I don't know what you'd call ordinary,' the cop replied. 'I've been coming to this diner for over thirty years now and nobody ever got shot here before.'

But the reporter had stopped scribbling.

Chapter Ten

The Governor's Ball. *The* post-Oscars party. The glitter, the glamour, the *bosoms*! There were bosoms as far as the eye could see, a great soft undulating shelf of bosoms that stretched from one side of the vast ballroom to the other. If anything was going to snap Bruce out of the irrational but uneasy sense of failure that his speech had cast across his great triumph, it was the Bosom Ball.

He stood at the top of the stairs that led down to the dance-floor and wallowed in the glorious display. From his vantage-point he could admire the thousand or so best cleavages in Hollywood, which of course meant the best in the world. What an admirable thought! Laid out before him were the planet's two thousand top tits, creamy white, coffee-brown, sun-kissed olive, all rising and falling to the rhythm of the night. The best that Mother Nature could build, the best that money could buy. Heaving against the silk and lurex and velvet and rubber of a thousand million-dollar dresses. Bosom upon bosom upon bosom, struggling to escape the surly

confines of the gowns that bound them. For the second
time that day Bruce felt the sap rise within his Calvins.
Was that an Oscar in his pocket or was he just extremely
bloody pleased with himself? The winner! The man of
the hour. The best director in town.

Intoxicated by the heady atmosphere of sex and
success, Bruce forgot his private sense of failure. Everybody made awful speeches at the Oscars: it was a
tradition.

Sure.

Absolutely.

In a way it was cool to be kitsch. Look at Elvis.

Right.

Buoyed up by this thought, Bruce waded into the sea
of bosoms.

'Thank you, thank you very much,' he heard himself
saying over and over again, struggling to address his
remarks to faces not bosoms. Cleavage etiquette was
something he had never been able to work out. Clearly,
a woman who was presenting her tits like the centrepiece
in some glorious bouquet would be saddened to think
that nobody had noticed them. On the other hand, if
you did stare appreciatively it looked a bit tacky. Bruce
thought about putting on his shades, but decided against
it. Instead he concentrated on being magnanimous in
victory.

'Personally, I thought so and so should have got it,'
he lied. Personally, he thought so and so's movie had
been an over-sentimental piece of crap which nobody
would have looked at twice if so and so hadn't been a
woman. But he was trying to be nice.

'No, really, I think she deserved it more than I did.'
Like hell.

'I'm just happy if someone goes to see my picture.'
Like double hell with mashed potatoes.

'Great to see you, pal.' Bruce pumped some handsome
star's hand fervently. 'I loved that cop thing you did. We
should meet. I'd like that. That would be fun.'

'Did you see the cop thing he did?' Bruce con-
fided to another firm-chinned wonder. 'Directed by
a moron, performed by a retard. I'm trying to be
nice here, but the guy has had a total talent trans-
plant.'

More bosoms. More congratulations. A couple of
drinks.

'I'm just glad for the cast, that's all. It's really their
movie . . . I just thought up the idea, raised the money,
wrote the script, cast it, directed it and told everybody
involved exactly what to do.'

More drinks. More bosoms. He was happy to address
them directly now.

'You are the wind beneath my wings and I flap for
you. God bless you all. God bless America. God bless
the world as well. Thank you.'

Bruce's voice wafted through the trees. The young
couple were lying on a blanket spread on the wet
ground. They had just made love in the warm but
drenching rain.

'Quiet, honey,' said the man, and he held his finger
to his lover's lips.

'Surely the most controversial Oscar choice in recent
times,' the radio said, 'particularly in the light of yet
another irrational murder thought to have been perpetrated by the notorious copycat killers known as the
Mall Murderers.'

The girl giggled with nervous excitement. 'Notorious!' she whispered into her boyfriend's ear.

'That's right, honey. No-fuckin'-torious.'

She lay back on the sopping rug and the rain splashed down on her fragile-looking body, forming shining beads on her white skin.

Notorious.

They laughed together at this reminder of their infamy. He ran his hand across her stomach and on to her breasts, collecting a ridge of water as he did so. Then they made love again, while the radio pumped twenty minutes of advert-free rock through the dripping trees. No chit-chat, no hard sell, just pure one hundred per cent heavy-duty rock cumminrightatcha!

'Well,' said the man, when they had finished for a second time, as he got up and pulled on his jeans, 'I guess the engine'll be cool by now. We'd best be moving on. We have some stuff to do.'

Bruce was drinking and he'd stopped trying to be nice.

Although he was something of a style junkie, the abstinence thing was one Hollywood fashion Bruce had never cottoned to. He was one of the new breed of 'Hey, I smoke – you gonna call the cops?' hard guys.

'I like to drink,' he would say. 'I like the taste and I like the packaging. It is an indisputable fact, aesthetically speaking, that a bottle of Jack or Jim on a dinner-table looks considerably more pleasing than a bottle of Évian. Trust me, I'm a movie director.'

Under normal circumstances Bruce was a happy drinker, not one of those sad Jekyll and Hyde characters who turn into social psychopaths with the third glass. But on this night, although (or perhaps because) it was supposed to be the biggest night of his life, the bourbon was not giving him that familiar warm glow.

It was all the people in his face.

His face was completely full of people – friends, admirers, job-seekers, gold-diggers – and yet suddenly, all he actually wanted was to be alone. He would have liked nothing more than to lean against a wall in solitary, half-drunk splendour, watch the bosoms and forget about himself. But he couldn't because people kept coming up and talking to him. Congratulations would have been fine, but they always wanted to justify their gushing praise with a conversation. Why couldn't they just tell him he was great and fuck off? Instead he had to be nice to them. He didn't want to be nice. He'd been nice on the podium, nice enough for a lifetime. That was enough nice; he was niced out. He should not be expected to spend the whole evening, *his* evening being nice.

'Thank you, that's kind, thank you. Well you know that's very kind.'

It couldn't go on for ever and it didn't.

'Look, I just made a movie. I didn't find the cure for cancer!' That shut them up.

'This Oscar means nothing,' he added grandly, warming to his theme.

'It's a tainted trinket.' . . . 'A statue without status.' . . . A bauble with no balls.' . . . Bruce loved that last one.

'Take a look at it.' He held up his Oscar, waving it about and pointing at the golden sword which coyly covered the relevant part of its anatomy. 'It's a bauble with no balls.'

People laughed – but nervously. You didn't come to the Governor's Ball and take the piss out of the Oscar statuette. It was like going to church and sneering at the cross. The Oscar was the most coveted glittering prize of them all, potent symbol of the greatest entertainment industry on earth. Cynicism was not only bad form, but utterly deceitful. Everybody knew that, balls or no balls, the Oscar was the ultimate goal and Bruce had wanted it like life itself. To grab it and then try to be smart after the event was appalling behaviour. Bruce knew this too, but he didn't care. Having failed to speak his mind in his speech, he was making up for lost time.

'Look, if a picture's good it does not require the approbation of a twelve-inch eunuch to legitimize it!'

It was the memory of the faces in the mirror pointing their accusing fingers at him. It was the dreadful, deluded MAD mothers with their sad stories of loved ones lost. It was Oliver and Dale and that smug little professor.

All of them lingered in the back of his mind, niggling away, trying to call him to account, to spoil his fun. Apparently it wasn't enough to make cool, slick, exciting movies that people got off on. No, he was also expected to try and second-guess some unknowable repercussions that his work might or might not have.

Absurd. Puerile.

Yet he'd had his chance to speak out and had said nothing. Worse, he'd made out that everything was fine. He felt such a hypocrite himself that he saw hypocrisy in everybody else. He couldn't bring himself to believe that any of the gushing praise people kept heaping upon him was sincere. Why should they be telling the truth? He hadn't. He'd cravenly failed to use the platform that the Oscars had given him to take on the censorship debate. To nail, publicly, all the dangerous, reactionary talk of copycat killings, protecting kids from themselves and whatever happened to Andy Hardy. He'd had the chance to take that famed twelve-inch golden statuette and shove it right up the collective ass of Professor Chambers, the Senate Committee on Taste and Decency, the Concerned Mothers of American Dimwits and every other God-bothering, mealy-mouthed, Moral Majority moron in the USA. He'd had the chance, but he'd blown it.

'Legs of fire', for Christ's sake!

'Give me another Jack Daniels.'

'Give me another Jack Daniels.'

The terrified shopkeeper reached down a second bottle of whiskey and added it to the box of booze and provisions that stood on the counter. The scrawny girl watched proudly as the pathetic man leapt to do exactly what her boyfriend ordered. Her boyfriend had such natural authority and command. She loved that about him. She felt that, even without the Uzi machine-pistol with which he was threatening the storekeeper, his commands would still have been obeyed.

They were in the process of robbing the store of a small country caravan park, which they had stumbled across after leaving the main highway.

'There'll be road-blocks,' he'd said, swinging the big, saggy old car on to a gravel road, 'and we ain't gettin' caught till we're good and ready.'

'Ready to be saved?' she'd asked eagerly.

'That's right, baby, ready to be saved.'

She slid across the big bench seat and put her head on his shoulder. The vast redwoods slid past the windows, and for a while she indulged in the fantasy of staying in the forest for ever. The trees looked so thick and friendly in the Chevy's lights that she thought maybe they could build a secret cabin among them and live off berries and venison.

It was a delicious thought, and as she peered out through the wet windscreen and deep into the dark shadows she could almost see the two of them, standing in the doorway of their little fairy-tale home, he with an axe in his hand, she with a tray of fresh-baked fruit scones. All alone in the world.

When the caravan park hove into view it seemed to her that perhaps they had chanced upon a halfway point between fantasy and reality.

'Let's rent a trailer, baby,' she'd pleaded. 'We could stay a few days. I'll bet they haven't even heard of us out here.'

For a moment the trees and the night and the smell of the rain had tricked her into imagining that she lived in some other age, one when people still hid out in woods, when you could still run and hide. When a person could still start again.

'Honey, we ain't more'n fifteen miles from the Interstate. You think they don't have TV and a phone?' her boyfriend said. 'Besides, everybody in the whole United States has heard of us.'

'Well, couldn't we just stay one night? Y'know, like a holiday?'

'Tonight ain't jus' any ol' night, hon. Tonight is *the* night. Shit or bust. We'll just pick up some stuff and move on.'

So they had pulled in off the gravel road and forced the old storekeeper to open up his shop. They should have been out again in a couple of minutes. It should have been the simplest thing in the world. After all, they had turned over country stores a hundred times before.

But this time the robbery was going wrong. This time there was a problem.

The storekeeper had no Twinkies.

No Twinkies? Every store had Twinkies.

'I *want* some Twinkies' the girl said, and she actually stamped her foot. 'You *said* I'd get some.'

'I know, I know, baby, but I can't just make 'em up outa dog food, can I?'

The sound of television commercials could be heard from the back room. The storekeeper had been watching TV when the robbery began.

'You're a modern girl. You know what you want and you want it now!'

'Don't take no for an answer.'

'Why wait, when you can have it all today?'

They could have been ads for anything. Even Twinkies.

'You get everything you want!' the girl shouted. 'Whiskey and pretzels and cigarettes and I don't even get no Twinkies!'

'I know that, honey, but what can I do? I'm sorry.'

'Don't shoot me, please.' The storekeeper could scarcely speak for fear.

'For me, freedom is about doing what I like to do when I like to do it' said the TV in the back room.

'What d'you say?' the young man asked the store-keeper.

'I . . . I said please don't shoot me . . . I just ran out yesterday. We're a small business. We can't carry no huge stock.'

'You think I'd shoot a guy for not having *Twinkies*?'

'I . . . I have Pop Tarts.'

'For Christ's sake, what kind of person do you think I am?' The young man was so offended that he shot the storekeeper anyway.

'C'mon, honey. We'll stop by a 7–11 when we hit LA.'

Chapter Eleven

There was a crowd of people round Bruce now, sensing scandal. Some kind of critic guy was in his face, a big noise, art editor on the LA *Times*, or maybe gardening editor, something he was pretty proud of anyway. Great Caesar's tits, the man was a pompous little pecker.

'I must say,' the pecker said, 'I found *Ordinary Americans* a wonderfully seductive piece of film entertainment.'

'Film entertainment'. What a phrase! Not 'work of art', not 'cultural benchmark', not 'celluloid reflection of the spirit of the age', but 'film entertainment'. As if Bruce made daytime soap or something.

Bruce did not consider himself conceited about his work. He was the first to admit that it was popcorn – but only if other popular and corny works like *Romeo and Juliet* and Beethoven's Fifth were popcorn too.

'And I will go to the wall,' the pecker continued, as Bruce's eyes glazed over, 'to defend your right to kill as many people as you like in your movies. The only question I ask is – that age-old bugbear – is it art?'

'Is it art?' said Bruce. 'Well, let me see now. That's a tricky one. Is shooting a whole bunch of people in a movie art? I think the best way I can answer that is to ask you not to be such a complete fucking jerk.' Not brilliant, perhaps, but it got the pecker to go away.

It brought Bruce no relief, though. One jerk was replaced by another. At least this time it was a lovely young actress. Lovely to look at, that is, not to listen to. She was a whiner, a spoilt brat. Her conversation had a banal self-assertiveness which was the result of rarely being contradicted, on account of the fact that she rarely spoke to anyone who wasn't trying to sleep with her. Bruce did not want to sleep with her and so listened to the young woman's conversation with a less indulgent ear than she was used to.

'No, actually, as a matter of fact I don't think I was emotionally abused as a child,' he said through gritted teeth. 'Well, I think I would know . . . Really? Is that so?'

According to the young woman, it was not necessarily the case at all that a person would be aware of having been emotionally abused. She herself had been blissfully ignorant of the appalling truth until it was uncovered via hypnotherapy.

'And what did he say to that?'

It was the following morning and the girl (whose name was Dove) was recounting the story of her party encounter with Bruce to Oliver and Dale on *Coffee Time USA*, the events of Oscars night having by that time turned anyone who had been with Bruce during the previous twenty-four hours into an important character witness and a sought-after celebrity. All across the air waves, hat-check girls and drinks waiters were offering their opinion on Bruce's state of mind during the five or six seconds they had spent with him 'one on one'.

'He said that I must be very relieved,' Dove replied, looking beautifully earnest and careworn.

'Hang on, let me get this straight here,' said Oliver, putting on his glasses. Oliver's glasses did not actually have any lenses, because if they had they would have reflected his autocue. Nevertheless he always kept them close by and put them on whenever he felt it necessary to make it clear that he was feeling deeply sympathetic and extremely concerned.

'Bruce Delamitri said you must be *relieved* to have uncovered hidden memories of emotional abuse?'

'Yes, he did.'

'How d'ya *like* that guy!'

'He said that it meant I was off the hook. That I could do what I liked – take drugs, sleep around, steal stuff, be a total loser – and none of it would be my fault because some hypnotherapist had granted me victim status. Can you believe somebody would say that? I cried all night.'

Dove twisted a handkerchief between her dainty fingers in anguish at this painful memory.

'Camera Four.' Deep within the control suite the editor issued his instructions. 'Extreme close-up on Dove's hands.'

Dale saw the shot cut up on her monitor and put her hand on top of Dove's.

'You're saying that Delamitri didn't believe your very real heartache was anything more than a ploy?'

'That's right. He asked me how much I'd paid my hypnotherapist and when I told him three thousand dollars he said it was peanuts.'

'Peanuts? Three thousand dollars?' said Oliver, who earned eight million a year. 'Well, I guess those Hollywood types never pretended to live down here in the real world with us ordinary folk, did they?'

'He said that a hundred thousand dollars would have been cheap. He said what price could you put on getting an excuse to screw up your life.'

'These guys just don't think the rules of common decency and good manners count for them, do they?'

'I guess not.'

'So what did you say?'

'I told him I had uncovered a deep and painful wound.'

'Way to go, Dove. Feisty stuff,' said Oliver. 'We'll be hearing more about Dove's deep and painful wound and millionaire Delamitri's cold indifference to her suffering after these messages.'

'Excess wind can blight your life,' said the sweet old lady standing in the park with her dogs.

'I have uncovered a deep and painful wound,' Dove said, attempting to fight her corner but making a pouty, sulky hash of it. She felt exposed and out of her depth. She did not really know how to handle men when they were not trying to sleep with her. Bruce just laughed. People were listening now but he didn't care. Having personally spouted bullshit to a billion people earlier in the evening, he was not going to put up with it from anyone else.

'Oh, I see,' he said. 'A deep and painful wound, but

not quite deep and painful enough for you to notice until you paid some guy thousands of dollars to point it out.'

'He didn't say that!' Dale said as Dove relived her terrible experience on the following morning.

'He did say it,' Dove protested. 'Everybody heard.'

'Let me get this straight here.' Oliver adjusted his glasses and peered at the imaginary notes he'd been making. 'He utterly denied the validity of the terrible emotional abuse you'd suffered? He accused you of making it up?'

'Yes, he did, Oliver.'

'Is that legal? I'm not sure that's even legal.' Oliver glanced about a bit. He liked to give the impression that behind the camera was a crack team of lawyers and researchers who would leap into action at the merest nod from the great man. In fact, behind the camera were a woman holding a powder brush and a woman holding a plastic cup full of water.

'So what did you do?' asked Dale. 'What did you say?'

'I said, "Mr Delamitri, just because you have made a lot of money exploiting the pain and suffering of others, that does not give you the right to exploit mine."'

'Way to go, girlfriend,' said Dale.

'Right on, sister,' said Oliver. 'We'll be back after this.'

'As a woman you have a right to firm, uplifted breasts, no matter what your age.'

Dove lied on *Coffee Time*. In reality she had not been so courageous. Actually she had just stood there, tears of confusion forming in her eyes, wondering why this man was being so *mean*.

'Anyway, what's a little pain?' Bruce said. 'I mean, what would you be without that pain?'

'Excuse me?' Dove sniffed.

'I'll tell you. You'd be the same pointless and self-indulgent idiot that God made you, but you wouldn't have anyone to blame it on.'

Dove was fighting back the tears now. What had gone wrong? People were supposed to cluck sympathetically when you told them about your emotional abuse, not emotionally abuse you.

'Take it easy, Bruce. You've had a couple.' An old friend of Bruce's tried to lead him away, having decided that both Bruce and the company that distributed his movies might regret this behaviour in the morning.

'And I shall tell you why I've had a couple,' Bruce answered triumphantly. 'Because I have an addictive personality, that's why. You know how I know? A court told me so. Oh yes it did, when I got busted for drink-driving. That was my plea. That's what I said. Not "I'm sorry your honour, I'm an irresponsible shit" but "I can't help it. I have an addictive personality". *I* drank the booze, *I* drove the car but it *wasn't my fault*! I had a problem you see and it saved me a prison term . . . Hey, Michael!'

A huge movie star was passing. He turned at Bruce's call, delighted to be hailed by someone of equal celebrity.

'Getting any at the moment?' Bruce enquired.

It was a cheap shot and it touched a nerve. The star had recently been exposed in the press as a serial adulterer. He turned away without further acknowledging Bruce.

'Addicted to sex,' Bruce explained to Dove. 'Did you read that? He said it to *Vanity Fair* after being caught in bed with various ladies to whom he was not married. He said he was addicted to sex. Not just a gutless, cheating little fuck-rat, you notice. No. A sex addict. He had a problem, so it was *not his fault.*'

A little crowd had gathered by now, which was a considerable relief to Dove. She was extremely pleased no longer to be the sole target of Bruce's anger.

'Nothing is anybody's fault. We don't do wrong, we have problems. We're victims, alcoholics, sexaholics. Do you know you can be a shopaholic? That's right. People aren't greedy any more, oh no. They're shopaholics, victims of commercialism. Victims! People don't fail any more. They experience negative success. We are building a culture of gutless, spineless, self-righteous, whining cry-babies who have an excuse for everything and take responsibility for nothing . . .'

'He mentioned shopaholics?' Oliver asked on the following morning. 'Do you think that possibly, in some weird, uncanny, unconscious way, he was connecting there with the Mall Murderers? After all, what are malls full of? Shops, right?'

'Right,' said Dove, but slightly hesitantly.

'And what are shops full of? Shopaholics!'

'And murderers,' Dale added helpfully.

'Exactly,' said Oliver. 'Maybe, in some weird, uncanny, unconscious way, Bruce Delamitri knew what was coming.'

'I am threatened by your attitude,' said Dove.

She could not have said a worse thing.

'Threatened? My God! So what? Who cares? I'm

crying here. We all feel threatened, babe. You should be threatened with a baseball bat sometime and get things into perspective. There was a time when if someone said something you didn't like you told them to shove it. Now you go to court and say you've been conversationally harassed.'

'Bruce, please.' His friend was still trying to calm him down, but Bruce wasn't talking to him, or to Dove. He was talking to Professor Chambers and Dale and Oliver and the MAD mothers and the two mad psychos who were out there somewhere, stealing his plots.

'Victims! Everyone is a fucking victim these days, and we've all got our victim-support groups. Blacks, whites, old, young, men, women, gays, straights. Everybody looking for an excuse to fail. Well, it'll kill us all, that's what it'll do. A society which defines its component groups by their weaknesses is going to die. We are losing more kids a year to violence than we did in the Vietnam war. But do we blame the violent people? No, we blame my fucking movies!'

'Go home, Bruce,' said his friend.

People were already drifting away. Dove had turned on her heel in disgust. His friend was right. It was Bruce's night but he'd spoilt it. He was bored and boring. He decided he should go.

Then he saw Brooke.

Through the glittering hordes, way, way out across the bosom shelf he saw her: Brooke Daniels. Coincidence or what? Synchronisity surely. Everybody has some special fantasy figure, a particular pop singer or actor that comes number one in the 'if you could have anyone for a night who would you have?' party game. Up until a couple of days before Bruce would probably have answered

Michelle Pfiefer in her Batwoman costume. Then he had happened to be glancing through a copy of Playboy Magazine at his agents office. Brooke had leapt instantly to the top of Bruce's league. And now here she was, in the flesh, looking even better without the creases and the staples.

'Excuse me,' he said to anybody who cared to hear it, and plunged into the crowd, pushing his way through to where the woman of some of his more recent dreams was talking to a small man in a hired tuxedo.

'Hi, pardon me for butting in but I won "Best Picture", so I can do what the hell I like.' All Bruce's angry petulance disappeared instantly and was replaced by his more familiar charm.

'Not at all, Mr Delamitri, and congratulations. I'm Brooke Daniels.' Brooke smiled, pulling back her shoulders the tiniest fraction in order to add further lift to her magnificent figure.

'I know who you are. I saw the *Playboy* spread – it was wonderful.'

'Thank you. I don't seem to be able to get away from that. I do acting too, you know.'

The little fellow in the borrowed tux shifted from one leg to the other, which was not a long journey.

Brooke remembered her manners. 'This is . . . I'm afraid I didn't catch your name.'

'Kevin.'

'Oh yes, of course, Kevin. This is Kevin. He's from Wales, in England. This is Bruce Delamitri, Kevin.'

'I know,' said Kevin. 'I saw *Ordinary Americans*. Bloody hell, I'm glad I didn't take my gran.'

There didn't seem to be an obvious answer to this, so Bruce didn't offer one. Brooke hastened to fill the silence that followed, feeling for some reason that the responsibilities of playing hostess lay with her.

'Kevin's a winner too, Bruce. "Best Foreign Animated Short". It's about a boy called Midget—'

'Widget,' Kevin corrected her.

'Yes, that's right,' said Brooke. 'And he has a pair of magic Y-fronts. What are Y-fronts, Kevin?'

'Underpants. They're called Y-fronts because they have an inverted Y on the front, which provides an orifice through which a bloke can poke his old fella.' Kevin hoped she'd find his British bluntness charming.

'Oh, I see.' It didn't look as if she did.

Bruce decided it was time to get rid of the Welshman. 'Wait a minute, you mean *you're* Kevin?' he said, light apparently suddenly dawning. 'The guy that makes the animated shorts? Jesus, are you a lucky guy! Sharon Stone is looking for you . . . Yes, that's right, she wants to talk about your Widget . . . No I'm not kidding . . . I don't know, maybe she likes Welsh guys, but she told me that when she saw your movie it made her nipples hard . . . That is what she said, word for word: it made her nipples hard . . . You'd better go talk to her.'

In a pub back home Kevin might have spotted that he was the victim of a less than elaborate hoax, but at the Governor's party? Talking to Bruce Delamitri? He *had* just won an Oscar, after all, so surely anything was possible, even the notion that the work of the Welsh Cartoon Collective (in association with the Arts Council of Great Britain, Channel Four Wales and some high street bank's Youth Initiative) could make Sharon Stone's nipples go hard. He thanked Bruce for the tip and scurried off.

'That was a little cruel, wasn't it?' Brooke enquired.

'No way. How many guys get to spend five minutes of their life believing Sharon Stone is interested in them?'

Bruce felt much better already. 'Great dress,' he volunteered, and of course what he meant was great body, the dress, such as it was, being merely what might be called garnish, or figure-dressing.

'Thanks. Bold, I'll admit, but it's tough to make an impact these days. Did you see the Baywatch Babes make an entrance? It was like silicone valley in earthquake season. It's getting so that the only women who get noticed are the tattooed lesbians from New Zealand.'

A little later they danced. It caused quite a stir, Bruce being nearly at the end of a very public divorce.

'Can I say something embarrassing?' Brooke asked.

'Sure.' Bruce hoped desperately she wasn't going to comment on the fact that he had been pushing his erection against her stomach for the past five minutes.

'I didn't see your picture. The one you got the Oscar for, *Ordinary Americans*.'

For some reason Bruce was pleased. 'That's OK, I don't insist. It's probably just as well, anyway. Maybe you'd have gone out and shot up a shopping mall.'

For a moment the bitter memory of his speech intruded on Bruce's burgeoning seduction. He forced such unhappy thoughts from his mind and concentrated on the extraordinary body he held in his arms.

For her own part, Brooke seemed to feel that some apology was called for. 'I can't imagine how I didn't get to see it.'

'Well, I guess you just never visited a movie theatre when it was playing . . .'

They danced for a moment in silence. Bruce had a thought. It was so long since he'd asked a girl to leave a party with him he'd been wondering how to broach the subject. Now Brooke had offered him the perfect opening.

'Maybe you'd like to see it now?'

'Now?'

'Sure. I have a print at the studio. We could grab some beers and dumb bits of cracker with blobs of caviare on them and go watch it on my editing machine.'

'My God, I've had guys ask me to the movies before, but this is the first time the guy with the Oscar offered me a private view. Quite a date.'

'So you'll come?'

'No, I have netball practice. Of course I'll come, for Christ's sake.'

'Great. I think you'll like the picture. One word of warning though: it does contain scenes of graphic violence.'

Chapter Twelve

INTERIOR. NIGHT. A 7–11 STORE.

A robbery is in progress. Terrified customers and staff lie on the floor with their hands on their heads. Standing over them are WAYNE and SCOUT, poor white trash murdering hoods on a killing spree. They are both heavily armed. Wayne is in his early twenties. He wears work boots, jeans and a torn vest, and has tattoos on his muscular arms. Scout is a waif-like girl in her late teens. She has on pink Doc Martens boots and a girlish little cotton summer dress. Clearly, there has already been a terrible incident: there is money scattered about everywhere, and two or three dead or dying people lie among the cowering customers. Wayne and Scout are both hysterically elated. He grips her to him.

                    WAYNE
               (SHOUTS WILDLY)
     I love you, sugar pie!

                    SCOUT
     I love you too, honey.

They embrace. A customer, a fat man lying face-down on the floor, still holding a half-eaten hamburger near his mouth, steals a glance at Wayne and Scout. Wayne is chewing on Scout's ear. Close-up on Wayne's face as he turns away from Scout's head to notice that the fat man is looking at him.

                    WAYNE
        You like to watch, fat boy?

The terrified man says nothing. His answer is to bury his face in the floor as hard as he can and wrap his arms around his head. Wayne's POV is now just the top of the man's balding head with his pudgy hand pressed against it, holding the half-chewed burger. There is a loud bang and a hole appears in the top of the bald head. Blood runs out as if from a tap, not a spurt but a silent, almost gentle, welling-up, a small flood, so to speak, which quickly forms a large pool, soaking into the hamburger and turning it completely red.

Cut back to Wayne, who is ignoring his victim completely, and is grinding his hips against Scout.

                    WAYNE
        Oh Sweet Jesus! Killing makes me horny! I'm going
        to screw you till your teeth rattle, baby.

Wayne's strong hands clutch at Scout's buttocks. It is almost as if his fingers will push through the flimsy cotton.

Cut to close-up of the dead fat man's hand gripping the blood-soaked burger. (NOTE: The impression should be that the burger and Scout's backside are just two different pieces of meat to be devoured by men.)

Cut back to full-length two shot of Wayne and Scout entwined in lust. Rock music is pumping in their heads and they seem almost to be dancing to it. If they are, it is a primitive, sexual dance, the dance of two wild animals caught between the two great life forces, survival and sex.

WAYNE

C'mon, sugar.

Wayne pulls Scout's dress up round her waist, revealing her panties, which are decorated with little hearts or cute cartoon characters. Despite her obvious sexual passion, Scout remains coy and childlike.

SCOUT

We are in a store, Wayne, a public place! We cain't do no lovin' right here now. There are people. They might see.

WAYNE

No problem, baby doll.

Wayne releases Scout and turns his machine-gun on the prostrate forms. They jolt like puppets as the bullets thud into them. Screams fill the air.
We cut to a series of close-ups.
A mother hugging a child hugging a doll, all suddenly riddled with bullets.
A businessman weeping as he dies.
A poster featuring a happy family shopping and saying, 'If you have a problem please ask our staff if they can help.'
A very wide shot of the whole store, a scene of bloody carnage with Wayne in the middle of it all, triumphantly spraying bullets. The muscles and veins on his brawny arms are taut with the tension of controlling the spitting machine-gun.
Close-up of Scout. She is staring at Wayne, transfixed with adoration. The shooting finally subsides.

WAYNE

Ain't no people now, cotton candy, leastways not any going to get offended none.

SCOUT
Oh Wayne, I surely do love you.

Scout embraces Wayne. One slender, coltish leg, fragile-looking and
vulnerable despite the big boots she wears, winds about him as she
reaches up an arm to draw Wayne's face to hers.

Chapter Thirteen

INTERIOR. NIGHT. THE LIVING AREA OF A RICH CALIFORNIAN HOME.

A beautiful but rather impersonal interior of vast white couches, glass and steel tables and shelves. Clearly whoever lives here had the place designed for them. Wayne and Scout stand in the middle of the room. Their cheap, dirty, blood-stained clothes are in stark contrast to the cold pastel colours that surround them. They are hot and high with excitement. They have recently broken in and Scout is staring in wonder at this opulence. They both carry machine-guns and have more weapons hanging from them.
Cut from the wide to a mid two shot as Wayne kisses Scout tenderly on the forehead.

> WAYNE
> (Sudden exuberant shout)
> Ain't nothing like killing, Scout. I done it all in my time, stock cars, broncos, gambling, stealing and I am here to tell you that there ain't nothing to touch the thrill of killing.

Close-up on Scout. Her eyes are closed; she is drinking in the
atmosphere.

> SCOUT
> Don't shout, Wayne. I was just enjoying the peace.
> Isn't it a beautiful home? Don't you just love the silk
> cushions and glass coffee tables and all?

Scout kicks off her shoes and walks about.
Close-up of her feet luxuriating in the thick carpet and rugs.
Pan up her legs. Her hands are against her thighs, playing nervously
with her dress. She absently pulls the skirt up a little. We see bruising
on her thigh.
Two shot. Wayne and Scout.

> WAYNE
> You know why they have those glass coffee tables,
> precious? You want to know why they have them?

> SCOUT
> So's they can put their coffee down, Wayne.

> WAYNE
> No it ain't, baby. It's so they can get underneath and
> watch each other take a dump.

Close-up on Scout, her jaw dropping in astonishment.

> WAYNE
> Yes it is, honey. I read that. It sure is.

Wide shot of room. Wayne has thrown himself on to a vast couch,
his big booted feet up on the table under discussion. His comments
have completely deflated Scout. She is very volatile; tears show in
her eyes.

SCOUT

That is not so, Wayne! It is just not so and I do not want to hear about it. Just when everything is nice, you have to start on about people going to the bathroom on their coffee tables.

WAYNE

That's the real world, honey. It's weird. People are weird – they ain't all nice like you and me. Aw c'mon, sugar, don't feel bad. I feel good. Do you feel good, baby doll?

Scout's moods change with alarming speed.

SCOUT

Yeah, I feel good, Wayne.

WAYNE

I always feel good after I kill a whole bunch of muthas. It's like a pick me up, you know. They should make a commercial . . . like for Alka Seltzer.

Close-up on Wayne.

WAYNE

Feeling low? Dull? Shitty? Don't waste a minute. Burn some muthafucka's ass. You'll feel great.

Pull out to two shot. Wayne is laughing at his fantasy.

WAYNE

You know what Dr Kissinger said, baby?

SCOUT

You didn't tell me you'd seen no doctor, honey.

Scout flops down beside Wayne on the couch. Her dress rides up; again we see the bruising, this time from Wayne's POV. He can not avoid seeing it. Embarrassed, Scout quickly pulls her skirt over it.

> WAYNE
>
> He wasn't no real doctor, he was the Secretary of State. A powerful man, killed a whole lot more people than we ever will, not matter how hard we try. Well, you know what he said? He said that power was an aphrodisiac, which means it gets you horny.

> SCOUT
>
> I know what an aphrodisiac is, honey.

> WAYNE
>
> Well, you ain't never gonna get more power over a person than when you kill them, so I guess killing is an aphrodisiac too.

> SCOUT
>
> I guess so, honey.

A joke occurs to Wayne. He sits up in excitement, which means he has to move the gun on his lap. Moving it makes a harsh metallic sound.

> WAYNE
>
> And get this, baby doll … if you kill a black guy, it's an Afro-American-disiac!

Wayne falls back, laughing, into the thick cushions. He makes himself more comfortable on the couch.

SCOUT

I don't know what you're talking about, honey, but you keep your dirty boots off that couch and be careful of all that blood on your pants. This is a nice house and I'll bet the people who own it are real nice people and we don't want to get no blood on their couch.

WAYNE

The blood is dry, pussycat. Blood dries real quick on account of it congeals. You know what, honey? If your blood didn't congeal you could die from just one little pinprick.

SCOUT

I know that, Wayne.

WAYNE

And you would be what is known as a homophobic.

SCOUT

Honey, a homophobic is a person who does not approve of carnal knowledge between a man and a person of the same sex. I believe you're thinking of a haemophiliac.

Sharp zoom in to close-up on Wayne. His change of expression is as fast as the camera movement. His face has turned from happy to sullen and sinister. Scout knows the signs.
Close-up on Scout, she attempts a casual smile.
Close-up on her hand, which is shaking.
Two shot.

WAYNE
(With ill-concealed menace)
Is that so?

                         SCOUT
                (A pitiable attempt to be casual)
          Yes, honey, it is.

                         WAYNE
          Is that so?

                         SCOUT
                    (Shaking now)
          I believe it is, honey.

In a sudden lunge Wayne grabs Scout by the neck with one hand and,
dropping the gun, pulls back his other hand, clenched into a fist and
ready to strike.

                         WAYNE
          And what d'you call a woman whose mouth is too
          damn smart, huh? A woman with a busted fucking
          lip, that's what.

Wayne pushes Scout off the couch and on to the floor. She
screams.

                         SCOUT
          No! Please, Wayne, don't!

Wayne drops off the couch on to Scout, straddling her on his knees.
Again he grabs her neck, ready to strike. Close-up on his fingers digging
into her neck.
Pan up from Wayne's fingers on Scout's neck to close-up on her face,
mouth gasping for air, eyes making a terrified mute appeal.
Scout's POV of Wayne's face directly above her, staring down, face
contorted with fury.

WAYNE
You think I'm dumb, sugar? Is that it? Maybe we'd
better see if your blood congeals!

Scout screams in terror.
Two shot. Wayne sits across Scout. It seems that he will beat her.
Instead he kisses her passionately. After a moment Scout returns the
kiss and embraces him.

SCOUT
Oh honey, you scared me.

WAYNE
I know that, cotton candy. I love to scare you,
because you're just like a little bird when you're
scared.

Now it becomes sexual. Wayne stretches out on top of Scout and
begins to kiss his way down her body.

WAYNE
(Through his kisses)
You like to live in a house like this, cotton candy?

SCOUT
Oh yeah, sure. Like I'm ever going to get the
chance.

WAYNE
We're living in it now, ain't we honey? I'll bet they've
got a real big old bed up them stairs. Stairway
to heaven.

Wayne is beginning to undo Scout's dress.

                    WAYNE
How about it, cherry pie? How about we go upstairs
and make some noise?

Scout pulls herself away and sits up.

                    SCOUT
I ain't doing no stuff in no stranger's bed, Wayne ...
Could be we'd catch Aids or something.

                    WAYNE
You can't catch Aids offa no sheets.

                    SCOUT
If they're dirty sheets, if they're stained.

                    WAYNE
Honey plum, these people are millionaires, billion-
aires even. They ain't going to have no stained sheets.
Besides which, even if they did you couldn't catch no
Aids offa them 'less you put them in the liquidizer
and injected them directly into your body! Now
I bet these people have satin and silk, and I do
not often get the chance to fuck my little girl on
satin and silk.

                    SCOUT
We do not ...
                    (She spells it out)
... F–U–C–K, we make love, and I don't care if
you're coming at me from behind in the restroom
of a greasy spoon, it's still making love and if it ain't
making love we ain't doing it no more because I do
not fuck.

Wayne nuzzles up to Scout. Close two shot.

WAYNE

You're right, honey, I stand corrected. And right now
I'm just about bustin' to make love your brains out.
So come on, honey.

Wayne draws Scout to him. Her resistance is weakening. His lips are
now at her ear. Close two shot.

WAYNE

Let's have us a party. I'll bet they've got a water
bed and a mirror on the ceiling and everything ...
You know something, baby girl? When I get a hold
of your ass, I guess I wouldn't let go of it to pick up
a hundred-dollar bill and a case of cold beer.

SCOUT

Oh Wayne, you know I can't resist your sweet-
talking.

WAYNE

Well, you don't have to, honey.

Wide shot. Wayne gets up and slings the various weapons over his
shoulder. Then he gathers Scout up in his arms. We linger briefly on the
tension in his impressive muscles. He carries her out of the room.

Chapter Fourteen

The first thing that struck Brooke as Bruce ushered her into the lounge of his fabulous Hollywood home was how designed it looked. It was beautiful but completely impersonal with its vast white couches, glass and steel tables and shelves sparsely decorated with extremely costly *objets d'art*. Like an enormous and incredibly expensive hotel. Brooke loved it.

The truth was that in the previous three or four years Bruce's workload had been so high and his ascendance so meteoric that he had had no time at all to arrange his personal life. He still owned his old apartment off Melrose Avenue, and in it were all his old framed movie posters and stuff like his *Star Wars* space gun. But it was just gathering dust. Perhaps one day he would move it all and re-personalize his world, but for the time being he was happy simply to decide upon a price and purchase a lifestyle appropriate to his rising status. Farrah, his nearly ex-wife, who had previously provided Bruce with the semblance of a private life, had long since tired of being married to a workaholic movie nut. She had retreated from his world, taking most of their stuff (which was hers anyway) and their daughter with him.

Bruce had never been very interested in personal lifestyle. Even as a student he had been famous for owning only one pair of jeans and one saucepan. He had always put all his huge creative energies into his work. There was none to spare for picking out cushion covers or visiting kitchenware shops. All Bruce required from a home was somewhere to wash and sleep. Of course, the more luxurious it was the better, and with his current abode he had pretty much reached the pinnacle of luxury. As far as he was concerned, he would be happy to stay exactly where he was for ever.

He was not going to get the chance.

The first thing he should have noticed as he followed Brooke into the room was a pair of pink Doc Martens boots lying on the carpet, boots that had not been there when he had left the house that morning. He should have spotted them instantly; there should have been a fast zoom to a close-up on the boots, and a sinister musical sting to inform him that things were terribly and dangerously amiss. But there was no sting and no close-up. Bruce scarcely registered the boots and remained oblivious of the fact that their presence indicated he was in very big trouble.

In the brief moment of thought he gave them, he imagined that they must be the property of his fourteen-year-old daughter, left under a couch on some past visit and only now dislodged by the cleaner. He kicked them back out of sight. The last thing a man wants in mid-seduction is to be reminded that the object of his lust is only a few years older than his own child.

Mid-seduction? Hardly. He hadn't even started yet and the sun was already up. He would have to get a move on.

A boyish grin, a nervous half-smile.

Extreme close-up on girl's lips.

Lips part slightly, revealing white teeth teased by tip of tongue.

Fuck music plays. Bang, they are at it like rabbits on E.

Not quite. Even Oscar-winning directors can't edit reality. The dull pre-sex preamble had to be gone through, and there was not a great deal of time to do it in. It was Bruce's own fault that they were so late. It was he who had suggested that they watch *Ordinary Americans*, a two-hour picture, and they had sat through the whole thing.

It had been worth it, though, there was no doubt about that, a real ego buzz. There is nothing quite like having a gorgeous girl gasp at your masterpiece. Brooke had loved his film, or at least she had professed to – and done so with sufficient conviction to satisfy Bruce. It had been a very curious sensation, sitting beside this girl, all wound up to make a move on her but not wanting to disturb her enjoyment of his great work. Which would be more exciting, hearing her gasp at his powers as a director or at his powers as a lover? Every time he had got himself ready to chance brushing a gentle kiss along her delectable bare shoulders, those same shoulders shook with mirth at one of the many dazzlingly witty ironic juxtapositions of image and dialogue with which the movie was peppered. Every time he was ready to slide an arm round her or 'accidentally' lay his hand on top of hers, the movie arrived at another of his favourite bits and he had to stop to let her concentrate.

Bruce had lots of favourite bits and vanity had been stronger than desire. He had let her watch the whole movie unmolested. Hence the lateness of the hour, the coldness of the approaching dawn and the fact that he was not even at the proverbial first base. He cursed himself for not having made a shorter film. He had always thought about cutting the discotheque sequence; after all seventies kitsch had been done and double-done. On the other hand, it was such a funny scene, the way the guy kept getting more and more stains on his white Travolta suit, first food, then wine, then puke and finally his own blood. Classic stuff. You couldn't cut it; it would have been a crime. Still, it had added eight minutes to the movie. Eight minutes in which he could have been making love to his favourite ever *Playboy* centrefold.

The movie had finally come to an end, however, and they were back at his home. It was time to make a move.

'It really is a wonderful picture,' Brooke said.

She had said it a hundred times already. She knew it and he knew it. The awkward pre-sex atmosphere had led them into one of those circular conversations in which nobody can think of anything to say and so instead they continually retread ground already covered.

'I can't believe you sat and watched the whole thing on an editing machine. That shows real dedication.' Bruce, too, had ploughed this furrow many times.

'Well, you know, like I say, it's such a wonderful movie,' Brooke said again.

'Well, I'm delighted you think so, but it still shows

real dedication to have watched the whole thing like that . . . and on an editing machine.'

Brooke simply could not bring herself to comment further on the wonderfulness of the movie. They lapsed into silence.

Bruce looked at his watch. 'Shit! It's nearly four a.m.' It wasn't meant to come out like that, but he hadn't realized it was quite so late. 'I thought it was about two thirty.'

'Is that a problem?' Brooke enquired. 'Did you have anything planned?'

'I'm afraid so. My wife will be here at nine.'

This was disappointing news. Brooke had not been one hundred per cent sure what she wanted when she accepted Bruce's invitation to come home, but meeting estranged spouses certainly wasn't it.

'I thought you said your divorce came through.'

It is true that Bruce had said this, in the car, as they left the Governor's party. It hadn't really been a lie. The whole world knew that he and his wife had parted irrevocably, and the thing really would be final in a day or two.

'We are, practically. That's why she's coming round – money stuff.'

Brooke shrugged. 'Oscar at night, alimony in the morning: life in the Hollywood fast lane.'

There was an uncomfortable pause. How could there not be? Two strangers already dealing with the difficult problems of whether to go to bed together and if so how to get to it, and now this. As chat-up lines go, 'My wife will be round in a couple of hours' is only one step from 'I am a regular drug-user and I always share needles'.

'Oh well . . .' said Brooke. 'It's been a lovely night.'

He had not even offered her a seat. They were both still standing, looking at each other across a vast couch.

'You really think so?' Weak, so weak. He had meant it to sound boyishly anxious, nervous and attractive, but it hadn't. How much better to have said, 'It could get lovelier' or 'Not as lovely as you' or even 'Never mind that, how about a fuck?' But no: 'You really think so?' Pathetic. For a moment Bruce recalled 'I stand here on legs of fire', and the erection that had been straining in his trousers for the previous three or four hours took a momentary dive.

Brooke was beginning to feel a little out of sorts herself. This big man, this Oscar-winning king of cool wearing pointy boots and Bogart's tux was just standing there. What did he expect? Was she supposed to offer herself unasked? Was it a power thing? Maybe he thought a bit of polite small-talk was beneath him. Maybe babes were expected just to climb aboard.

'Yes, I do think so. It's been a lovely night.'

This was absurd. She said something dumb, he said is that so? and she said yes, it was so. How long could they keep this up?

Brooke summoned up all her powers of imagination in an effort to advance the dialogue. 'Kind of like a first date. You know, we had a dance, we saw a movie . . .'

'That's a nice thought. It's been a long time since I had a first date.'

They were getting there.

'Me neither,' Brooke agreed, and then, after a tiny pause, she looked him in the eye and said, 'Brings back the old first-date question, doesn't it? How far do you go on them?' Well she couldn't do any more than that.

Not without actually taking off her clothes. Now it was up to him.

'So . . . What's the answer to that, then?'

She was annoyed. She certainly was not going to beg him to make a move on her. He had picked her up at the party, he had brought her to his home. He had to make some of the running, if only for form's sake.

'Well the rule in school was the boy gets a feel of the boobs but only from outside the bra.' Her voice showed traces of the irritation she felt. 'These days I tend to think the rule depends on the guy.'

She sat down. Bruce had still not offered her a seat but she sat anyway. Elegantly, beautifully, a vision. She crossed her legs and Bruce took a personal close-up on the slashed skirt of her dress falling either side of her knees.

'Nice table,' she said, studying her reflection in the shiny glass.

'I like it.'

'I can think of a good use for it,' said Brooke.

'Help yourself.'

She took some cocaine out of her bag and began to chop it up on the table. 'Just to keep you bright and cheery for your wife,' she said pointedly.

Belatedly Bruce recalled his duties as a host. He put on some music and fixed a couple of drinks. Now he was getting somewhere. He sat down beside her.

'It's so great that you liked my movie.'

Back on the damn movie. How the hell did that happen?

'It really means a lot to me.'

He said it quickly, trying to coat his boring platitude in a cloak of sincerity. It sounded *so* lame. After all, he'd only known this woman for four or five hours and here he was trying to suggest that they had some kind of intellectual bond. 'It really means a lot to me.' Oh yeah? Why? He'd just won an Oscar, the entire industry had come together to honour him, and here he was trying to tell a nude model he'd picked up at the party that her opinion was of particular significance to him. Of course, Brooke knew he was bullshitting, and he knew she knew.

'There was one thing I didn't like about your movie,' she said.

Bruce sighed to himself. He had provoked this gorgeous creature into feeling she had to justify herself intellectually. He'd told her that her opinions mattered to him and they both knew she'd had offered no opinion at all beyond 'neat movie'. Now she was obliged to think one up. He would have to sit through some desperate, second-hand, pseudo art-babble about derivative imagery, or some such thing, culled from the cover of last month's *Premiere*.

'Here it comes,' said Bruce trying to affect good-humoured indulgence. 'I knew your enthusiasm was too good to last. What's the beef?'

'I didn't like the sex scene.'

That surprised him. 'What are you, a nun? That was the sexiest scene I ever made. I edited it with a permanent erection.'

Brooke shrugged and took a sniff at one of the little white lines on the table. 'Sure it was sexy, sort of. But it wasn't true. Everything else in the movie was so real – the guns, the attitude, the blood all over everything, the guy's skull exploding when that big statue of Mickey Mouse fell on his head . . .'

'That's my favourite scene, by the way, because it's all about irony.'

Brooke handed Bruce the straw and he too took a sniff.

'So why couldn't the sex be real too?' she asked. 'The only place overacting is still encouraged is in sex scenes. Did you ever see *Nine and a Half Weeks*? Jesus, you only had to tap that woman on the shoulder and she had an orgasm. Why can't the sex be convincing? Convincing is sexy. Girls wear pantyhose, you know, not stockings. When they get laid they have to take off their tights. I never saw a girl take off pantyhose in a movie.'

'That, I'm afraid my dear, is because pantyhose is not sexy. It is impossible to remove pantyhose in a sexy manner.' Bruce rather regretted the 'my dear'. It was verging on rude and Brooke was, after all, his guest. But really! Trying to tell him how to make movie.

Brooke snorted up the last of the lines and stared at Bruce for a moment. He wondered if she was going to ask him to call a cab. Instead she got up off the couch, stood before him and, to his astonishment, began to dance. The music was sexy and the lights were low and she was dancing. In fact it was more an undulation than a dance, a kind of slow shiver that seemed to go up her body from her toes to her head and then slowly down again.

'Wow,' said Bruce.

The standard of his conversation was actually deteriorating, but Brooke no longer seemed to care. She was into her own agenda. Her hands were on her thighs now, slowly massaging the exquisite creamy material of her dress, her long fingers gently clawing at the cloth, ruffling it up against her legs before letting it fall back into place. Except it did not fall quite back because she retained a little of the dress beneath the palms of her hands, pressed as they were against the splendid outline of her thighs. Bruce realized that bit by bit, a centimetre or two at a time, Brooke was drawing up the long skirt of her dress, very slowly revealing her legs. And such legs. Bruce was entranced as shapely ankle gave way to shapely calf, then delightful knees and on, up past her equally exquisite thighs. It must have taken her more than five minutes to bring the skirt up to her panty line. Somehow she contrived to collect the folds of the material about her hips in a bouquet-like cluster, and it looked for a moment as if she was wearing a ra-ra skirt, or a rather flamboyant tutu. Then in one quick movement, almost a jerk, she brought the handfuls of cloth right up high, pulling the folds of skirt to just under her breasts, revealing all of her pantyhose and some of her bare midriff besides. Her hose was, of course, of finest quality. No ladders or frayed gussets here. High-waisted, covering Brooke's whole stomach (such as there was of it), ending a few inches below her ribs in a wide black, delicately embroidered waistband. Her whole lower body was now on show, from diaphragm, down past her navel to the shadowy half-hidden panties, her long legs and on down to the silver stilettos she wore. All encased in sheer black nylon splendour. Above all of which she held her dress in great silky folds. Not necessarily a very elegant pose, but undeniably sexy. The look on her face was slightly sullen, almost indifferent. Her legs were four-square, feet about nine inches apart. She seemed to be saying, 'This is what I've got. Do you want it?' A bad little girl showing you hers.

Now she had her thumbs under the waistband of her

hose and was pulling the material slightly away from her soft skin. Still contriving to hold up her dress, she began slowly, fold by fold, to wind her pantyhose downwards, not pulling, or tugging, but neatly peeling them floorwards, with elegant thumb and finger, one fold over another. The whiteness of her belly appeared first, followed by more black, the black of her panties, then white again as the very tops of her legs appeared, and then more perfect skin as the hose descended.

She stopped for a moment.

'Go on, please!' croaked Bruce. He couldn't remember the last time he'd seen anything so erotic.

Brooke raised one glorious limb and put her foot on the glass table. This caused the hose, which were now pulled down to a few inches below her crutch, to stretch out taut between her thighs, lending the tiniest suggestion of bondage and constraint to her sultry pose.

Her stiletto heel made a sharp tap on the table top. 'Unbuckle it,' she instructed Bruce. Her voice was cold and firm: it was an order. Bruce leant forward, his stomach pushing down on the top of his frankly spectacular erection, and did as he was bidden. The movement brought him so close to the partly revealed tops of Brooke's thighs, crowned as they were by the bouquet of her dress, that he wondered for a moment about kissing the exposed flesh. He resisted the urge. She was in control. She would tell him what to do. Brooke brought the unbuckled shoe back to the ground, and with equal balance and elegance raised her other leg.

'Again,' she snapped. Again he obeyed.

She kicked off her silver stilettos and stood for a moment on the rug, holding her dress and the folded top of her pantyhose before folding the latter a little bit further towards her knees. Her arms were now at full stretch, so she could lower her hose no further by this method.

She sat down. In one athletic movement, she lowered herself to the floor, simultaneously pulling her tights down to her knees. As her bottom touched the soft carpet she continued her movement, rolling over on to her back, and bringing her knees up to her chest. Keeping her thumbs in the band of the tights all the while, she released her dress, letting its folds fall back on to her and on to the floor around her. Her backside pointed straight at Bruce like the centre of a silk flower. For fully fifteen seconds she let him stare at the triangle of black panties that separated the flesh of her rear upper thighs from the flesh of the small of her back as it curled down into the folds of her dress on the carpet.

Then the endgame. Still lying on her back, and keeping her knees close to her chest, she rolled the tights down past her calves to her ankles and along her feet until they covered only her toes, which pointed seductively at Bruce above the eye magnet of her knicker-covered bottom. One final push on the tights and they fell down past her backside and lay crumpled on the carpet beneath the black triangle. In the same movement her long white legs shot upwards until they pointed straight and true towards the ceiling. Still lying on her back Brook gently parted her legs to make a glorious upright V through which, by raising her head, she could see Bruce.

She smiled, lowered her legs and, picking up the tights, got to her feet. Her toes clenched at the luxury of the carpet. She took a step towards Bruce and dropped the still-warm hose into his lap.

'So?'

Bruce did his best to say something cool and classy. 'So I hope you don't expect me to be that good with my socks.'

It was certainly better than might have been expected on the basis of his previous form.

Bruce drew Brooke towards him on to the couch and they drifted into an embrace. Within moments all the pent-up sexual tension of the evening seemed to explode. Their mouths writhed against each other. Cool seduction was replaced by hot, lustful passion.

Then Brooke broke away. 'Let me get some protection.'

She reached down to her handbag and for a moment Bruce imagined himself in love. What a woman! He had just been wondering, himself, how to bring up the subject of protection, and here she was, all ready and prepared, doing it for him.

However, when her hand emerged from the chic little bag it was holding not a packet of condoms but a small hand gun.

Chapter Fifteen

'Touch me again you bastard, I swear I'll kill you.'

Bruce leapt away from Brooke as if she had pulled the trigger and it was a bullet rather than sheer shock that thrust him backwards against the arm of the couch.

She glared at him, he glared at the barrel of her gun. What the hell was going on? Had he transgressed some new pre-sex rule? Was he guilty of attempted date rape? He had heard of such things of course, horror stories of college boys who had attempted to follow a goodnight kiss with a hand up the jumper and the next morning had found themselves the subject of a poster hate campaign all over campus. But come on. The woman had just removed her pantyhose in front of him. That had to be an invitation, hadn't it? Maybe not. Oh Christ, maybe not. If a woman hoicks up her dress and flashes her knickers at you, does it mean 'yes' or 'perhaps' or even 'no'? Should he have waited for a formal invitation? Should he have asked her to state her sexual requirements, if any, clearly and concisely? Should he have got it in writing?

'Listen, Brooke . . . please, I'm sorry, but . . . but . . . what's going on?'

'You think just because I'm a model I'm some kind of whore?'

'No! My God no! Of course I don't. I . . . I . . . Look, if I've misunderstood the situation I'm very sorry. But really . . . I mean . . . I thought—'

'I know what you thought, prick-for-brains!' Brooke's trigger knuckle whitened. 'You looked at me and you saw sex, right? From the first fucking second we met I've been just a piece of meat as far as you're concerned. Well, you're going to pay, you bastard.'

She was mad, Bruce knew that. Not just angry or hysterical, not just perversely politicized in an aggressive and unpredictable manner, but stark raving *tonto*. Unbalanced like the global economy was unbalanced, or a seesaw competition between a mouse and an overweight elephant. She must be mad. It was the only explanation. Their whole evening had been one of mutual compliance, Bruce knew there was no way he could be accused of forcing the issue. He hadn't got her drunk or used his superior body weight to coerce her or done any of the other things that were apparently unacceptable to do to a woman unless you were a lesbian. No, this woman was crackers. A mad bitch of the 'seduction is just rape with champagne and chocolates' variety. But what do you do when a lunatic is pointing a gun at you? What do you say?

'Please, Brooke, please, this is not necessary.'

He was trying to turn his eyes into limpid pools of calm and compassion. It didn't seem to be working.

'Kiss my fucking feet, muthfukka!' she shouted. Screamed, in fact. Her voice cracked with forced volume so that the 'fucker' ended up a rasping squeak – which in no way diminished its furious power.

Kiss her feet? Bruce had to concentrate. Of course he must kiss her feet immediately, but how did she want them kissed? Hard? Soft? Should he take one gently in his hand and turn his lips into tiny butterflies fluttering all over them from toe to ankle? Should he prostrate himself before her and suck her toes like a hungry animal at its mother's teat? If he let his tongue explore between the digits, would that make her melt and lower the gun or would it add flames to her fury and cause her to lose what was left of her fragile self-control?

'I said kiss my fucking feet!' Brooke demanded again.

Bruce dropped to his knees without any particular plan of approach in mind and nuzzled vaguely at her toes.

'I said kiss 'em, not wipe your nose on them,' she barked.

He attempted to raise his game. He kissed her big toe, then her little toe, then he kissed them all in a row, one by one. What next? Back again? He kissed back down the row. Then maybe repeat the whole process on the other foot? He did that. Then he did the whole thing again.

That was it. He had kissed her toes. He was at a loss how to proceed. 'Would you like me to lick them?' he asked tentatively.

'Don't make me puke.'

Bruce's neck was beginning to ache. He went through his kissing routine again but after that he did nothing. What could he do? He listened to Brooke's breathing, trying to get a clue to her mood. Was it getting calmer?

Could she be reasoned with? Could he somehow win her confidence, her trust, ingratiate himself? He had to be very calm and kind. Flattering even.

'What do you want, you mad fucking bitch?'

It wasn't meant to come out that way. Fear had blocked up his brain. He cringed on the floor, waiting for the punishment which must be his.

'Are you scared?' he heard her say.

What a question. 'Yes, I'm scared.'

'How scared?'

'Very' – pause – 'fucking' – pause – 'scared.'

'Good' was all she replied.

Bruce's neck was really aching now. 'Look, Brooke, please tell me what you want.'

Brooke removed her foot from under Bruce's lips. He could sense her kneeling down in front of him. Her hand appeared under his chin and gently brought his head up until he could look her in the eye again. What now?

'I . . . want' – her eye was steady but he could feel her hand shaking under his chin – 'a . . . a part in your next movie.'

It took a moment to sink in. It wasn't until he took an extreme close-up on the nervous look in her eyes that he started to believe it.

'Put away your gun,' he said, by way of a tester.

Brooke put her gun back into her handbag. It was obvious that she really was nervous now: her hand was shaking.

Bruce was nearly speechless. Not quite, however. 'You mad, crazy fucking bitch!' he shouted.

It was Brooke's turn to be scared. Bruce's fury was only just beginning, but clearly when it erupted fully it would be mighty indeed. She had to talk fast.

'Your pictures make people horny and scared. What did I just do to you? Come on, be honest. I did it all in half an hour, first horny, then scared.'

'Pamela Anderson makes me horny, Pat Buchanan makes me scared. I'm not going to put either of them in my movie.' Bruce couldn't believe he was even bothering to debate with this outrageous woman. 'You made me kiss your feet! At gunpoint! I ought to call the cops!'

'I've sent you fifty letters. Fifty! Did you see them? Did you read them?'

'Have you any idea how many actresses and models write to me? I don't see any of that stuff. I have people.'

'Yeah, I guessed you didn't. That's why I decided to do what I did. I'm just a dumb model. Nobody would take me seriously as an actress.'

It dawned on Bruce that he had been playing patsy for the last five hours. 'Have you been planning this all along?'

'No. It occurred to me while we were watching *Ordinary Americans*. I had seen the film before by the way, five times, but I said I hadn't because I wanted to look cool.'

'Well you don't, you look fucking insane. I ought to throw you out.'

'I made you horny and I made you frightened. Be fair – I did. Give me a chance.'

Bruce looked at her, barefoot, scared, breasts heaving with the tension of her own audacity. It was true. She had made him horny, she was, after all, spectacularly attractive, and she sure had frightened him.

'Supposing I said it depended on your sleeping with me?'

'No,' Brooke replied. 'I don't screw on a professional basis.'

'Pity.'

Bruce was not a dishonourable man. Having made the pass, he knew he had in a way committed himself. Besides he didn't want to look cheap.

'OK, I'll give you a screen test anyway. Maybe you're half as good as you think you are. Have your agent call me next week. Believe me, there is no chance that I will forget you.'

'Thank you, Bruce, thank you very much. I promise I won't disappoint you.'

'You can't disappoint me any more than you already have. I'll call you a cab.'

'What's the rush? We still have some hours before your wife gets here.'

'But you said . . .'

'I said I didn't screw on a professional basis. I already got my screen test.'

Bruce wondered for a moment if it was another trick. You don't get over the kind of shock he'd had in a moment. If he embraced her, would he suddenly find himself with a knife at his throat? Brooke could see he was hesitating. She stepped forward, took his arms, folded them behind her and turned her face up towards his. Bruce hesitated no longer and within a moment they were welded together like an old steamboat. It was a great relief for both of them finally to reach the point towards which the whole evening had been heading. Bruce crushed his chest against hers, she crushed her thighs against his. Inevitably they lost their balance, but they didn't care because the huge couch was ready to take their fall.

Now their lovemaking could begin in earnest. Bruce was on top of Brooke, his hands kneading her breasts through the delicate fabric of her gown. He could feel her nipples hardening and slipped his fingers beneath the silk in order to tease them further. Brooke had one hand on Bruce's behind and one thrust down between their bodies, struggling at his fly zipper.

Close-up on Brooke's face.
Her expression changes from passionate lust to shock mixed with horror. (She is staring upwards, past Bruce's head, the back of which occupies the corner of the shot.)

BROOKE
(Struggling to maintain her calm)
Bruce ... Bruce ... For Christ's sake, Bruce.

Whip pan to take in Brooke's POV. Bruce's face is in the foreground of shot. Over his shoulder we can see Wayne standing behind him, an automatic weapon balanced casually on his shoulder. Bruce is unaware of Wayne.

BRUCE
Listen, Brooke, I really don't think I can handle any
more of your games. Are we going to make love
or do I call you a cab?

Bruce's head drops out of shot as he leans down to kiss Brooke's bosom. Wayne stands alone in the vacated shot which is Brooke's POV. He smiles and gives her a little wink.
Overhead three shot. Bruce on top of Brooke, Wayne standing over them both. Bruce is the only thing moving. Brooke is staring at Wayne, Wayne is looking back. Bruce's back and back of head writhe about a little as he nuzzles into Brooke's cleavage. Brooke finds her voice.

> BROOKE

Bruce. For Christ's sake. Behind you.

Bruce raises his head to address Brooke. Close-up on his face, chin
and cheeks, framed by Brooke's cleavage.

> BRUCE

Sure, honey, sure.

A voice intrudes upon his complacency. It is Wayne's.

> WAYNE

Morning, folks.

Chapter Sixteen

B ruce swung round and recoiled. In doing so he dug
an elbow into Brooke's stomach. She yelped in pain.
Despite the terror of the situation she could not help but
protest: 'Be careful, for Christ's sake.'

Bruce didn't apologize – he was too surprised, too
scared. He allowed himself a momentary crumb of hope.
'Brooke, do you know this guy? Is this part of your joke
thing?' But even as he said it, he knew that this was
no joke.

'I do not know this man, Bruce.' Brooke's voice
betrayed her status as his partner in terror.

Neither she nor Bruce could think of anything more to
say. The three of them just stared at each other. Wayne
brought the gun down from his shoulder so that it hung
casually from his hand, pointing towards the luxurious
rug. He had a pistol stuck in the waistband of his jeans
and another machine-gun slung across his back; he also
had a huge hunting knife at his belt. So heavily armed
was he that it would not have surprised a casual observer

to be told that he had a hand grenade clamped between his buttocks, a bazooka lodged behind his ear and the nuclear button hidden in the holdall he carried in his non-gun hand.

Wayne took a step towards the couch and, leaning over, stared hard at Bruce. He put his face right into Bruce's, drinking in every detail at extremely close quarters. Bruce held his ground, but he had never in his life felt so uncomfortable or so intimidated.

After what seemed like a whole minute (which it was), Wayne whistled slowly, as if unable to believe what he saw.

'I don't believe this. I do not be-fuckin'-lieve this! Sheeee-IT!' Wayne exclaimed, shouting the final expletive as he turned away from Bruce in his wonderment. 'I mean I knew it was the right house n' all on account of the scripts and stuff in your bathroom, but I still can't believe it . . . I am actually here, I am actually meeting Bruce Delamitri. Bruce Dela-fuckin'-mitri. The man! I am talking about the fuckin' MAN here!'

He dropped the holdall and shook Bruce's hand hard. Bruce was still sitting half on top of Brooke, so all three of them shook slightly with the force of it. 'I can not tell you what a pleasure it is to meet you, sir. Scout!' Wayne shouted. 'C'mon in here and say Hi. Oh yes, this is a real thrill, sir. This is awesome. Scout, get your dumb ass in here right now! Don't make me come get you, now!'

Scout appeared nervously in the doorway. Her hair was tousled at the back from having just had sex, her cotton print dress gaped open a little at her breast from hurried dressing. Her bare toes were twitching again at the carpet, still unused as they were to such a luxurious sensation. There was a pistol at her hip, a huge pistol, a Magnum or something like that. It seemed to have been chosen deliberately to accentuate the smallness and birdlike, girlish quality of her body. Scout also carried a machine-gun, hanging from her hand as a little girl might hold a teddy bear. If she was trying to look like an innocent but sexy, childlike but womanly, vulnerable but dangerous, slightly imbalanced cutie pie, she was succeeding. If she wasn't trying, she was a natural.

She stared at Brooke and Bruce with what seemed to be something approaching awe. It was almost as if she was more scared of them than they were of her. This was naturally not the case, but that was how it looked. Her big eyes were sad and troubled, and there was a hesitant, almost ingratiating, smile on her lips. She wanted them to like her. She raised a hand and nervously tried to arrange her hair.

'Hi!' She giggled nervously, embarrassedly even, as if she knew she'd been naughty but hoped they were pleased to see her anyway.

Bruce and Brooke could only stare.

'C'mon in, hon. Join the party.' Wayne was as brash and confident as Scout seemed reserved. She stayed where she was, rubbing one bare foot nervously against the opposite calf.

'We messed up your sheets some,' she said, 'but you know, with modern detergents there shouldn't be any problem.'

Wayne did not feel that this was the right note to strike. You do not introduce yourself to your new hosts by owning up to having just stained their sheets. 'It don't matter about no sheets, sugar. We can buy more sheets. This is Bruce Delamitri. You are looking at the man here. *The* man.'

Wayne gestured flamboyantly towards Bruce. He seemed to mean it friendly enough, but since the hand with which he gestured was holding a gun it was something of an alarming movement nevertheless.

Seeing Bruce recoil in terror, Scout hastened to reassure him. 'Wayne's a real big fan of your pictures, Mr Delamitri. He saw you on *Coffee Time USA* with Oliver and Dale yesterday, and he's seen all your movies dozens of times . . . Me too, I like them for sure, but Wayne, he just loves them.'

'Hey, Scout, quit it. I'll bet Mr Delamitri gets real tired of people telling him all that stuff.'

A glimmer of something which, if not hope, was at least a positive and coherent thought crossed Bruce's mind. There was a great deal in Wayne and Scout's behaviour that Bruce recognized, that he had dealt with before. They were basically acting like a couple of fans, Scout shuffling her bare feet and casting shy sidelong glances at Brooke, while Wayne stood with his head held high in a 'Hey, I know you're famous but you're just a regular guy like me' pose. Bruce had met these couples a thousand times. The girl is all embarrassed, while the guy struts up to you and says, 'I guess you really hate being bothered,' and then proceeds to bother you. As if by 'being bothered' the guy means Bruce would hate to be bothered by schmucks and assholes, not by regular guys like himself. Bruce's work had always attracted these chippy, arrogant male fans, the sort of person who asks for an autograph and then says, 'You can have mine if you want,' adding with a sneer, 'Except you wouldn't want it, would you, because I'm not famous, I suppose.' As if Bruce had gone out and become a celebrity simply in order to score a cheap and easy point over a person

who is clearly his equal if not a slightly better person
than himself.

Oh yes, Bruce knew Wayne's tone of arrogant approbation; he had found the same thing in his face many
times. What he was not used to was finding it heavily
armed and having broken into his house.

'Do you want money?' Bruce found a voice of sorts.
'I have money, about two thousand dollars in cash, and
there's some jewellery . . .'

Wayne raised one booted foot on to the coffee table
and leant his weight upon his knee, bending towards
Bruce, his boot crushing the residue of the white powder
that Brooke had placed upon it. It would have made
a good close-up for one of Bruce's ironic moments,
symbolizing virile, honest mayhem kicking aside pre-
tentious decadence.

'Mr Delamitri . . . May I call you Bruce?'

Bruce nodded. He hoped the nod was firm and dignified, politely showing that he was following events
closely and considering his options. In fact he nodded
like a toy dog on the rear shelf of a family saloon, a
panicky movement which suggested that Wayne could
call Bruce anus-breath if he wished, so long as Wayne
refrained from killing him.

'Bruce, we don't want no money. We got money, we
got more money than we can spend, and we don't spend
nothing anyway because we steal all our stuff. We just
came around to visit with you. Is that OK? If we visit
with you? How about we all sit down? Maybe we could
have us a drink? Would that be OK? I like bourbon and
Scout here'll take anything sweet.'

Wayne stepped back to the couch opposite the one on
which Bruce and Brooke still sat, and collapsed casually

on to it. Scout joined him, but with none of his showy confidence. She perched on the edge of the cushion, as if anxious to show that she did not wish to intrude or be the cause of any inconvenience. Bruce got up and went to his drinks cabinet, leaving Brooke alone on the couch. She had been half lying on it since being disturbed in mid-embrace, and she seized the opportunity to sit upright and adjust her clothing. Brooke, like Scout, was barefoot and Bruce had been on the point of liberating her bosom from her dress when they were interrupted. She put her shoes back on and did her best to cover herself up. A highly revealing evening dress is not the most comfortable garment in which to confront armed intruders.

There was an embarrassed pause. Nobody knew what to say. Socially the situation could not have been more difficult.

Scout turned to Brooke in an effort to make polite conversation. She felt, perhaps rightly, that though she was a guest, the burden of social responsibility lay at least partly with her. 'You're Brooke Daniels aren't you?'

It was like two people forced into conversation in a doctor's waiting-room. Brooke's face twitched in a reply of sorts; she was clearly in no mood for small-talk.

'Yes, you are,' Scout continued. 'I'd know you anytime from all the magazines you've been in . . . *Vogue* and *Esquire* and *Vanity Fair* . . . I love all that stuff, it's so glamorous and nice . . . I've been in a magazine too . . .'

'Sure, Scout, *America's Most Wanted*.' Wayne laughed and slapped Scout's thigh.

'It's a magazine! Isn't it Brooke? . . . Brooke? It's a magazine, isn't it? *America's Most Wanted* is a magazine, isn't it?'

'Yes, it's a magazine.' Brooke's throat was so dry she was surprised that the words came out.

'Of course it's a magazine, and I was in it and you said I looked cute, Wayne.'

'You always look cute, honey. Don't need no magazine to prove that.'

Bruce brought Wayne his bourbon. He had agonized over how much to pour. A lot? A little? Would Wayne be a violent drunk or a mellow one? If shitfaced, would Wayne start singing 'Danny Boy' and collapse, weeping, on Bruce's shoulder, swearing they would be buddies for ever? Or would he puke up on his boots and spray the room with bullets? Bruce had eventually opted for rather a short measure, which he had attempted to pad out with ice. Wayne knocked it back in one, but to Bruce's relief did not immediately ask for another.

'Hear what I said, Bruce? I said Scout here's cute enough for any damn magazine, and I'm right, ain't I?'

Bruce didn't answer, preferring to make another attempt to establish Wayne's agenda. 'Look ... if you don't want cash, I have a customized Lamborghini parked right outside and—'

'Bruce, I don't want your damn car.' Wayne's voice was calm but suddenly sinister. He addressed his reply to the ice in the bottom of his glass. 'Matter of fact, I got a car.'

'I see.'

'An American fuckin' car. Made in the motor city US-fuckin'-A, out of sweat and American steel' – Wayne's voice began to rise – 'not some fuckin' wop, faggot, greaseball-built pile of tin shit for queers! A Lamborghini! Bruce, I am surprised at you. When you drive a foreign car you are driving over American jobs.'

Bruce was silent. It did not seem the right time to discuss the relative merits of free trade and protectionism. He gave Scout her drink, thankful to have a diversion, even such a small one.

'This is *crème de menthe*,' he said. 'It's sweet.'

'I love cocktails.'

Bruce returned to the drinks cabinet and collected two small bourbons for himself and Brooke. He sat down beside her on the couch, sipping at his; she did not touch hers.

Again an uncomfortable silence descended. Having so completely misfired with his last attempt, Bruce was reluctant to have another go at establishing what these lunatics wanted. Brooke had nothing to contribute either. It fell once more to Wayne and Scout to keep the nervous, desultory conversation going.

'Why'd you do that *Playboy* spread, Brooke?' Wayne asked. 'I mean, I ain't saying it wasn't beautiful, because it was, but hell, I wouldn't never let Scout do a thing like that. I'd kill her first, and Hugh fuckin' Hefner too.'

'Oh, come on now, Wayne,' said Scout coyly. 'As if anyone would ever want to see me in *Playboy* magazine!'

She was clearly fishing for compliments. Bruce wondered about attempting to ingratiate himself by assuring her that she was certainly centrefold material. He was glad he didn't.

'Sure they would, honey,' Wayne said. 'Oh yes they would. Excepting I wouldn't let you do it, on account of the fact that my rule is that if a man even looks at you with lust in his eyes, I have to kill him. So if you was to be in *Playboy* I'd have to kill just about half the men in the United States.'

'You're getting there anyway, honey!' Wayne and Scout laughed at this.

Wayne turned to Bruce as if to explain some small private joke. 'Scout's exaggerating of course, Bruce. Why, I bet I haven't killed more than forty or fifty people.'

Again an embarrassed moment, as Scout's laughter died away into silence.

'So why'd you do it, Brooke?' Wayne returned to his theme. 'I'd really like to know.'

Brooke could only stare. It would have taken a less astute judge of character than she to have failed to notice that Wayne was unpredictable. She had noticed the traces of bruising on Scout's leg where Wayne's marauding hand had pulled away her thin cotton skirt a little. Brooke decided that the more desirable of two deeply undesirable choices was to say nothing. Scout spoke for her. She knew the answer; she had read it in a magazine.

'Brooke did it, Wayne, because being an in-control woman does not mean denying one's sensuality. Isn't that what you said, Brooke? I read that.'

Brooke nodded.

'She didn't do it for men, Wayne, no matter what you and your bar-room pals might think,' Scout scolded. 'She did it for herself because she is proud of her body and proud to be beautiful and there is nothing wrong or dirty in celebrating that. In fact, it's an assertive thing to do, a feminist thing to do.'

Scout finished her little speech and turned, smiling, to Brooke, clearly hoping to have won her approval.

'That's right, um . . . Scout, it's all those things.'

Wayne got up and helped himself to another drink. 'Well, I guess that makes me feel a whole lot better about jerking off in the john over it, Brooke. I must confess, I never realized I was doing such a fine and empowering thing.'

Scout looked as though she wanted to die with embarrassment. But before she could apologize to Brooke, Wayne pressed on. 'I want to ask Brooke something now, Scout, and I don't want you getting mad at me. OK?'

'Well, it depends on what you ask her, Wayne.'

'What I want to ask is how'd those girls in *Playboy* magazine get their hair the way they do? It always looks so damn perfect.'

Brooke managed to steady her voice. 'Well . . . you know, I guess it's just a question of styling really. They use a lot of mousse and they back-light it and sometimes they put in extensions . . .'

'Brooke, I do not mean that kind of hair.'

Scout's pale skin blushed a deep red. She could not believe what her boyfriend was asking – and them guests in someone else's house and all.

'Wayne!' She punched his ribs.

'Well I want to know!' Wayne protested. 'Ain't never going to get a better chance to find out. I mean we tried shaving yours, didn't we, sugar, and you just ended up like some kind of damn Mohican with a rash!'

Mortified, Scout turned to Brooke. 'I am truly sorry, Brooke I—'

Wayne was not going to drop it. This was clearly a subject that had always bothered him. 'But in *Playboy* magazine those girls just have a little tuft, like that was all that ever grew. It don't look shaved or nothing. These are adult women, not little girls, but all they got's a tiny little tuft. How'd they do that?'

Strangely, the turn the conversation had taken was no less embarrassing for the terrifying circumstances under which it was being conducted.

Scout stared at the carpet, clearly wishing that she could crawl under it and hide. Brooke simply did not know where to look. She tried to stare straight at Wayne to show she wasn't scared, but unfortunately she was and so she didn't have the nerve. She couldn't look at Bruce – she had nothing to say to him, even with her eyes. In the end she leant back on the huge couch and looked at the ceiling. Between the two of them, Scout and Brooke had the room covered from top to bottom.

'I said, how'd they do it Brooke?' Wayne repeated, his voice hardening.

'Well, Wayne one has a stylist.'

This was one of the funniest things Wayne had ever heard. 'A stylist! A pussy hair stylist! Now that would be one hell of an occupation! Yes sir, I guess I could get to like that kind of work!'

'Wayne that is enough!' Scout was mortified.

But Wayne did not care. In his opinion he was mining a rich comic seam. 'Oh, yes, sir! I'd work weekends and all the overtime the boss'd give me. I'd be saying, "Can I shampoo that for you madam? And how about I massage in a little conditioner?" I'd work hard and get me my own salon . . . There'd be a whole row of women sitting reading magazines with little hair driers on their—'

'I am not *listening* to this any more!' Scout grabbed two cushions, held them to her ears and began to scream. 'Aaaaaaahhhh!'

'Oh come on, honey,' Wayne pleaded through Scout's shouting and his tears of laughter. 'You cannot deny that the notion of a snatch stylist is hill-fuckin'-larious. I mean, would they talk to their clients while they worked? Say, "How was your vacation, ma'm?" and . . .'

But the more Wayne talked the more Scout screamed, adding drumming feet to her efforts to block out his comic monologue. The mad cacophony was enough to jerk Bruce out of the lethargy of terror. He strode across the room and plucked an internal phone from its bracket on the wall.

'What you doing, boss?' Wayne enquired, still smiling at his own wit.

'I'm calling my security guard. He's in the lodge at the gate. If you leave now, he won't hurt you but if you harm us, he'll kill you.'

'*He'll* kill *me?* Well ho, fuckin' ho.'

Wayne levelled his gun at Bruce. For a moment Bruce believed his hour had come.

'Bang!' said Wayne, who was still in a merry mood. 'You give that guard a call, Bruce. Yes sir. If it makes you feel better, you give that ol' boy a call.'

Bruce punched the button on the intercom and awaited a response. Scout took the opportunity to apologize to Brooke. She was still mortified over Wayne's comments.

'Brooke, I am so sorry that Wayne has gotten to prying into your personal stuff. He does not understand that a woman likes to keep her special private places special and private.'

Bruce punched the button on the wall again. He was getting no reply. Wayne looked up from the gun with which he was still playing.

'He ain't answering you, Mr Delamitri. Maybe he can't hear you . . . Here, let's see if we can't get him a little closer to the phone.'

Wayne and Scout were sitting together on the couch. The holdall he had been carrying when he entered was on the floor between his feet. Wayne reached his hand down into the bag.

If Bruce had been shooting the scene, he would probably have started on a two shot of Wayne and Scout, then taken a close-up on Wayne's hand and panned down with it as it disappeared into the bag. Perhaps he would then have covered himself in the edit by picking up a reaction shot from Scout, who knew what was in the bag; then back to Wayne's hand as it emerged from the bag pulling a severed head by the hair.

But Bruce was not shooting the scene. He was in it and his heart nearly stopped. He had to clutch at the wall to keep from fainting.

Brooke opened her mouth to scream but scarcely a sound came, only a rasping gasp, dry and painful. She felt as if in a dream, paralysed by a complete and immovable fear.

Wayne raised the head and held it next to his own.

It would have made another lovely two shot. The grotesque, blood-drained, death-head and the handsome, grinning young face beside it.

'Surprise!' Wayne said, and he laughed.

There was a sheepish grin on Scout's face too. Half pleased with the major effect her boyfriend was having, half apologetic and embarrassed, aware that they had done a very bad thing.

Wayne got up, still holding the head by the hair, and carried it across the room to where Bruce was standing. Bruce gasped and recoiled, backing himself against the wall, almost as if trying to force himself through it.

'Huh huh huh.' Bruce tried to speak but it was as much as he could do to draw breath. He still held the intercom phone in his hand, although so lifeless was his grip it was surprising that the phone had not fallen. Wayne took it from Bruce's numbed grasp and held it up to the ear of the severed head.

'Hallo! Hallo!' Wayne shouted. 'Oh Mr Security Guard! . . . He don't hear so good, does he, Bruce?'

Wayne let the phone drop and held the head up so that its face was in front of his own, so close that their noses were almost touching.

'Hey! You hear me?' Wayne shouted into the dead face at the top of his voice. 'The guy who pays your salary wants to talk to you, you fuckin' jerk!'

The head swung about on its hair. Wayne turned its face away from his in disgust.

'How much did you pay this guy, Mr Delamitri? Was he expensive? Because if he was you are being ripped off, Bruce my friend. He wasn't worth shit as a guard. He just sat there in his hut with his big dog and we crept up behind him and killed him.'

Scout looked across at Brooke. 'We didn't kill the dog.'

The little caravan-park store in the redwood forest turned blue then red then blue again then red.

There was no particular call for the police car to be so garishly illuminated as it pulled up outside the shop. It was scarcely dawn yet and there had been no other traffic on the gravel road leading through the woods from the Interstate. Cops, however, will be cops. The few guests slumbering in the darkened trailers were lucky they hadn't turned on the siren.

Astonishingly, it was the storekeeper himself who had raised the alarm. Wayne had shot him only once and that had been in the shoulder. The force of the impact had spun the victim back through the open door and into the parlour behind, and Wayne could not be bothered climbing over the counter to finish the job.

The storekeeper was lucky. Such is the terrible damage done by modern weapons that even a shoulder wound can be deadly. The man's flesh, however, was old and weak and put up little resistance to the bullet as it passed through his body. In fact, the projectile had caused nearly as little damage on its exit as it had on its entry. Nevertheless, there had been considerable loss of blood, and the old man, who lived alone, had lain semi-conscious on the floor in front of the television for several hours before summoning the strength to crawl to the phone. The telerecord of the Oscars ceremony had been playing throughout, and the old man's troubled dreams and hallucinations had been further disturbed by talk of legs of fire.

While waiting for the arrival of the ambulance (which did deploy its siren and woke everybody up), the police questioned the storekeeper. They soon realized that he was another victim of the celebrated Mall Murderers, who were clearly no longer restricting their activities to malls.

'A young man and a scrawny kid of a girl,' one of the officers said into his radio. 'Same description as at that motel this morning ... All they took was some Jack Daniels, some cigarettes and some pretzels ... oh yeah, and one of those maps of the movie stars' homes . . . I don't know why. Maybe they wanted to go visit Bruce Delamitri and congratulate him on his Oscar.'

Chapter Seventeen

Wayne was still swinging the severed head about in disgust. He was clearly moved by the tawdry service Bruce was getting from his employees. He saw it as symptomatic of a national malaise, and held the head up as evidence of declining standards in general.

'I mean, shit, man! That's what's wrong with this fuckin' country. People just don't do the damn jobs they're paid for. No wonder we can't get ahead of the fuckin' Japs. Wouldn't catch no fuckin' Jap screwing up on his duty like that, man. No way! This motherfucker deserved what he got, Bruce. I did you a fuckin' favour.'

On the table stood a lava lamp in the shape of a rocket. In a gesture which amply summed up the contempt he felt for the dead security guard, Wayne impaled the head on the lamp.

Bruce gulped down his rising nausea and Brooke began quietly to weep. They stared, transfixed, as the great misshapen tumours and globules of red lava slowly rose upwards through the electric-green liquid in the lamp and disappeared into the severed neck, waited a moment and then slowly re-emerged from the head and dripped down again.

'Please,' Bruce muttered.

'What's that, Bruce?'

'Please,' he repeated. 'I don't know who you are but—'

'Oh, we're just no-count white trash, Bruce,' Wayne said, crossing over to rejoin Scout on the couch. 'We ain't nothing. Nothing at all. The only memorable thing I ever did in my whole life was kill people.'

But it was plain to see that Wayne rated himself rather highly. He was puffed up with pride like a psychotic peacock. He gripped Scout's thigh proudly, as if to reassure her that he was only being self-effacing out of politeness.

Scout was proud too. 'We're the Mall Murderers,' she said. 'I'm Scout and this is Wayne.'

Bruce and Brooke said nothing. Scout was a little disappointed. She had hoped her announcement would have more impact. Fearing that they hadn't understood her properly, she repeated the main point. 'We're the Mall Murderers.'

Scout need not have worried. They had heard her the first time.

They should have guessed, of course, Bruce particularly. Two insane murderers? A man and a woman? Big fans of his work? People whose own activities had been consistently linked with his own for the previous month and now *in his house*? It had to be them. But why? Their connection was entirely an invention of the media. In reality, Bruce had nothing whatsoever to do with the Mall Murderers. This was small comfort, though, because murdering people with whom they had nothing to do was the Mall Murderers' stock in trade.

'Are you going to kill us?' Bruce asked.

'Now what kind of question is that? Me and Scout here never know who we're going to kill till we done it.'

'It just happens,' Scout added, swinging her legs like a little girl talking about some game – although little girls don't tend to have guns lying on their laps, except sometimes in Bruce's movies and now, of course, in his lounge.

Silence returned.

Conversation was getting no easier. Again Scout felt it incumbent on her to try and oil the social wheels.

'This is so great, isn't it?' she said. 'I mean, us all here together, just sitting talking.'

Bruce was scarcely listening. His mind was racing. If these were the Mall Murderers, then he and Brooke could be dead literally at any moment. He had to do something: every second left alive with these two psychos was borrowed time. He looked at his big desk, which was positioned across the room, behind the couch on which Wayne and Scout were sitting.

In one of Bruce's movies there would have been a close-up on the top right-hand drawer and a music sting: *that drawer matters.*

Scout's voice rattled on, scarcely penetrating the edge of Bruce's thoughts.

'Because Bruce here is Wayne's hero, and I've always admired girls like you, Brooke. So beautiful and all. Except I can't deny I think it's a shame about all this cosmetic surgery you ladies get done, because these days you don't know who's really beautiful and who's just a nasty old rich bitch.'

Had Bruce moved? If anyone had been looking they might have thought he had. Before, he had been standing by the wall intercom. Now, he seemed to be a little closer to the desk.

Wayne was talking now. 'Hell it don't matter none about cosmetic surgery, does it, Scout?' he said. 'I mean, if you look beautiful, you are beautiful, don't matter how it happens.'

'I just think it was kind of nice when a girl was what she was and that was it,' Scout protested.

Bruce was definitely moving now, if incredibly slowly. He was making his way around the room towards that desk, that drawer. He glanced around to see if anyone was watching. Wayne and Scout were still concentrating on each other, their voices just babble inside Bruce's head. Brooke was staring at the floor. Only one pair of eyes seemed to be fixed on Bruce, the eyes of the security guard, popping out of his severed head. It was almost as if the head was willing Bruce on. Like some creature in an insane Frankenstein experiment, it seemed to sense a man who might avenge its bloody murder. For a moment Bruce caught those eyes and they stared at each other, sharing two extreme close-ups. For that moment Bruce half imagined those eyes alert in a living head, a head kept functioning by the great bloody globs of life-giving lava that journeyed up its neck and down again.

Bruce made a supreme effort to pull himself together. His terror was making him light-headed. The voices of Wayne and Scout, the bright eyes in the dead face and the near-certainty that death was just a heartbeat away were all crashing about his head and preventing him from thinking. Bruce was not a weak man: his glib exterior concealed a steel core. Still only in his mid-thirties, he was currently the most successful movie director in the USA. This was not something that could be achieved without considerable strength of character. None the less, Bruce's current situation was on the verge of defeating him.

'It's a movie,' a voice inside him whispered. 'Just be in a movie.'

Bruce told himself he'd seen it all a hundred times before. He was in control. He was always in control. 'It's just another movie.'

He tore his gaze away from the dead head and viewed the room in a wide shot. Nobody was looking at him. He was in deep background. Infinity focus.

'How about Brooke here? Do you reckon she's real?' Wayne was saying. He leant back into the cushions of the couch, relaxed, and clearly feeling at home. Scout cast a critical eye over the woman sitting opposite.

Brooke shrank before her gaze. An observer might have thought it strange how absurd a really sexy evening dress can look when the person wearing it is cowed and scared. One has to carry glamorous, sexy clothes off with confidence, otherwise it's possible just to look like a sad, desperate tart.

'Real? Get out of here!' Scout exclaimed. 'Why, Brooke here'll have been cut up and stretched back and sucked out and pumped up and I don't know what. Ain't that right, Brooke? . . . I said, ain't that right, Brooke?'

The star of Bruce's movie was nearly at the desk now, nearly at that special drawer. All he needed was a few more moments of inattention from his tormentors.

Bruce did not realize it but he had a co-star in his drama. It might not have appeared that Brooke was aware of his tortured journey across the room, but she was. While staring at the floor, she had caught fleeting shots of Bruce's feet moving across the back of frame. She knew that Bruce had some kind of plan and that

Wayne and Scout must remain diverted. She knew that it was up to her, that she must enter the conversation and enter it arrestingly. She raised her head and stared Scout in the eye.

'It's none of your fucking business.'

Scout and Wayne were certainly surprised. Brooke had shown little spirit up to this point, but now she was coming out punching. Her voice was hard and tough; it commanded the room. Bruce seized the opportunity and advanced a whole step.

Wayne glared at Brooke. 'Now that is where you are wrong, Miss High and Mighty fuckin' bald snatch Daniels. It is our business on account of the fact that you belong to us. You hear? You be-fuckin'-long to me 'n' my baby. Now, answer my baby's question. Unless you think you're too good to talk to her. In which case, you can talk to this.'

Wayne raised his machine-pistol to his shoulder and pointed it at Brooke. Her POV was the gaping end of the barrel with Wayne's grinning face behind it, chin resting against the stock.

But beyond Wayne's head, in deep background, Bruce was still edging through the rear of frame.

Brooke knew she must keep Wayne's attention. Bravely she met his stare, fixing on to his eyes as they hovered above the black-hole snout of the gun.

Slowly he closed one eye in a cheerfully grotesque wink. He was taking aim.

Brooke attempted not to flinch, which was not an easy task. 'All right, pervert, if you must know' – it was terrifying to risk annoying him in this way, but she knew that above all she must keep the focus on herself until Bruce got to that desk – 'I've had the wrinkles round my eyes and lips dealt with, some cellulite removed from my thighs, I have had breast implants and my navel has been remodelled.'

As she spoke Bruce opened the drawer. Wayne was never going to be more distracted than he was at that moment. It was Bruce's best chance, and he took it.

He watched his own hand in close-up, pulling open the drawer. He watched the hand disappear inside.

The drawer was empty.

As Bruce frantically felt to the very back, there should have been a musical sting. Something harsh, like a scream, or, seeing as it was Bruce's movie, perhaps something ironic, like a sit com 'wah wah waaaah' but discordant and sinister. There was no sting, however, because Bruce had stopped playing his desperate little movie game. His defeat was too real, too complete.

'Oh, Bruu-uuce.' It was Wayne's voice, nasty and sarcastic. 'Is this what you're looking for?'

Wayne had not even bothered to turn round to face Bruce. All Bruce could see was the back of Wayne's head above the cushions and his hand protruding over the arm of the couch. From one finger of Wayne's hand hung a small pistol.

'You see, Bruce, I can *smell* guns,' Wayne said, still without bothering to turn round. 'I smelt this one a while ago. I went over to fix me a drink and I thought, mm-mm, what's that smell? I like it. I do believe it's a gun. And guess what? It was! Can you believe that?'

Bruce did not answer. Not for the first time that night, he was incapable of speech.

'Also, I must confess that it is not uncommon for a man to keep his piece in the top drawer of his desk. For an Oscar-winning film-maker, Bruce, you are not very original.'

Bruce shrank a little inside. For a moment there he'd been a fighter, he'd had a plan and a chance. Now he was a fool, casually outwitted and out-manoeuvred by the dregs of a small town truck stop.

It was six a.m. and Bruce's appointment with nemesis was well under way. His old life was already over. Even if he survived his ordeal, nothing would ever be the same again.

Outside in Los Angeles, of course, and America-wide, like him or loathe him Bruce remained the lion of the hour. His Oscar triumph was still a top story on the morning news. Sadly, not *the* top story. It would have been so under happier circumstances, but the massacre at the 7–11 store was necessarily number one on all the channels. Even in California, fourteen dead while doing a bit of shopping is big news, particularly if surviving witnesses are prepared to swear that after they had committed the massacre the perpetrators actually coupled, like two wild animals on heat, against the Slurpy Pup dispenser.

'Sex and death in America today,' said the reporters, as the ambulances squealed off into the dawn. 'It could come straight out of a Bruce Delamitri picture.' An observation which coincidentally segued very nicely into the pre-edited Oscars report.

'I stand here on legs of fire,' said Bruce.

'Why'd the guy have to make such a vacuous speech?' the news editors complained. 'My God, if he'd said something about violence and censorship, would we have had *him* this morning!'

Chapter Eighteen

Wayne did not bother turning to Bruce even now. He was more interested in the conversation he'd been having. He put the little pistol he had taken from Bruce's drawer on Scout's lap, and strolled casually round the glass table to stand over Brooke. As he passed the severed head, it seemed again for a moment as if it might rotate on its gory plinth in order to follow Wayne's movements with its bulbous dead eyes. It didn't.

'You know something?' Wayne said, standing over Brooke, leering at the curiously unnatural semi-circular definition of the top of her breasts. 'I've always wanted to know what fake tits feel like. Well, I guess there ain't a working man in the United States who hasn't thought the same thing. Like, you know, are they hard? Soft? Can you feel that bag of stuff they put in? Do they move around?'

Wayne's right hand had been resting casually on the butt of the pistol stuck in his waistband. Now, he let go of the gun and blew on his fingers to warm them, clearly making ready for an inspection. Brooke did not look at him. She brought her knees up to her chest, clasped her arms round them with her shoulders hunched forward, and stared straight ahead, her chin on her knees.

'Don't you dare fucking touch me.' Her voice was quiet and shaky; she was almost muttering.

'Pardon me, ma'am,' Wayne replied, 'but I guess I didn't hear you right.'

Wayne placed the barrel of one of his guns against Brooke's forehead and with his free hand ready, fingers outstretched, he slowly bent forward, clearly intent on investigating inside the top of her dress.

Across the room Scout took up her gun. 'Wayne, you leave her bosoms alone, now. I don't want you touching her bosoms none.'

It was a stand-off, Wayne pointing a gun at Brooke, Scout pointing a gun at Wayne, Wayne's hand hovering above Brooke's cleavage.

Wayne cracked first. 'Jesus, there ain't nothing more irritating than a jealous woman,' he said, returning to his seat.

Brooke remained hunched up in her defensive position, breathing deeply. 'Just hold on,' she said to herself, 'just keep it together.'

She knew that the number-one enemy of survival was panic. The moment one gave in to that oxygen-consuming, energy-sapping, adrenalin-pumping surge of blind fear, one was done for. Only the day before, she reminded herself, she had been swimming off Malibu and had got caught in a rip. It had been a sucky one, and without warning Brooke had been pulled under, turned over, filled with water and dragged out to sea about twenty metres.

'You nearly died then,' Brooke told herself concentrating on her breathing. 'Only yesterday you were as close to death as you are now, but you made it.'

It was true. Brooke had been in mortal danger, although it would not have been the rip which killed her. Rips don't kill people. Panic does. The first instinct of the swimmer caught in a rip is to try to head back to shore. This is disastrous: no one can swim against the sea and the mildest undertow will defeat the strongest swimmer. But this suicidal instinct is strong and, although Brooke had been swimming in the Californian waters since girlhood and should have known better, she succumbed momentarily to the desperate desire to get back to beach by the shortest route possible.

Even at the first stroke, as she raised her arm over her shoulder and thrust her fingers into the foam, she could feel her panic rising. She was a very strong swimmer, but her efforts got her nowhere and within seconds she was exhausted. It happens that quickly. A couple of mouthfuls of salt water, a few flailing strokes and suddenly the toughest mind becomes clouded with despair. It is at this point that swimmers either pull themselves together or drown. Brooke had pulled herself together.

She knew the rules. Never head into your trouble. Head out of it, sideways along the shore, or, if necessary, right out to sea. Rips are always relatively confined and once the swimmer is out of them, no matter how far from shore they may be by this time, they have the opportunity to recover their energies, consider their position and calmly make their way to safety. Brooke, like any decent swimmer, was capable of keeping herself afloat for hours and yet panic could have killed her in two minutes.

That was the lesson she reminded herself of now. Rips don't kill people (breath), panic does (breath).

In his own way Bruce had drawn the same conclusion. By pretending to be in a movie, he had so far avoided being consumed and defeated by the horror of his surroundings. He had avoided panic. Just.

'What's this guy's weakness?' he said to himself, no longer in a movie, but in a script conference, reading over Wayne's character breakdown, which had been prepared for him on Popcorn's headed notepaper. 'Why does he kill?'

'He kills irrationally,' Bruce answered himself.

Inside his head, Bruce leapt to his feet, the cool, decisive producer, waving the studio memo about triumphantly.

'Here's how it is, right? The guy's stock in trade is murdering strangers, right? Well then, surely safety lies in forming some kind of relationship with him. Maybe these guys don't kill people they know.'

All this had been running through Bruce's head while Wayne was attempting to investigate Brooke's breasts. In the hiatus that followed the silicone stand-off, Bruce made his pitch.

'I'd like to ask you something if that's OK, Wayne. May I ask you something?'

'I would be honoured, sir.' Wayne appeared genuinely pleased.

'Well, I guess I'm interested in what it's like to kill someone.'

'You want to kill someone? Hell, man, do it, it's easy. Kill Brooke.' Wayne took his pistol from his belt and opened the chamber. He removed all but one of the bullets from the drum and offered the weapon to Bruce.

Bruce hesitated. One bullet. Could he achieve anything with that?

Wayne read his thoughts. 'Take it, man. You don't have to kill Brooke. You could kill me, or Scout here – 'cepting, of course, if you did vengeance would be not be a long time a-comin'.'

'I don't want to kill anyone, Wayne. I just wanted to know what it's like.'

Wayne put the gun back in his belt and thought for a moment. This was a tough one. He'd never really thought about it before. It was like asking what's it like to eat or to make love, it was just stuff you did.

'You might as well ask what it's like to make a movie, Bruce. It depends. On the circumstances, on the victim. I can tell you what it ain't like. It ain't like you show it. For one thing, there ain't no music playing.'

'No, I imagine not.'

Despite the terror of the situation Bruce felt slightly annoyed at this. People were always pointing out to him that in real life nobody died to a sexy backing track. Like they were saying something really original and astute. It was one of the Moral Majority's favourite points. They always took particular exception to the rock soundtracks Bruce assembled to accompany the mayhem he depicted. They said it was manipulative. Well of course it was. Bruce put fuck music behind his love scenes too and nobody minded that.

'I'll tell you another thing,' said Wayne. 'It ain't witty.'

Witty? It seemed a strange word for a truck-stop hick like Wayne to use.

'Like in *Ordinary Americans*, when the two guys put

the little short-order cook's hand in the food-processor. You remember that scene?'

Of course Bruce remembered it. It had been a triumph of dark, brittle humour. 'Film-making for a new generation', he seemed to remember somebody saying, and if they hadn't they should have done.

'Now that was witty,' Wayne said. 'They put the guy's hand in the blender and it whizzes up blood and stuff all over their suits, and one of the tough guys says, "Shit, this suit is Italian," which was so funny because, like, the poor little cook's screaming on account of he's only got a spurting stump on the end of his arm and this guy is worrying about his suit!'

Wayne howled. 'Neo-Gothic', they'd called it, 'post-modernist pulp noir'. Wayne just thought it was cool.

'But that was only the start, right? It got better, because we knew that the boss man had told the two heavies to go to some real swank hotel to waste this black dude and they know that there is no way they are going to get into no swank hotel with all blood and pieces of bone and skin on their suits. But if they don't make the hit, the boss will burn them. So they have to go to the dry cleaners and strip off to their underwear and the dry cleaner guy is this little faggot in tight shorts and he says, "That's OK fellas, I'm used to shifting stubborn stains from delicate fibres. I have satin sheets," which is a very funny line in itself, but it's even funnier because we know that one of the killer guys just hates faggots, he hates them like a fuckin' religion, so he just digs out this huge Magnum from his underpants and wastes the faggot dry cleaner guy completely, like half his head comes off. But then the other killer guy is real annoyed and says, "Shit, man, how we gonna clean our suits now?" So they have to try to figure out how to work the machine and when they get to the swanky hotel to kill the black dude their suits is all tiny like kids' suits, because they shrunk. Now that was one classy scene, Bruce. Like I say, witty.'

Bruce did not reply. Normally when people enthusiastically repeated his work back to him, as they often did, he would say, 'Thank you, that's very kind,' at the earliest opportunity to try and shut them up. But this time he said nothing. There was an awful fascination in just how well this terrible man knew his work.

'I don't know how many times Wayne watched that movie,' said Scout.

'A shit load of times, let me tell you,' Wayne added. 'It said on the poster that the *New York Times* reckoned it was ironic and subversive. I just thought it was classic the way everybody got wasted. It was so witty.'

Bruce was getting nowhere. He had been attempting to get to know his persecutor, to get inside his head. All he got was his own imagination quoted back at him.

For a moment Bruce remembered something from before. Mirrors. Something about mirrors. Then that thought, too, was interrupted.

Buzzzzz . . . Buzzzzz.

They all jumped, even Wayne. After all it was only seven a.m.

Buzzzzz. The entryphone intercom on the wall was not going to shut up.

'Now who's that coming calling, Bruce?' Wayne took up his gun. 'It's Oscars morning. Everybody knows you're liable to have a head sorer than a hog's ass on a country farm. You ain't pushed no alarm button or nothing, have you, Bruce? Because if you have, I'll kill you inside'a one single breath.'

'No, Christ, no!' Bruce said quickly 'I think it's my wife, my ex. We have a settlement to discuss. Christ, she's an hour and a half early.'

Scout squealed with excitement. First Brooke Daniels, now Farrah Delamitri. It was like being in her very own edition of *Entertainment Tonight*. 'Farrah Delamitri! My God, I'd love to meet her. Didn't I read somewhere you wished she was dead?'

'It's a figure of speech,' Bruce replied 'I was quoted out of context.'

The buzzer sounded again, more insistently this time.

Bruce turned to Wayne. 'So I leave it, right?'

There was very little love lost between Bruce and his nearly ex-wife, and on occasion he had wished many horrid things upon her, but inviting her in to visit with the Mall Murderers went beyond any desire for revenge he might have had. Unfortunately the decision wasn't up to him.

'You've made an appointment, you keep it,' Wayne said. 'I guess she can see your big old Italian Lambor-fuckin'-homosexual parked out in the drive. She knows you're here and I don't want her getting suspicious about nothing.'

Again the buzzer.

'Look, surely we don't need to bring anybody else into this. I mean . . .'

Wayne was trying to be patient. 'Ain't going to drag nobody into nothing, Bruce. You just have her come on up here, do your business like you would anyhow, and then she can go.'

With great reluctance Bruce crossed again to the wall intercom and picked it up. There was a harsh New York voice on the other end.

'For Christ's sake, Karl,' said Bruce, 'have you any idea what the time is?' He put his hand over the receiver and turned to Wayne. 'It's not my wife, it's my agent, a guy called Karl Brezner. He says he has to see me right now. It's urgent.'

'Now if me 'n' Scout wasn't here, Bruce, and it was just you and Brooke here, would you let him up?'

'I . . .' Bruce knew he had hesitated too long to lie. 'I guess I would, if he said it was urgent.'

'Tell him you're sending someone down,' said Wayne.

Wayne put all the bigger guns behind the sofa cushions where Scout was sitting. He put one handgun in his pocket and Scout kept one ready under a cushion on her lap. 'I'm going to go down to the gate and let Karl in so we can visit with him for a while. Now he don't have to see no guns or nothing but Scout and me are going to be ready, and anybody who tries to mess around with us is going to get very dead, d'ya hear? So you all just sit tight till I get back. Like I say, this guy don't need to see nothing suspicious.'

He was about to leave when Scout stopped him. 'Wayne, honey, what about the head?'

He laughed. Turning back, he plucked the head from its stand on the lava lamp and dropped it into a wastepaper basket.

Chapter Nineteen

'Did you see that movie *Ordinary Americans*?' the detective, whose name was Crawford, enquired through a cloud of blueberry-muffin crumbs.

'*Please* close your mouth when you're eating,' his partner, Detective Jay, replied. 'It makes me sick to my stomach.'

'You make me laugh, Frank. Most days you get to see the insides of some poor fuckin' dead guy or a smackhead drowned in his own puke and yet still my spit offends you.'

'Just because we work in a pigsty doesn't mean we gotta act like pigs.'

'So did you see the movie?' Another deposit of muffin crumbs.

'Yeah, I saw the movie.'

'And?'

'And when they finally blow me away, I hope I look half as good. Look, I don't care about any movie right now. I'm thinking, OK? Working. Remember work? Or maybe the city pays you to redistribute food.'

'Oh my God, that's funny. I can't wait to have grandchildren so I can tell them how funny you are.'

Detective Jay ignored his partner. 'These two psychos, they're in LA, you know that?' He was looking at the map he had made of Wayne and Scout's most recent atrocities, plotting their course. 'Look, they were heading straight down the interstate. Sure they left it after they did the motel murders, but if you plot a path between the caravan park and the 7–11, they are clearly heading for town.'

'Maybe they turned around.'

'Sure they did. They're in LA, I'm telling you.'

'Like we didn't have enough psychos in LA already, for Christ's sake,' Crawford said. 'You think they're looking to go to ground?'

'I doubt it. These wackos are attention-seekers. Serial show-offs. I mean, for Christ's sake, making out against a Slurpy Pup in front of a bunch of bullet-riddled shoppers! They think they're some kind of twenty-first-century Bonnie and Clyde. I don't see them wanting to lose themselves in a big city.'

'Maybe they're visiting relatives.'

Detective Jay looked again at the crime report on Wayne's attempted murder of the old storekeeper.

'Bourbon, smokes, pretzels . . . and a guide to the movie people's homes.'

On the desk in front of him was a copy of the LA *Times*, the front page cover of which carried a picture of Bruce holding his Oscar, alongside a picture of a corpse-strewn 7–11 and the obligatory piece on violence influencing kids and copycat killings.

'Movie people's homes,' Detective Jay repeated. 'Hey

Joe, that picture, *Ordinary Americans*. Who were the stars?'

'Kurt Kidman and Suzanne Schaefer, although there were a lot of cameos. Anyhow, I thought you didn't care about no movies.'

'Yeah, well, I changed my mind.'

Chapter Twenty

How much time did Bruce have? His was a very big house and the drive was a long one. If Wayne intended to go all the way down to the gates, he would be gone perhaps ten minutes. If he let Karl come up the drive, and met him at the front door, the whole thing would take no more than five. Either way, not really long enough for much delicate negotiation.

'All right, young lady,' Bruce barked, trying to summon up the voice with which he cowed cinematographers and hordes of extras, 'this has gone far enough. If you hand over your gun now, it is just possible that I may be able to speak on your behalf at your trial.'

Scout did not look at Bruce but she slid the cushion from her lap, revealing her gun. 'I don't want to have to kill you but I will.' She said it quietly, almost sadly, but she clearly meant it: both that she didn't want to kill him and that she would.

Bruce was at a loss to know how to proceed. He hadn't really hoped that schoolmasterly authority would bear much fruit, but it was the only idea he had.

Brooke had completed her programme of breathing. She was centred now, in control and ready to attempt a different approach. She stared at Scout. Her face wore a strange expression; she looked interested but slightly perplexed. She tilted her head one way, then the other, all the time looking at Scout as if trying to get a better angle, trying to work her out. Scout knew she was being studied, and reddened. She stared down at the cushion, which she had now put back in her lap to cover the gun.

'Scout,' Brooke said, 'may I do something?' Almost without waiting for an answer, she leant forward, took a lock of Scout's hair which was hanging down in front of her face, and gently pushed it behind her ear. 'You're a pretty girl, Scout, you know that? Real pretty.'

To Bruce this seemed such a transparent ploy that he expected Scout to shoot them both on the spot, but she didn't. She just kept on staring at the cushion in her lap and said, 'Oh I don't think so.'

'Oh yes you are, Scout,' Brooke insisted. 'A very pretty girl. Except you don't make as much of yourself as you could. Like, for instance, you have beautiful hair, but you've done nothing with it.'

Scout shyly explained that there had been all blood and bits of brain and stuff in it from a regrettable incident which had occurred recently in a 7–11. She had been forced to rinse out her hair in the ladies' room, which was why it was such a mess.

Brooke knelt on the carpet in front of Scout. 'Well, I'll bet I could help you with that kind of thing, Scout. Maybe we could do a little make-over on you. I have my beauty bag and I'll bet Bruce's daughter has left some great clothes in the house – we could pick something out. You could look like a movie star. Don't you think so, Bruce?'

Bruce was amazed. Scout seemed to be taking Brooke's interest seriously. At least, she hadn't shot her.

'Yes, Scout is very pretty,' he answered stiffly.

Scout's attention still appeared to be riveted to the cushion.

Brooke addressed the top of Scout's head. 'You could have so much going for you. I bet any agent would love to have a cute little girl like you to look after.'

Scout raised her head a little. 'You think so?'

'Of course I do. You said yourself how nice you looked in that magazine.'

Bruce was stunned at Brooke's audacity. Was it possible that this pathological murderess could be taken in by such an obvious ploy? Quietly, he began to pray that it was.

'Why would any agent notice me? I mean, I ain't saying I ain't pretty, because I know a lot of men have taken a shine to me from time to time, including my own father. But there's a heap of pretty girls in this town.'

Bruce's heart sank. His prayer, scarcely delivered yet, was already being returned to sender, unanswered. He had been foolish to allow himself to hope. Scout was not an imbecile: just because you're psychotic does not render you moronic. The woman would have to have had her brains sucked out with a bicycle pump to believe that a bit of make-up and a borrowed dress were going to turn her from a sad, sick psycho into a glamorous celebrity.

But Brooke was a lot smarter than Bruce gave her

credit for – and braver. She took Scout's chin and gently but firmly raised her head so that she could look her in the eye.

'OK, Scout, I'll be straight. You're right, ordinarily why would anybody notice you? Just one more pretty girl in a town that's full of them. But you know very well that you're not just one more pretty girl. You're a killer's girl, already famous . . .'

'I'm a killer too,' said Scout.

Brooke conceded the point. 'Well sure, but the world is going to know that he made you do it and meanwhile, if I make you as pretty as can be . . . who knows? You wouldn't be the first person to get away with stuff just for being cute.'

Scout had a faraway look in her eyes. Her toes were twitching at the carpet harder than ever. 'You really think I could be a star? You mean you'd help me?'

'Of course I'd help you, Scout. I like you and I think you like me. We could be friends.'

Scout finally raised the point that Bruce had been nervously awaiting from the outset. 'That's easy for you to say while Wayne's threatening to kill you.'

Bruce cursed inwardly. Brooke's progress thus far had been so astonishing that he had dared to think she might actually win Scout's trust. This remarkable woman had got from nowhere to serious buddy-talk inside two or three minutes. Now, however, it seemed that Scout had finally spotted the rather obvious point that Brooke's affection might be influenced by an ulterior motive.

But Brooke was a fighter, and hit back. 'Maybe you're right, Scout, but think about it. Seems to me that Wayne is always going to be threatening to kill somebody or other. So how you ever going to make any friends, huh? Y'ever think 'bout that, now?'

Not very subtly, Brooke's voice was going both down-market and in-country. It had left the upper echelons of West Coast society and was meandering gently along Route 66 towards the Heartland.

'I don't know,' Scout replied softly. 'Sometimes I do wonder about it.'

Brooke took Scout's hand. 'Listen t'me Scout. If ever a person needed friends right now, it's you. We could help you, but you have to help us. Don't you want friends?'

'Sure I want friends. 'Course I want friends. I ain't a freak, I'm just an ordinary American.'

A loud New York accent intruded on the scene. Instantly Scout's demeanour hardened. She pulled away from Brooke and her hand tensed under the cushion. For the time being at least, Brooke's heroic efforts to divide the enemy would have to be suspended.

Chapter Twenty-One

The unmarked police car pulled up outside the Beverly Hills mansion. The sun was out now, and the automatic sprinklers hidden beneath the perfect lawns had sprung to life. As he looked about him, Detective Jay could see a hundred rainbows shimmering in the spray which hung above the deep green grass. Everything looked so peaceful and so *rich*.

Jay wondered if inside that glorious colonnaded house unspeakable mayhem had already been perpetrated. It was just a hunch, after all. On the other hand, nobody had cut up a major Hollywood star since Manson.

'You know,' said Crawford as they approached the vast front door, 'this guy was a daytime soap star for years, started as a kid. That's what's so clever about Delamitri. He makes weird moves, like, you know, doing the unexpected, casting against type. Making uncool cool.'

'What, like murder?'

'You don't buy that copycat crap, do you? What? Are

we all going to have to go and watch Doris Day movies?'

Buzzz. Buzzzzzzz.

At first Kurt didn't hear it. The pounding of the treadmill and the Van Halen in his headphones blotted out any outside sound. He rarely answered the intercom himself, anyway. The staff arrived by public bus at nine, and nobody ever visited before that.

Except today.

If he hadn't stopped for a swig of salinating energizer drink and five minutes under the sun-lamp, he'd never have heard it at all.

'LAPD,' said the intercom. 'Sorry to call so early, sir.'

In contrast to the characters he played, Kurt Kidman was as dull as old brown paint. Like many people in LA these days, all he ever did was work and exercise. He had certainly never been visited by the police at six fifty in the morning.

'The *police*?' said Kurt. 'But . . . but why?' The receiver actually shook in his hand.

He had never done anything illegal in his life (although some of his acquaintances considered that squandering his huge wealth and fame on a boring, healthy lifestyle was something of a crime). None the less, Kurt was a nervous sort of fellow and anybody suddenly confronted by the police tends to feel an irrational sense of guilt, particularly at so early an hour. Had he done anything wrong? Was it possible that he'd gone over the speed limit when he drove back from the Oscars on the previous night? Or else maybe, like Dr Jekyll, he had a terrifying subconscious alter ego, who roamed the night committing terrible murders of which his conscious self had no memory in the morning.

'Good morning, officer,' Kurt said, attempting to sound calm, as he answered the door. He had tried to communicate with them only over the intercom, but they had asked him to come down in person. He half expected to be brutally handcuffed the moment the door was open.

'How can I help you?'

Should he have said even that without his lawyer being present? Kurt couldn't remember the rules. Was saying hullo incriminating? He longed to tell them that his copious sweating was the result of an hour on the treadmill, not because he was desperately attempting to cover up some guilty secret. But would that sound like protesting too much? Probably.

'Just a routine enquiry, sir,' said Detective Jay 'Have you been visited or contacted during the night? Have any strangers attempted to speak to you?'

'No,' said Kurt.

'In that case we won't bother you further. Sorry to have interrupted your work-out, sir.'

Detective Jay gave Kurt his card and asked him to call if anything out of the ordinary occurred, and then he and his partner departed.

Kurt worried about it all day.

Chapter Twenty-Two

In the doorway to Bruce's lounge stood Wayne and Karl Brezner, Bruce's agent. Karl was a tough, hardbitten operator from New York. He had been in the business for thirty years, but judging by his manner it did not seem to have made him happy.

'Here's your man, Bruce,' said Wayne.

Karl threw a questioning glance at Bruce. Understandably he was wondering who the lowlife might be.

'Hi, Bruce. Sorry to call so early,' he said. 'Coupla real important things. So, having a party?'

Karl looked round the room. Brooke was still kneeling on the carpet in front of Scout. Wayne was also taking in the scene. Both he and Karl were surprised to see the two women in this position.

Brooke got up from the rug with what dignity she could muster and returned to her seat on the couch.

'Yeah, a party, kind of,' said Bruce. 'This is Brooke Daniels.'

Karl had eyed Brooke appreciatively as she crossed

the room. He would have had to have been made of stone not to. She was extremely beautiful at any time and if anything she was even more fascinating now, looking sad and vulnerable in her increasingly absurd evening gown.

'Brooke Daniels!' said Karl with delight. 'Well, well, well. Miss February, I didn't recognize you with your clothes on. Great spread, by the way. I'll bet the nozzle of that gas pump was cold, am I right? Who're these two, Bruce?'

Karl spoke as if Wayne and Scout did not exist. He was not actually quite as rude as he appeared. He came from a brusque culture, in which good manners were commonly interpreted as bullshit and prevarication. His style would not have gone down well in Japan or over tea at Buckingham Palace, but in New York show-business circles it had served him well.

Bruce struggled for a reply to his question.

'A couple of . . . actors. I saw them in an improv' night out at Malibu . . . thought I'd talk to them. Might be right for *Killer Angels*.'

Killer Angels was the project that Bruce and Karl currently had in development. It was again to be about people who killed strangers, but this time for a reason, anti-abortion, the environment, wiping out a sporting rival, whatever; the idea being to show that all murder is in fact arbitrary. Or something like that, anyway. They intended it to duplicate the enormous success of *Ordinary Americans*.

'Seeing actors in the early morning after Oscars night? That is dedication.' Karl turned to Wayne and Scout. 'No offence to you guys, but for me talking to actors is only one step up from visiting with the dentist.'

As with most agents, being rude about actors was Karl's favourite joke. He patronized them behind their backs, calling them childish and mad. He was, of course, just jealous. No matter how rich and powerful an agent gets, he still finds it difficult to jump queues in restaurants.

Bruce pursued his hasty improvisation, in the hope that detail would make it more convincing. 'I just thought they had, you know . . . maybe they had the right look.'

Karl cast a doubtful glance at Wayne and Scout. 'Well, I'm just the schmuck who counts the money, but these kids look about as much like psychopaths as my grandmother, God save her soul.'

Bruce was pleased at this response. The less interest Karl showed in Wayne and Scout the better.

'You want a drink, Mr Brezner?' Wayne asked.

This gave Bruce further cause for relief. Wayne appeared to be prepared to play along with the fiction.

'Are you kidding?' said Karl. 'A drink? At seven fifteen in the morning? Have you any idea how much my current liver cost me? Body parts do not come cheap, my friend, particularly those of which the donor only had one and was hence reluctant to part with it . . . Only kidding. Since we're celebrating, get me a scotch, kid.'

Karl sat down on the couch beside Brooke, taking the opportunity as he sat to cast an appreciative glance down the front of her dress.

His mentioning the time reminded Bruce that Karl had no business being there at all. 'That's right Karl, it's only seven fifteen. What do you want?'

'Lemme get this drink, then maybe we can talk down in the snooker room.'

'We'll talk here. I'm busy.' Bruce hadn't meant to snap. The last thing he wanted was to raise any suspicions in Karl that something was wrong. Wayne caught the wrongness of the tone too and shot a warning look at Bruce from where he was standing at the drinks cabinet. Had there been a musical sting at this point, it would have suggested that Bruce had better be damned careful.

'Well excuuuuse me,' said Karl. Even tough New York agents with skin thicker than an elephant sandwich can be offended. 'I forgot for one moment that you just won an Oscar and therefore are professionally obliged to treat with contempt those whom formerly you have loved and respected.'

Bruce knew he must remain very calm. If Karl's suspicions were even slightly aroused he would never leave the room alive. 'Karl, I didn't sleep yet.' He attempted a weary matter-of-fact tone. 'Could we do this another time?'

'Another time? Maybe you didn't see the papers today.'

'Of course I didn't see the papers – it's seven fifteen in the morning.'

Karl took his drink from Wayne without even glancing at him, let alone thanking him.

'Well, I don't want to be the shit-delivery boy here, Bruce, but yours is not a popular Oscar choice. Frankly, the editorials would be kinder if they'd given it retrospectively to *Attack of the Large-Breasted Women*.'

Bruce shrugged and he meant it. 'Who gives a fuck what those parasites think?'

Just a few hours earlier he would have been obsessed with what they thought, but that was a few hours earlier. Things had changed. Changed for ever. Karl, of course, was still living in the old world.

Or at least he thought he was.

'We give a fuck, Bruce,' he said. 'It's the violence thing. It's the big deal of the moment and it's getting a little serious. These fucks are talking up *Ordinary Americans* like it was some kind of training manual for psychos. Newt Gingrich was on the *Today Show* this morning—'

'All politicians are scum,' Wayne interjected. '*Ordinary Americans* is a fuckin' masterpiece.'

Again Karl ignored him. 'He says you're a pornographer and you shouldn't get honoured for glamorizing murderers.'

Scout was bored. She didn't like Karl and she didn't care what Newt Gingrich thought. She had been having a much more interesting conversation before Karl arrived. She turned back to Brooke.

'Brooke, will you put my hair up like you said you would?'

Rather nervously Brooke nodded and, taking her handbag, she crossed over to where Scout was sitting and started to do her hair. Karl was not a little surprised to be interrupted in this way by out-of-work actors, but he let it go. That he should care if this little runt showed him disrespect. In his life she did not even exist.

'I think the Republicans want to turn it into a mid-term election issue. We need to make a plan.'

Again Scout barged in with her own agenda. 'You know what I love? I love the way hair mousse comes out of the can. Like, how do they get it all *in* there?'

'It expands, honey,' said Wayne.

'I know it expands, dummy. Because it's bigger when it gets out. But I don't know how it happens. It's the same with cans of whipped cream. How do they *do* that? I mean cream is cream – you can't crush it up.'

Karl looked at her, astonished. He hadn't been ignored like this in twenty-five years.

'Excuse me,' he said, 'did I become invisible? I'm talking here.'

Scout seemed suitably admonished. 'Sorry,' she said.

'You are very far from welcome,' Karl replied with ill grace, before turning back to Bruce. 'They're thinking about reclassifying for over-eighteens. That's half our box office gone at a stroke, to say nothing of actual bans, particularly in the South. In retrospect, I think the crucifixion scene was a mistake.'

'Awesome scene, man,' said Wayne.

Again Karl ignored the interruption. 'It's these fucking Mall Murderers, Bruce. Those two little punks are in danger of getting our picture pulled, Oscar or no Oscar. Do you know they just shot up a 7–11? Christ, what kind of pointless sickos are these people?'

Brooke and Bruce froze. Karl's conversation had suddenly taken an unimaginably dangerous turn.

'Well, you know,' Brooke said casually, while teasing at Scout's hair, 'I mean, you have to try to be a little understanding, see things from their point of view.'

Karl was not an understanding type of person. 'What, you mean the point of view of a socially inadequate jerk-off? *Please*.'

'I really don't think you can dismiss them that easily.' Brooke was doing her best but it was a hopeless task.

'Pardon me, miss, for appearing rude, but that I should give a fuck what you think. Wayne Hudson and that weird, scrawny little bitch he drags around with him are screwed up trailer-park white-trash nobodies who have mashed potato instead of brains. The sooner they get burnt, fried, decapitated, castrated, lobotomized, liquidized and generally fucked over, the better. I would gladly take a mallet to the little fucking scumbags myself.'

Bruce and Brooke braced themselves. Surely now the mayhem would begin. Wayne had moved to behind the couch where Scout was sitting. He had only to reach down into the cushions at her back to produce a machine-gun, and this appallingly provocative man would be dead. Scout herself need merely brush aside the cushion on her lap. Surely it was all over for Karl?

'You talk big, Karl, but you'd never do it.' Bruce's laugh was wooden as a daytime soap. 'You always end up on the side of the underdog.'

'Underdog? Those scum?' Karl replied.

Bruce was now convinced that Karl had a death wish.

'Like I would waste my tears on such syphilitic maggots? I would puke on their graves and those of their mothers, who no doubt were whores.'

Shut up! Every fibre of Bruce's being willed this loudmouthed oaf to shut up. Brooke, too, was desperately trying to reach somehow into his mind and stop this fool from digging all their graves with his violent language.

How often had Brooke spoken in the past about auras and third eyes? While not actually holding a season ticket on the New Age Traveller bandwagon, she had always claimed to have a palpable connection with the mystic. She believed firmly that thought-transference was possible. She was getting a painful crash course in Old Age reality.

Wayne's voice was cold, although in comparison to his eyes it was positively balmy. 'You think the Mall Murders are fucked-up white trash, Mr Brezner?'

'He does not think that!' Bruce almost shouted.

'You can't just dismiss them' was Brooke's desperate plea.

'Weird, scrawny little bitch?' Scout said to herself, a faraway look in her eyes. 'That weird scrawny little bitch *he drags around with him*?'

'Karl didn't mean that!' Bruce forced himself to laugh again; it sounded like a razor-blade cutting through a tin can. 'You should hear the way he talks about his wife.'

Karl, oblivious of the terrible agenda swirling around him, was mystified by Bruce's attitude.

'Excuse me? What is this right now? Oprah? Are we having some kind of *debate* about these fucking filth? Of course they're fucked-up white trash. What else would they be? I'd like to take that pair of pointless, gutless, no-brain, no-dick, asshole insults to the intelligence of a wet fart and—'

'Karl! What do you want?' Bruce leapt to his feet. 'I'm busy here. I have stuff to do and you are getting in my face.'

He had not wanted to confront Karl quite so bluntly. If he acted too strangely, Wayne would know that Karl's suspicions must inevitably be aroused. On the other hand, he had to shut Karl up and get him out before he talked them all to death.

Karl studied Bruce for a moment, but decided not to rise to him. Karl was, after all, an agent and Bruce was his top client.

'OK, Bruce, OK. You're the artist. I just negotiate the obscene and disgusting amounts you get paid. Now, like I say, I think we have real trouble here. This is an important moral issue and we can't be seen to duck it. We have to react to this thing responsibly. What we have to do is get out there immediately, say fuck you, and announce a sequel to *Ordinary Americans.*'

'Everybody died at the end of *Ordinary Americans,*' Bruce replied.

'Bruce, yours is not a pedantic audience. Look, you have to rise above this thing. Get out there today and work the chat shows. You did great on *Coffee Time* yesterday. Tell the world that these killers are not your responsibility and—'

Wayne walked across the room and plucked Karl's whisky glass from his hand. 'OK Bruce. I'm sick of this guy now. We have things to talk about. Get rid of him.'

Bruce jumped out of his seat in his eagerness. 'Right, good, OK. Karl, I appreciate you coming round and I'm going to think over what you said, but right now I'm busy, OK, so . . .'

Karl was astonished. He had known Bruce for years. They were friends. 'You want me to go?'

'Yes, I do.'

'Because you have stuff to do with these people?'

'Yes.'

Karl looked from Wayne to Scout and made no attempt to conceal his distaste. He was very worried. These types were clearly no good. There was trouble here. He had no idea just how much trouble there was, or indeed what kind.

'Look, Bruce' – Karl lowered his voice – 'if you want something rough to mess around with, you should talk to me and I'll get it for you. This kind of thing is dangerous. You're going to end up blackmailed.'

'Karl, go,' Bruce replied. 'Now.'

Karl turned away. He could do no more. 'OK. See you.'

WAYNE

See you.

Wide shot, taking in the whole room. Karl is walking towards the door. Wayne reaches down behind Scout and pulls out a gun.

BRUCE
(Shouting)

No!

Almost simultaneously, before Karl even has time to realize that something is wrong, Wayne has shot him in the back. Karl begins to fall forward, dead.
Two shot of Brooke standing over Scout, doing Scout's hair. Brooke screams.

SCOUT

Ow! You pulled my hair!

BROOKE

I'm sorry.

Wide shot. Everything is happening at once. Karl is still falling to the floor. Slow motion. An expulsion of blood and guts flies out from the front of the falling body as the bullet explodes through.
Close-up. On the wall in front of Karl's falling body, a framed print, a poster for *Ordinary Americans*. Karl's lifeblood impacts upon the poster in a bloody splat. A buzzing sound is heard.
Whip pan from bloodstain on the poster, across the wall to a close-up on the wall intercom, which is buzzing again.

Chapter Twenty-Three

Detectives Jay and Crawford stood on another sweeping drive outside another gorgeous colonnaded mansion. As before, all around them the false rainbows shimmered above the lawns.

'You know, if your theory's right,' Crawford said, 'this door's going to get opened with lead.'

'Hey, you get paid, don't you?' Jay replied, and he rang the bell again.

Inside the house there was panic.

Susan Schaefer had only recently arrived home, having spent the night with a new acquaintance whom she had met at the Oscars. But it was not this that had thrown the movie star into a frenzy of confusion. She was a forthright modern celebrity, and press revelations about her latest boyfriend held no fears for her. In fact, if anything she was rather proud of her exhausting private life. That was not the reason that the sound of the buzzer had created this agony of indecision in her.

The problem was simply what to do with her breakfast.

She had arrived home famished, and had instantly stuck six streaky rashers under the grill. When they were perfectly crispy, she put them on a plate, added maple syrup and some double choc ice cream from the freezer, and wolfed the lot. She had been on her way to the bathroom to puke it all up again when the buzzer buzzed.

This was the reason for the panic. Every moment that the food remained in her stomach her traitorous gastric juices would be digesting it. She had to get to the toilet and hurl.

But the buzzer kept buzzing.

'Later. I'm busy,' she shouted into the intercom.

'Police,' Jay shouted into the microphone.

'Police?' A shaky voice asked.

'That's right, Ms Schaefer. We need you to come and speak to us.'

Susan rushed down the stairs and flung open the door in an agony of haste. She could almost feel herself getting fatter as she faced the cops. Six rashers, about a barrel of maple syrup and two scoops of double choc! She *had* to get it out of her stomach! Already half of it must have attached itself to her hips.

'Yeah?' She said, looking so panicky that the detectives believed immediately that they had scored a bullseye.

Carefully they asked her the same questions they had asked Kurt.

'Look, I've only been back half an hour,' she answered breathlessly, 'and I have not seen any psychos.'

But she was sweating, shaking even. She was clearly not happy. Jay tried to keep her talking. He asked her where she had been, where she would be going later in the day. Had she checked her answering service?

'A friend's. The gym. Whadaya think? Of course I checked my messages.' All the time Susan could feel the fat caking on to her thighs, swinging from under her chin, piling up on her bottom. Eventually she could stand it no longer.

'Look, just come in and search the fucking house!' she shouted.

'Thank you, ma'am,' said Jay.

Was it an ambush? Had this poor, terrified woman been coerced into luring two cops to their deaths? They had no choice but to risk it.

Drawing their weapons they crept past Susan and entered the house. Without a word they split up and began their search. Both were on tenterhooks, listening for the slightest disturbance which would, they were sure, be the precursor of terrible violence.

It wasn't long before their worst suspicions were confirmed.

'*Ugh ugh hooor aaarrrrghh!*'

Behind them, they could hear Susan Schaefer croaking and gasping in agony. The psychos were killing her for allowing them in. It sounded as if she was already in her final death throes. Both officers rushed back through the house the way they had come. There was a small door leading off the hall: it was clear that the noise came from there.

'LAPD!' shouted Crawford, and assumed the firing position as Jay tore open the door.

There on her knees before them, head in the toilet, fingers down her throat, was the female star of *Ordinary Americans.*

'What's the matter with you guys?' she shouted. 'Can't a girl finish off her breakfast in peace?'

Chapter Twenty-Four

The buzzer was still buzzing. Karl lay dead on the floor.

'Answer it.' Wayne walked calmly around the couch and sat down beside Scout.

Bruce protested that it was bound to be Farrah, his wife. He said that Wayne could do with him what he wished but that he had no intention of inviting anyone else in so that Wayne could murder them.

Wayne shrugged. 'So tell her to go away. But make it good. If she comes back with the cops, we all cross Jordan together.'

The buzzer rang again. Bruce tried to focus his thoughts. What excuse could he use to send Farrah away? It was difficult to concentrate; his mind was still ringing with the sound of the shot that had killed Karl. The insistent noise of the door buzzer seemed to magnify the memory, as if the shot was still being fired and Karl was still dying.

Bruce looked down at the body of his murdered friend.

'Why?' he asked Wayne. 'We could have got him out.'

'Why? *Why?*' Wayne's emotional barometer swung once again from casual indifference to blind fury. 'Because he called my best girl a weird, scrawny little bitch, Bruce. That's fucking why. What the fuck would you have done? What would Mr Chop Chop have done?'

Mr Chop Chop? Who was Mr Chop Chop? Bruce remembered his other life, the one that was now definitely over. He remembered Mr Chop Chop. How could he forget him? Mr Chop Chop's image was emblazoned on a million T-shirts and lunch-boxes.

What would Mr Chop Chop have done?

'Mr Chop Chop is a fictitious character that I invented. So he wouldn't do anything, because he doesn't exist, you insane bastard!'

It was not bravery that led Bruce to abuse Wayne, but fear and loathing. He was in a state of shock.

The door buzzer sounded again, this time even louder and longer. Wayne looked hard at Bruce. He did not like Bruce's attitude; he felt patronized.

'I know that Mr Chop Chop is a fictitious character, Bruce. That don't mean he don't exist, now, does it? You gonna tell me Mickey Mouse don't exist? Huh? Fictitious characters got a life inside'a the fiction and what I'm asking you is, what, inside of his personal fiction, would Mr Chop Chop do to any fucker who fucked with his baby and called her names? Now you know as well as I do that Mr Chop Chop would chop chop that fucker good, which is what I did. Now stop working yourself up into ten types of asshole and answer the fucking buzzer.'

Again Bruce struggled to overcome his panic. He had to

stay calm. Christ, how could he? He took the phone from the wall and, mastering his shaking voice, attempted to send his nearly ex-wife away.

He told her she was early. That he couldn't see her. That he had a woman with him. 'I'm partying here, Goddamnit. I just won an Oscar.'

If Canute thought he had problems, he never tried to turn back a Beverly Hills spouse intent on discussing alimony.

Bruce put down the phone, the life draining from his face. 'She's coming up. She has a key.'

Wayne shrugged, indifferent once again. He wasn't much bothered either way. He got up and began to drag Karl's corpse towards the door.

'Well, I guess I'd better move ol' Karl, then. You don't want to be having no discussion about who gets the wedding presents and the CDs over a dead body.'

'I'll get her to leave,' Bruce shouted. 'Tell me you'll let her go, tell me you won't kill her.'

Wayne paused at the door. He was holding Karl's corpse under the arms. The dead face of the ex-agent was staring straight up Wayne's nose.

'Maybe. Long as she don't call us no names. Now I'll just take ol' shit-for-brains here down into the kitchen, huh? Jes' tidy him away, so to speak. Scout, you're in charge.' He departed, taking the corpse with him.

Scout looked up at Brooke. 'I'm sorry I shouted at you, Brooke.' She was contrite. 'I didn't mean nothing, it's just you pulled my hair.'

Brooke knew she had only minutes in which to attempt to complete the task she had begun when Wayne had last exited from the room. Scout's attitude, at least, was encouraging. She seemed to care what Brooke thought of her, which was the best start Brooke could hope for. She knelt down beside Scout.

'Scout, listen to me. This can't go on. Sooner rather than later you're going to get caught, and the more trouble you cause the worse it's going to be.'

Scout's stare found its familiar focus on the cushion in her lap underneath which she held her gun.

'We know we're in trouble, Brooke. Big trouble. But Wayne's got a plan.'

'What plan can he possibly have?'

'I dunno, Brooke, but he's got one. "I got me a plan, hon," he says, "and everything is gonna be just fine." That's what he said. He has a plan for our salvation.'

Brooke had no time to be gentle. 'His plan is to get you both killed, that's what his plan is, and that's how it's going to happen. The cops will come, Wayne'll fight and you'll both be shot to ribbons. Us too.'

'He's got a plan.'

'To get you killed.'

'Well, if that's his plan, then it's OK with me. We'll go out together, in a hail of blood, love and glory.'

Brooke's mind raced. She had only minutes – maybe less – to connect. What could she say? Where was Scout vulnerable?

'Love and glory,' Scout repeated. 'Me 'n' Wayne gonna get that tattooed on us one day. It's our motto.'

Brooke plunged. 'And you do love him, don't you, Scout? You love him very much.'

She had connected. This was a subject about which Scout could talk for hours.

'I love him more than my life, Brooke. If I could pull down a star from the sky and give it him I would. If I had a diamond the size of a TV I'd lay it at his feet. I got feelings bigger than the ocean, Brooke, deeper than the grave.'

It was now or never. 'Wayne needs help, Scout. If you love him, you won't let him die. If you love him, you have to let us be your friends, Scout, let us be *his* friends.'

Brooke took Scout's free hand. Scout stiffened a little but allowed herself to be held.

'Will you help us to be his friends?'

'If they take him, they'll put him in the chair,' Scout whispered. 'They'll melt his eyeballs. That's what the chair does t'ya. I read it.' A tear began to steal its way down her cheek.

'But it doesn't have to be that way,' said Brooke, gently squeezing the small hand she held. 'Maybe if we bring him in peacefully they'll put him in a hospital. They'll try to find out why he get's so angry. Bruce is a big man in this state, Scout. He can help.'

Bruce was transfixed. Could Brooke pull it off? There could be only moments left to do it in. She was close, very close. Ask her for the gun! He wanted to scream it. Every sinew of his body was taut like a dog on a straining leash. *Just reach under the cushion and grab the gun.*

Scout raised her head to look at Brooke, her eyes as big as fists. 'You know what I think, Brooke?'

'What's that, Scout, honey?'

'I think you think I'm dumb.' She seemed to say it more in sorrow than anger, as if she desperately wished it was not so.

Brooke hurried to reassure her. 'No! No, it's not true. I don't think you're dumb, Scout. I like you, I think you're smart and you've got to be smart now. You don't want to die and you don't want us to die either. Above all, you don't want Wayne to die. One day you're gonna to lay diamonds at his feet. Give me the gun, Scout.'

Scout sighed. It was almost wistful, almost as if she was day-dreaming. 'You want me to give you my gun?'

'It's best for us all, Scout, including Wayne.'

Bruce realized he was holding his breath. He'd been holding it for quite some time. He tried to let it out slowly so as not to make a sound. If he intruded on the moment it could be disastrous. Scout was still day-dreaming into Brooke's face.

'If I give it to you, will you be my friend?'

'I said I would be, didn't I, Scout?' Brooke replied. 'And I keep my word. Give me the gun.'

This was it. Bruce stared at the cushion that hid Scout's hand. Was her hand moving? Was she going to bring out the gun? Her hand was moving.

Scout's voice was quiet and scared. 'OK,' she said, the sweetest two letters Bruce ever heard.

Close-up on Scout's hand emerging from under the cushion, hold-ing a gun.

Close up on Scout's face, which has totally changed. No longer docile and teary, it fills suddenly with naked hate and fury.

Wide-profile two shot. Scout on the couch, Brooke kneeling before her. In one extremely fast, shockingly sudden movement, Scout pulls back her gun hand and then slams the butt of the gun into Brooke's mouth. There is a nasty crunch as metal connects with gum, bone and tooth. Brooke is propelled backwards out of shot as Scout rises.

Pull back and pan across to bring Scout fully into frame. She is standing over Brooke, hand raised to strike again. Brooke is bleeding heavily at the mouth.

SCOUT

I sure fucking gave it to you, didn't I, you bitch? You

my friend now? Huh? You always keep your word, don't you! So now you're my friend, right?

Cut to Brooke's POV of Scout's face, contorted with fury, staring down at her.

                    SCOUT
        Say it!

Cut to Scout's POV of Brooke, lying face up on the carpet, bleeding, struggling to reply.

                    BROOKE
        I'm your friend.

                    SCOUT
        Well I don't want you for my friend, you whore!
        Because you tried to turn me against my man and
        that is unforgivable! Maybe you want him for yourself.
        Is that it? Are you coming on to my Wayne? If you try
        it, bitch, I'll kill you.

While Scout was working herself up over the unlikely idea that Brooke might ever make a pass at Wayne, Detectives Jay and Crawford, having left Susan Schaefer to her breakfast, were pondering their next move.

'Well, I guess we drew a blank,' Crawford said sympathetically, for he knew how seriously Jay took his work. 'Don't feel bad, though. It was kind of a cute idea. I mean, the papers have been linking our murderers with that movie for weeks.'

'We have one more call to make,' said Jay. 'The Oscar guy.'

'Delamitri?'

'Yeah. In fact, thinking about it, I guess we should have tried him first. I mean, the directors are the damn stars these days, aren't they? They get to be more famous than the actors.'

'That's true. Did you see Delamitri at the ceremony? He made a beautiful speech. You could see he really meant it. You know, like he'd really given it some thought. My wife nearly cried.'

Chapter Twenty-Five

Bruce had scarcely had time to assimilate the catastrophic collapse of Brooke's brave attempt at dividing the enemy when he was faced with a further and even greater nightmare.

Standing at the door were not only his nearly ex-wife, Farrah, but also his beautiful and beloved daughter, Velvet. Velvet was the apple of Bruce's eye. This had not always been clear to Velvet, possibly because Bruce habitually wore shades. None the less, it was the case. Bruce loved Velvet very much. Also, deep down and in a strange way, he still loved her mother.

What a couple they had been.

Fifteen years earlier Bruce had scored his first directorial assignment and his first (and so far only) wife on the same day. The job was a used-car commercial, one of those sad, no-budget nasties, made purely for local TV, in which the owner of the business is himself the star of the ad.

'You want bargains? I've got bargains. *Crazy* bargains!'

At which point the script called for a jump cut so that the client/star could put on plastic novelty glasses, a comedy moustache and a day-glo green bowler hat with a spinning helicopter blade sticking out of the top.

'That's right, you'd be crazy to miss 'em. And I'm *crazy* to give 'em, ha ha!'

The picture froze on the client/star's amusing grin (his laughter soundtrack continued, but speeded up: hahahaheeheehee) and the address of the used-car lot appeared across the screen.

The one bonus for Bruce as he faced that gruesome morning's work was that throughout his pitch the star was to be surrounded by a bevy of gorgeous babes in bikinis. The original script had stated that after the jump cut these babes would also suddenly be wearing crazy masks and hats. However, the constraints of the budget meant this idea had to be vetoed.

Farrah had been one of the babes, and Bruce would never forget the first time he saw her. She had arrived for the shoot on her own Harley, which roared throatily as she gunned the throttle preparatory to dismounting. All heads turned, of course, and she got off the bike as if she had just fucked it. If Bruce had been a cartoon character, his eyes would have been on foot-long stalks by this time, because Farrah had arrived already in costume and ready to work. Under her studded leather jacket she wore only a bikini and bike boots.

He was utterly smitten, and that very night Velvet was conceived.

Bruce and Farrah had had a good marriage, and a long one by Hollywood standards, supporting each other as they climbed their respective career ladders. Eventually, however, their pretensions and aspirations diverged. As

Farrah got older and could no longer do bimbo parts, she started to put on intellectual airs, attending drama classes and pitching for 'proper' roles, something which Bruce found excruciatingly embarrassing. Likewise, as Bruce became more and more the doyen of hip culture his pose got tougher and sneerier (to the point where he had even considered a tattoo), which frankly turned Farrah's stomach, knowing him as she did for the nerd he secretly was. Basically, the marriage eventually failed because she was genuine street pretending to be boulevard, and he was genuine boulevard pretending to be street. They ended up loathing the sight of each other.

But no matter how many times in recent years Bruce had wanted not to see his wife, they were all as nothing to how much he did not want to see her now. On this terrible morning when the psychopath ushered the rest of his sad, dysfunctional little family into their own private hell.

For a moment longer, though, Farrah and Velvet were to remain in ignorance of their danger. Wayne had concealed his gun and Scout had quickly enveloped hers in the folds of her dress before putting the ever-present cushion back on her lap. Was it possible that Wayne might be prepared to let these two new arrivals pass unmolested through the drama he had created? Bruce could scarcely bear to hope.

Even without the weaponry, the scene that greeted Farrah and Velvet as they paused momentarily in lounge doorway was disconcerting.

A gorgeous woman lay on the floor in a grubby, bloodied evening gown, her lip bleeding badly. A strange wild-looking creature was just rising from where she had clearly been sitting astride the prostrate woman. And the young man hovering behind them was the worst of the lot: cocky and sneering, he had nasty, violent-looking tattoos on his heavily muscled arms and what looked alarmingly like bloodstains on his vest and jeans.

'Bruce, your old lady's here,' the man said.

Farrah raised a questioning eyebrow and stuck a piece of gum in her mouth. She didn't much care for such dismissive familiarity, particularly from so obvious a piece of rough trade, but it took more than a couple of tats and a bit of attitude to throw her.

'What the hell's going on here?' she said, striding into the room. 'Some kind of disgusting orgy?'

Velvet was equally unimpressed. 'Oh Daddy, this is so-o-o gross. I mean, you have really lost it. What're you into now, drugs or something?'

Velvet was alarmingly self-assertive for a fourteen-year-old, although to be fair, as a product of the Beverly Hills private schooling system she was no more cocksure than the majority of her contemporaries.

Bruce could scarcely speak. He was still trying to adjust to his daughter's horrifyingly unexpected arrival. 'It's just a . . . a rehearsal, precious.'

Velvet's face expressed some doubt. In fact, it expressed complete and utter contempt for such an absurd excuse.

'Oh yeah?' she laughed. 'What are you rehearsing, a remake of *I Spit on Your Grave*?'

Brooke picked herself up off the floor, dabbing at her bleeding mouth and coughing from the blood she had swallowed.

Farrah eyed her with naked hostility. 'Listen, sweetie, if this is some kind of S & M thing and he's been beating up on you, you make your claim out of his share of our property, not mine.'

Brooke did not reply. There was nothing to say.

Suddenly, without really thinking about what he was doing, Bruce grabbed Velvet and pushed her back towards the door.

'Get out, Velvet. Right now, get out.'

He didn't care if he was acting suspiciously. He just wanted his daughter to run.

'Please, Daddy, don't try and order me around. It's embarrassing. I'm a grown-up woman now. I've made an exercise video.'

This was true. *Teen Workout with Velvet Delamitri* had been something of a success, partly because as many sad old men as teenage girls had bought it.

Thus rebuffed, Bruce turned on Farrah. 'What the hell did you bring her here for? Send her away now. Get her out. She has no business being here.'

'No business?' Farrah sneered 'Well thank you, Bruce, you've just proved my point. I brought *our daughter* here to remind you that she and I are *two* and you are *one*, and that fact will have to be amply reflected in the final settlement.'

Bruce could scarcely contain himself. The woman was talking about money. They were all about to die and she was talking about money! Farrah might be unaware of her predicament but, hell's tits, what was wrong with the woman?

For the umpteenth time since the nightmare had begun, he tried to calm himself. 'Look, Farrah, you'll get a fair settlement, I swear. You can have whatever you want, just you and Velvet leave—'

Huuuurgh, glob. Wayne spat. It was a big spit. He

cleared his throat loudly, grollied up hard and gobbed the lot into a vase. It was a spit which announced that he was still there, and still in charge.

Bruce understood. Wayne did not like what Bruce had said. Offering Farrah whatever she wanted in settlement was bound to sound strange, and Bruce's job was to be normal. That was the only way his daughter was getting out of that house in one piece. But how? How to be normal? Bruce could no longer remember what normal was.

Velvet could, though, and this wasn't it. What is more, whatever it was, she didn't like it. 'Daddy, who are these people? Are they your friends? Can't they go now?'

Wayne strolled across the room and eyed Velvet up and down. Velvet, as most of her contemporaries did, wore the sexy teen version of conservative grown-up clothes. Today it was a smart, tight little two-piece woollen suit in pink – tiny mini-skirt and figure-hugging little jacket – white tights, high heels, lots of make-up. A scrummy little bundle all trussed up in pastels. Cute and clean and shiny as a ripe cherry. Wayne whistled appreciatively through his teeth.

'Mm *mm*, I'll bet you're proud of this one, Bruce.'

Velvet set her jaw against his leering stare, but she was acting more confident than she felt.

Scout looked at Velvet too, but she did not appreciate what she saw. It was strange, she thought, how rich girls had that way of looking that was just so clean and fresh and *undamaged*. Scout knew that Wayne would just love to dirty up that little girl's life. He wouldn't do it, of course, because she'd kill him if he did and he knew it. All the same, she didn't like him leering that way, and she didn't think much of Velvet.

'It's just like you said, precious.' Wayne was still staring at the girl. 'We're friends of your ol' man's. I'm Wayne, this is Scout and the bitch with the fat lip is Brooke Daniels.'

'Brooke Daniels?' Velvet was now convinced that she'd caught her father in the middle of some disgusting post-Oscar debauch. She was half relieved and half horrified, relieved to discover that the situation was not more sinister, horrified because it was so disgusting. Overhearing one's parents having sex is enough to traumatize some kids, so walking in on one of their orgies was a tough call, even for a diamond-hard Hollywood brat like Velvet.

She made an ugly face. 'Oh Daddy, *Playboy* bunnies? Pur-lease! That is so-o-o trashy and also just totally nineteen eighties.'

'I was never a bunny, I was a centrefold. What's more, I'm an actress,' Brooke said quietly.

Bruce had to try again to make Farrah leave, whatever the risk of arousing Wayne's anger. The alternative was to let Velvet prattle on, and Bruce knew it would not be long before she made dangerously obvious her distaste for the company she found herself in. Karl had been killed for showing disrespect, and when it came to showing disrespect tough New York agents were not in the same class as cocky little Hollywood princesses.

'Farrah,' Bruce barked, pointing his finger at her, 'I'm busy! Get the girl out. Now!'

Farrah wasn't going anywhere. It was clear to her that Bruce was worried, even flustered. This suited her; she'd rarely ever seen him anything other than calm and in control. His current mood was likely to bring forth further financial concessions in her favour. She held Velvet to her.

'Bruce, you are speaking about your own daughter. Trying to throw her out of what *was* her home. You disgust me. You'd rather be with sluts and street trash than—'

'Excuse me.' It was Scout who interrupted her.

Bruce froze, fully expecting his little family to be instantly cut down in a hail of vengeful bullets. But Scout was happy to ignore the insult. She was in a curious mood.

'Mrs Delamitri? Can I ask you something now?'

'No, you may not,' Farrah replied, with enough haughty disdain to cool a chili pepper, haughty disdain which was entirely lost on Scout, who pressed on regardless.

'Is it true you got so puke drunk one time that you miscarried? That you retched up so hard you done lost your baby?'

For a moment, even Farrah was lost for words. Her battle with the bottle had been long and public. She was naturally aware of the numerous disgusting myths that circulated about her, but she had never been so rudely confronted with one before.

'*What* did you say?'

'Well, that's what I read in the *National Enquirer*,' Scout protested.

'Well, I heard a better one than that,' said Wayne. 'I heard Mrs Delamitri here got stopped in her car one time by the cops, and they asked her to blow in the bag and she offered to blow the cops instead. And she did! Ain't that right, Farrah?' Wayne had recounted this anecdote often before, but it still made him laugh.

'I don't know about no cops and unhygienic acts,' Scout said primly, 'but it sure did say she got puke drunk and lost her child.'

'And that Velvet here had her first blow-job when she was seven,' Wayne added.

Velvet had read the article in question. 'It said *nose* job! And it wasn't true!'

Farrah turned on Bruce in fury. 'What is going on here, Bruce? Is this some kind of pathetic tactic? Are you trying to scare me or something? Because it won't work.'

'No, Daddy, it won't,' said Velvet, standing beside her mother in fiscal solidarity. 'Mommy and I want this house, plus the New York apartment.

'Otherwise it's trial by talk show. I'll tell Oprah you used erection creams—'

'Mommy! Don't be gross.'

Wayne roared with laughter and poured himself another drink. This was better than he could ever have hoped.

Bruce was desperate now. He threw caution aside. 'You can have what you want, Farrah, everything, the last cent. I'll sign today. Just get Velvet out now.'

At last it dawned on Farrah that something might be wrong. She was hardly the most sensitive of souls. She lived in Hollywood, and other people's problems were other people's problems. She had been born with a thick skin, and it had been pulled so taut by cosmetic surgeons that these days bad vibes tended just to bounce off it like dried peas off a drum. But when Bruce started talking about handing over everything, she knew something was very wrong. Also, clearly it must have something to do with the dangerous-looking people who seemed to have invaded Bruce's life. She decided to pursue her claims at a later date.

'I'll have my lawyer call. Come on, Velvet. We're outa here.'

But alas the penny had dropped too late. Wayne was already blocking the doorway.

'No need for them legal parasites to get involved, Mrs Delamitri. Fuckin' lawyers are eating away at the soul of this country. So fuck 'em I say. Fact is, I'll be handling Mr Delamitri's side of the negotiations from now on. Is that OK with you?'

'Come on, Velvet. We'll talk with your father another time.' Farrah took Velvet's hand and tried to push past Wayne, but he held his ground.

'Truth is, Mrs Delamitri, Bruce here wants you dead.'

He let this sink in for a moment before continuing, 'He's said so himself, and I have decided, in view of all the pleasure your husband has given me in the past, to fulfil his wish.'

With this he produced his gun and smiled a big smile.

'For God's sake, Wayne, let them go. You said you'd let them go.'

Wayne raised the gun to his shoulder and aimed it at Farrah.

Velvet screamed, shedding about thirty-five years in three seconds and turning into a fourteen-year-old girl.

'Daddy, do something!'

'Wayne, please!' Bruce shouted.

Wayne kept his eye trained along the barrel and straight into Farrah's face.

'You said you wanted her dead, Bruce. You said that. He admitted he said that, didn't he, Scout?'

'I heard him.'

'You don't go saying stuff you don't mean, do you, Bruce?' Wayne did not take his eye off Farrah.

'It was a figure of speech,' Bruce pleaded, his voice cracking with fear. 'For God's sake, man, it was a figure of speech.'

'Bruce, Bruce, calm down, buddy. It is not such a big deal. People get killed every few seconds. Listen, in South Central LA they're pleased if they make it through lunch. Man, if you live to see your balls drop, you're a survivor, you're an old man! C'mon, let me waste the bitch. I'll take the rap and you get to keep everything.'

Bruce's brain was thumping. He had to think of something, say something.

'*C'mon*, Bruce,' Wayne continued, 'this is the luckiest night of your life. I'm a wanted killer, dropped a hundred people. One more or less won't make any difference to me, but for you . . . Hey, you'll never have to hear this bitch's voice again, never have to put up with that scrawny fuckin' skull-head in front of your face. You *said* you wanted her dead, Bruce, you know you did.'

Wayne hadn't taken his eye off Farrah. It was still trained along the barrel of his gun, while he spoke his killing pitch.

'Look, Wayne.' Bruce spoke slowly, every syllable a miracle of mind over fear. 'I said I wanted Farrah dead because I was imagining something that in thought might or might not be desirable but in reality is obnoxious. Like, have you ever said, "I could eat a horse"? I'll bet you've said something similar. Now of course you don't actually *want* to eat a horse but—'

'Bruce.' Wayne finally looked up from his gun.

'Yes?'

'Are you patronizing me?'

'No, I'm just—'

'You think I don't know the difference between a figure of speech like "I could eat a horse" and a man who's telling the truth, even though he's such a spineless, unAmerican, Lamborghini-driving faggot that he don't have the guts to admit it? You hate this bitch. If she'd got killed in her car coming here today, you'd have been dancing a jig, I know you would. If fate was to take this fuckin' fossilized Barbie doll bag o' bones out of your life, that would be just fine. Well, fate's working good for you here. The bitch has met a psycho killer. Ain't your fault, so don't fight it. Watch me drop her, and count your blessings.'

Wayne took aim again. Farrah screamed and covered her eyes.

Bruce stepped in front of Wayne's gun. 'Look, I don't want her dead, all right? I don't care what I may or may not have said in the past but I'm telling you now, I don't want her to die and I don't hate her! So if my opinion means anything to you, which you keep saying it does, I'm begging you, pleading with you, don't kill her. Just leave her alone. *Please!*'

Wayne lowered his gun. 'OK OK, just trying to do you a favour. No need to get worked up about it.'

At this point, to everybody's surprise Brooke, who had appeared to be something of a spent force leapt across the room and jammed a pistol into the side of Scout's head.

While all attention was focused on the debate about whether to kill Farrah, Brooke had been preparing to mount a counterattack. She had reached down into her bag, which still lay on the floor beside her crumpled pantyhose – the hose which she had removed so beautifully in an earlier and happier life. In the bag was the pistol with which Brooke had scared Bruce and won herself the promise of an audition for his next movie.

Brooke's movement had been so surprising and so sudden that Scout had had no time to produce her own weapon from under the cushion and so was now very much at Brooke's mercy. The balance of power in the room had suddenly shifted considerably.

'Drop your gun right now, Wayne, you sadistic bastard,' Brooke shouted, 'or I'll blow this sick little fuck's brains clean across the room!'

Brooke was an intimidating figure, with congealed blood caked around her beautiful mouth, her glamorous gown torn and grubby, her body heaving with tension beneath the soiled satin. She had come a long way in a short time, and as Bruce could testify she had not been exactly without spirit in the first place. Now she seemed genuinely capable of anything.

Wayne certainly took her seriously. 'Don't you go pointing no gun at my baby, now.' Slowly he swung his own gun away from Farrah and Bruce in order to cover Brooke. In reply, Brooke pushed her own weapon harder into Scout's head. Scout winced.

'Brooke, girl,' said Wayne 'you do know that if you kill Scout, you and Bruce and these other two will not get to draw one more breath.'

'Maybe so, Wayne, but you love Scout, and I don't love any of these shits. What is more, killing us will not bring your baby back if I have just put a bullet through her tiny brain – that is, always presuming I don't fucking miss it altogether!'

It was a classic stand-off. Any decent movie-maker

would have spent a good two minutes lingering on every aspect of the scene. The tense trigger fingers, the narrowed, steady eyes, Brooke's heaving bosom.

Wayne smiled. 'You know, when this kinda thing happens in the movies – when two people are pointing pieces at each other and sweating and all – I always think to myself, what's the problem? Why doesn't one of them just quit talking and pull the trigger?'

Then Wayne shot Brooke.

The impact threw her backwards against the drinks cabinet like a rag doll, except rag dolls don't have blood pouring from between their ribs.

'I mean that has to be the sensible thing to do, hasn't it?'

Brooke's valiant fight back had ended as quickly and as surprisingly as it had begun. Now she really was a spent force. The gun had flown out of her hand as her body hit the cabinet, and she clearly would not be picking it up again. Indeed it seemed a good bet that Brooke would not be picking herself up again either.

Bruce wondered whether he was going mad. Two people had now been shot in his lounge inside one hour.

'When is this going to end, Wayne?' he asked.

For the moment, his sorrow was greater even than his fear. This splendid person, whom he had only just met, was dying. She had fought and fought again, far better than he had done himself, and now she was going to die before him, her only crime being to have left a party with the wrong man.

'It's gonna end soon, Bruce. 'Cos what I got, you see, is a plan.'

Wayne crossed to the window and peered out across the magnificent grounds of Bruce's mansion towards the outer gates.

'And here they come.'

Chapter Twenty-Six

D etectives Jay and Crawford got the surprise of their lives.

A few moments earlier, just when Brooke was confronting Wayne, the two officers had turned their unmarked car into Bruce's drive. The main gate was open, which aroused their suspicions immediately, and they had driven up the long gravel road slowly and with caution.

'Nobody leaves their gate open these days,' Crawford opined nervously.

As they turned the last corner and quietly halted before the vast frontage of Bruce's mansion, they both knew that Jay's hunch had been right and that they had found the Mall Murderers. There were three cars slewed casually outside the house, Bruce's Lamborghini, Farrah's Lexus, with FARRAH spelt out in silver on the numberplate, and a big old '57 Chevy.

Very gently Crawford slipped the car into reverse and pulled back round the corner and out of sight.

'Detective Jay to control,' Jay breathed into his radio, struggling to contain his excitement. 'Request urgent support.'

No sooner had he said the words than behind and above them they heard a rumble which turned almost immediately into a roar. They turned round to look out of the rear window.

'Son of a bitch!' exclaimed Crawford. 'That was quick.'

A convoy of trucks and cars was piling through Bruce's gate. Some had the markings of various TV news stations on them, some bore the badge of Los Angeles's finest. The noise of chopper blades joined the cacophony as a couple of helicopters appeared, swooping overhead. Both aircraft were owned by the media; the police had taken a little longer to scramble theirs, but they would be arriving soon.

The two detectives watched from their car, and Wayne watched from the window, as the convoy surged up the long drive and spread out dramatically on to the immaculate lawns (crushing the sprinkler system) and started to disgorge hundreds of people. Within no more than three minutes the quiet solitude that Jay and Crawford had so recently enjoyed was just an impossible memory. There was a marksman behind every wall and hedge, and a news reporter plus his or her crew on what seemed like every available piece of open ground. The only things missing were the gawping sad-acts who like to stand in the background waving and grinning whenever an event is occurring and news reports are being filed.

Within the besieged house, Bruce joined Wayne, uninvited, at the window. Suddenly, just when he had nearly given up, hope was dawning. They were no longer alone.

'They've found you,' he said 'like they were always going to.'

'Found me Bruce?' Wayne responded without taking his eyes off the extraordinary amount of activity going on outside. 'Found me? They didn't find me, man, I told them where I was. I told them to get on up here right now.'

Wayne turned away from the window, grabbed the TV remote control and began channel-hopping.

It was not difficult to find what he was looking for. Basically, the choice was either kids' morning cartoons or Bruce's house. It divided up at about twenty channels each.

Wayne flicked through the news shows.

'. . . notorious mass murderers, Wayne Hudson and his beautiful young female companion, Scout . . .' the first channel said, its reporter standing against a backdrop of Bruce's prime orange grove.

'They never know my whole name,' Scout remarked petulantly, although secretly she was delighted to be called beautiful by a genuine Hollywood cable TV news reporter.

Wayne flipped to one of the network channels, the *Today Show*, or *Good Morning America*.

'. . . the criminals appear to have taken refuge at the home of Bruce Delamitri, the renowned film-maker, the man who is said to have inspired their brutal killing rampage . . .' The immaculately groomed young reporter was making her report from beside Bruce's pool.

'Daddy, that's our pool!' Velvet exclaimed in astonishment.

Bruce stared at the screen. He scarcely knew what to think. There were so many things *to* think. The danger his daughter was in . . . Brooke bleeding to death on his carpet . . . His murdered agent and the security guard . . . Wayne's inexplicable behaviour in telling the authorities of his whereabouts . . .

But despite all these thoughts, any one of which could have stood some considerable mulling over, Bruce's paramount preoccupation at that point was one of intellectual outrage. 'They're blaming me. Jesus! Those facile morons are blaming me!'

'I sure hope so, man,' Wayne remarked, and hit another channel.

'. . . Mr Delamitri, last seen leaving the Oscars ceremony in the company of nude model Brooke Daniels . . .' A couple of photos from Brooke's *Playboy* spread appeared on the screen. Somebody at the TV station been doing some excellent and very speedy picture research.

Astonishingly, despite the fact that Brooke's whole body was in shock and she was already semi-delirious, she was still able to take in the sense of what was being broadcast. 'I'm a fucking actress!' she gasped from her position on the floor.

'Keep it down, Brooke, I'm watching TV here,' Wayne said, and flipped to another channel, where another immaculate, hairsprayed head appeared, this time standing in front of Bruce's garages.

'. . . leaving a trail of pillage, mayhem and death, murdering indiscriminately in the manner of the fictitious anti-heroes of Bruce Delamitri's Oscar-winning movie, *Ordinary Americans* . . .'

'They're blaming me! Jesus Christ, they are blaming *me* . . .' Bruce was astonished. This reporter was in front of *his* garage, literally only yards from where he himself stood, broadcasting live from outside *his* house, where he was being held prisoner by armed killers, and she was blaming *him*. Blaming him for the mayhem going on, mayhem which, as he had been assuring people for many months, had *nothing to do with him*.

Wayne changed channel again.

'Homer, I've been reading Bart's report card,' said Marge. 'It says our boy is academically challenged.'

'Really?' said Homer, drinking some beer. 'Academically challenged, huh? That sounds good. He probably gets it from me.'

'It mean's he's stupid, Dad,' said Lisa.

'Eat my shorts,' said Bart.

'Sorry about that,' said Wayne, and flipped to another channel.

'Leave it on,' Scout protested. 'I like *The Simpsons* and I don't think I ever saw that one.'

'Later, precious pie.'

Another reporter was speaking out of the screen. '. . . and so these two "Ordinary Americans" have taken refuge in the home of the man who foresaw their coming, who, some might even argue, brought them forth . . .'

Bruce shouted at the TV, 'Nature makes killers not movies!'

Wayne turned the television off.

'Well, I guess if you're just going to keep on talking we might as well have the damn TV off. Can't hear it none, anyways.'

Farrah spoke up. It had taken her some time to recover from the terror of staring down Wayne's gun barrel, but her spirit was returning. There were already hundreds of police officers outside. Maybe they were going to make it after all.

'Look,' she said, lighting a very long, very thin cigarette, made with pink paper and a golden filter, 'if the cops are here you can't escape—'

'I told you already, lady, I don't want to escape. I asked them to come here. I called them when I came down to get you.'

Bruce could make no sense of this at all. 'You called the cops?'

'Well, no, as a matter of fact I called NBC, told 'em to get all the stations down here. I guess they must have called the cops as well. It don't matter none. Me and Scout here are used to ignoring cops.'

There were now so many cops in the grounds of Bruce and Farrah's mansion that Wayne would have had to have been Buddha himself in order to ignore them. There were nearly as many cops as journalists, and more were arriving all the time. Detectives Jay and Crawford passed them as, with heavy hearts, they themselves left the scene of the action.

'Nothing more for us to do here,' Jay had been forced to admit.

It was a bitter pill to swallow. Having pulled off a brilliant piece of intuitive police work, locating two desperate and elusive felons, he was now forced to accept that virtually the whole force had been only seconds behind him. There was nothing left for them to contribute and so, as the helicopter and trucks disgorged squad after squad of paramilitary human gunships, the two detectives retired from the scene with what dignity they could muster.

One of the helicopters swooping overhead contained the chief officer of the LAPD, and he was in a hurry. Chief Cornell had been woken with the thrilling news that the Mall Murderers had Bruce Delamitri and his family held hostage in the Delamitri mansion. Chief Cornell had immediately decided to take charge of the operation himself.

He had no choice. He desperately needed the air time.

Thirty years before, when he had joined the police, Cornell had not done so in order to turn into a showbiz tart. But that was what had happened. He, who as a boy had dreamt of catching crooks, now spent half his time having lunch with them. In fact he had become one himself. His actions were no longer governed by the need to uphold justice as laid down by law. They were governed by the necessity of balancing the various social and political consequences of whatever action he took. He wasn't a cop any more, he was a politician – and a crooked one at that. All city officials were, whether they liked it or not, because the whole sad, crumbling edifice was built on lies and half-truths. Nobody could tell it straight any more because there was no straight to tell. Every group, be it defined racially, financially, geographically, sexually, by religion or by choice of knit-wear, had its own truth. And that truth was diametrically opposed to everyone else's truth. More than that, it was threatened by everyone else's truth. The city was out of control and the police chief's number one job, like that of every politician, was to persuade people it wasn't.

For that he needed profile. He needed air time.

And today he was going to get it. The chopper landed and Cornell stepped masterfully and purposefully into a barrage of clicking cameras. He was a general in a war zone, and beyond the cameras he could see the might of his army manoeuvring into position. It felt good. This was a dream come true. Suddenly, when he had least dared to hope for it (which is to say, three months before the city elections), Cornell had a real, one hundred per cent macho, shit-kickin', butt-whippin', ass-kissin' siege to deal with. A genuine proper piece of high-rolling, high-octane, high-profile police work, which above all, above double all, above all and hallelujah, was *race-free*! A race-free crime! In election year! Chief Cornell thanked his stars. He thanked his God. He would have happily conceded that somewhere in his youth or childhood he must have done something good, because all his Christmases (or holiday seasons, as the city now referred to them) had come at once. For the first time in a long time he was dealing with a crime of city-wide, state-wide, national and international significance in which race was not an issue. He had never dared to dream he would see its like again.

Chief Cornell was himself black. He had experienced plenty of racism in his life and he hated it. But his particular private and current hatred of racism was to do not with his colour but with his job. He was the city's top cop. He was proud of that and he wanted to do a good job, but racism, from whichever hue it emanated, had made that impossible. Proper police work was no longer an option available to him. Every day he encountered what appeared to be open-and-shut cases. The man killed the woman, the gang beat the guy. Simple, it would seem, but no, then it turns out that the main protagonists are of different races and suddenly the open-and-shut case turns into an impenetrable maze in which what people actually do is irrelevant. What matters is what the jury, and ultimately the public, *feel* about it.

But now, glory of glories, he had a race-free case.

Victims and villains were the same colour. Imagine, Chief Cornell thought, if those had been black or Asian punks in there, shooting white *Playboy* centrefolds and holding little white girls hostage. Absolutely everything about the case would be different. Nearly as bad would be if the director or the model had been black and the punks white. Either way, the case would already be a political football, there would be pickets and protestors at the gates. It did not bear thinking about.

But the chief's luck was in. Fate had delivered to him the perfect case in which to do, and above all be seen to do, a bit of proper policing, and by hell, Hades, glory and damnation, he was going to make the most of it.

Unfortunately for Chief Cornell, there was another chief on the scene and he was equally excited. Brad Murray, Chief of NBC News and Current Affairs, recognized the Delamitri siege as probably the sexiest bit of news and current affairs it had ever been his extreme good fortune to preside over.

'If this one wasn't true,' Murray remarked to his gorgeous power PA as they stepped off their own helicopter, 'I'd never have dared to invent it.'

But it was true, and what was more the principal villain appeared to understand the central and overriding principle of news and current affairs: that the most important element in any drama is television.

In an armoured police command vehicle the two chiefs met: an irresistible force and an immovable object. Their quarrel was over who should put the call through to Bruce Delamitri's house and open up negotiations with the villains. Understandably, Chief Cornell felt that it was a matter for the authorities. Chief Murray, however, reminded Cornell that Wayne Hudson had called the networks, not the cops, and had been most specific that he wanted to talk to a top news man.

A decade earlier, Cornell might have had a couple of his constables throw the NBC guy off the truck but not now. Not with elections looming, not with a city perpetually on edge. The police chief knew he had to co-operate with the media every bit as much as they had to co-operate with him, and so a compromise was reached. Having instructed AT&T to block all incoming calls to the Delamitri mansion (every acquaintance Bruce had in LA was of course trying to call him), the two chiefs agreed that they would call Wayne together, on a party line.

As it happened, they need not have bothered arguing about it because Wayne did all the talking anyway.

'OK, shut up and listen up,' he barked into the phone, without even bothering to enquire who was calling. 'This is Wayne Hudson, the Mall Murderer. Now me and my baby are in control here, you understand? We got Bruce Delamitri, we got Brooke Daniels, who is an actress by the way – you tell your reporters that, you hear? Also we got Bruce's wife and their daughter, Velvet, who is as cute as a button and will make very good TV, whatever I decide to do with her. Now you just give me a number right now where I can call you back when I'm ready with my demands.'

Police Chief Cornell gave the number, and having done so began to try and negotiate. He was, after all, trained in this type of thing.

'OK, Wayne,' he said. 'I think you want to make a deal.'

'What I want is for you to shut the fuck up, OK?' said Wayne. 'I will talk to you when I'm ready, and when

I do it will be me that says what's what. Understand? You know what I'm capable of. Don't call back now. Meantime, you have a nice day.'

The police chief and the NBC chief put their respective phones down and looked at each other.

'Guess we'll have to wait, Chief,' said the cop. 'Maybe this would be a good time for them to put a little make-up on me?'

'You got it, Chief,' said the newsman.

Inside the house, Wayne too had replaced the receiver.

'What did you mean about me being good TV?' Velvet asked, her voice understandably rather shaky. 'What are you going to do to me?'

'It's OK, baby,' said her mother, though it clearly wasn't. 'Are you holding us hostage?'

Wayne poured himself another drink; he felt he'd earned it. Scout was still sipping at her first *crème de menthe*. She was not a big boozer.

'In a manner of speaking, you're hostages,' said Wayne. 'Basically, what I got here is a plan.'

'Wayne's had a plan right from the start,' Scout said proudly.

'What plan?' Bruce was angry. He shouted at Wayne, 'What are you talking about?'

'Well, I guess a plan to avoid being executed for murder, Bruce. I can't think of an agenda more immediate than that for people in the position me and Scout find ourselves in.'

Brooke was still conscious. Velvet had briefly attended the Guides during her extremely short childhood, and knew a little first aid. Showing a composure that would have surprised her classmates and teachers, she had done her best to manoeuvre Brooke into the correct position and pad her wound with cushions, so that for the time being at least Brooke was still capable of following the conversation.

'Plan? Fuck you,' she said. 'You're going to die, you bastards. You don't stand a chance.'

'Don't talk,' said Velvet. 'Your wound is real big and any physical activity at all will screw any chance of the blood starting to clot.' She turned to Wayne. 'She's got to have a doctor. Can't we ask them to send in a doctor?'

'Maybe. I don't know yet,' Wayne replied.

'But she'll die.'

'Miss Delamitri, I thought you might have understood by now that I don't mind none if people get dead.'

Bruce was still standing at the window. Media cars and trucks and police vehicles continued to pour through his gate. He had eight acres of grounds and it was all already crowded. Incredible. A veritable village had sprung up in twenty minutes. Satellite dishes, tripods, fabulous hair-dos, four-wheel-drives, a million metres of electric cable. The hum of the massed mobile generators could be heard for miles.

Bruce struggled to get a handle on what was happening to him.

His security guard was dead, Karl was dead. Brooke was dying. He'd just won an Oscar and the entire LA media community plus half its police force were camped out on his lawn. What was more, the man who had brought all these things about (except the Oscar, although even that was apparently connected, according to the TV) was standing in Bruce's lounge, calmly sipping Bruce's bourbon and covering the room with a machine-gun. How could all this have happened? And in so few short hours?

What was going on?

'What's your plan, Wayne?' Bruce asked. 'Please tell me your plan.'

'OK, Bruce, I'll tell you. As you know, Scout here and me have committed murder and mayhem across four states. We can't deny it, 'cos we done it and it's true. Now I wish I could tell you that every one of those corpses we left lying all over America deserved to die. I wish I could say it was like the movies, where rapists, rednecks, bad cops, hypocrites and child-abusers get just what the fuck they deserve. But it just ain't so.'

Scout felt that perhaps Wayne was being a little hard on himself. Why should all the burden of proof lie with them?

'They might have been all those things, Wayne,' she said. 'We never knew any of them long enough to find out.'

'Well, whatever, honey. The point I'm making here is that we are in deep shit. They know who we are and they're going to get us. We've been caught on about one hundred security videos. On top of which, Scout could not resist sending her picture to her home-town local paper, for which I forgive her, even though it was dumb.'

'They all said I was trash and wouldn't amount to a hill of beans. Well, I showed them.'

'Yes, you did, baby doll. You sure showed them. So basically what I'm saying here, Bruce, is that whatever we do we are going to get caught damn soon now, and when we do I guess we have a higher than average chance of getting fried in the chair.'

Brooke gurgled at this from her position on the carpet. A gurgle that could be roughly translated as saying, 'The sooner the better, pal.'

Wayne ignored her. 'And that, Bruce, is where you come in.'

'What do you mean? What can I do?'

'We need you, Bruce. You're going to save our lives.'

'You're our saviour,' Scout added. 'That's why we came to you. You can make it different.'

'Give them what they want, Bruce. Anything – just give it to them!' This was from Farrah, for whom hope continued to dawn. Was it possible that they would be able to buy their way out of this? And did Bruce have insurance for hold-ups?

'I don't know what they want!' Bruce shouted at her. He swung back to Wayne. 'What *do* you want? Tell me, I'll give it to you, whatever it is.'

'We need an excuse, Bruce.' Wayne said.

'What we're looking for here is someone else to take the blame.'

Chapter Twenty-Seven

D own on the lawn the news reporters were repeating over and over again what little information that they had on the situation: '. . . the Oscar-winner . . . the Mall Murderers . . . the beautiful model/actress . . . the cute teen . . . the estranged wife . . .'

Their reports were punctuated on air by re-run footage from the previous night: Bruce on the red carpet . . . Bruce, standing on legs of fire, accepting his Oscar . . . Bruce dancing with Brooke at the Bosom Ball.

Then it was 'back to the studio', where the anchor men and women solemnly repeated the whole thing 'for those of you who've just joined us': '. . . the Oscar-winner . . . the Mall Murderers . . . the beautiful model/actress . . . the cute teen . . . the estranged wife . . .'

After this, the studio anchors threw back to the reporters on the ground. 'And let's go back to the Delamitri mansion, to see if there are any further developments.'

'There have as yet been no further developments,' replied the reporters on the ground. 'All I can tell

you is . . . the Oscar-winner . . . the Mall Murderers
. . . the beautiful model/actress . . . the cute teen . . .
the estranged wife . . .'

'In that case,' said the studio anchors, 'let's turn now
to our panel of criminal psychologists and show-business
experts.'

In TV studios all over LA, and indeed all over the
country, hastily summoned 'experts' were bundled into
their seats, having been hurriedly powdered down, miked
up and handed their cheques.

'Exactly what in your opinion is going on in there?'
the studio anchor asked the experts gravely.

'Well, this is a classic case,' the experts chorused, 'many
aspects of which are discussed in my latest book, which is
of course available in all good bookshops.'

Chapter Twenty-Eight

Wayne and Bruce stood together, staring out of the window at the instant city below. There were a hundred rifles trained on Wayne, but, unless the police could be sure of hitting Scout as well, no order to fire would be given.

'Someone to take the blame?' Bruce asked. 'What the hell do you mean, someone to take the blame? Some kind of magician, who can explain that the whole thing was an optical illusion and that actually someone else shot all those people?'

Bruce was feigning astonishment, but in the back of his mind a terrible suspicion had dawned.

On the floor, over by the drinks cabinet, Brooke coughed. Maybe she was trying to say something, maybe she was just coughing.

'This woman has to have a doctor,' Velvet pleaded. 'You have to let her have one.'

Wayne swung his gun towards Velvet, suddenly angry again. 'Listen, I did not ask that bitch to threaten my baby, OK? She is in this dire situation by her own choosing, on account of the fact that she pulled a piece on my girl. So shut the fuck up, because me and Bruce are talking here. Or maybe I should shut you up. Huh?'

He advanced a step towards the girl and raised his fist. Velvet burst into tears.

'If you hurt her,' said Bruce, 'I swear that whatever you want from me you will never get.'

'You'll do what the fuck I tell you to, whether I bust this bitch's head or not.' Wayne's mood swings really were most alarming.

'Please don't hurt me,' Velvet sobbed.

'There's no need to go beating up on no little girls, Wayne,' Scout remarked. 'It's beneath you.'

'This ain't no little girl, precious pie. Kids're born old in Hollywood. Why this little slut musta spent more money already in her few short years than your sweet momma woulda earned in fifty lifetimes. She *deserves* to get slapped around some.'

'I've told you,' said Bruce, 'you'll get nothing from me if you hurt her.'

Wayne lowered his fist slowly. 'I want you to know, Bruce, that I am minding the wishes of my baby here and not yours. Because I can assure you that you will do whatever I tell you to do, whether I hurt your little girl or not.'

Bruce seized upon the point. 'And what is it you want me to do?' He was almost begging. He had to know the worst, deeply fearful of it though he was. Fearful because in truth he had already guessed.

'I want you to plead on our behalf. I want you to speak up for us and save us from the chair.'

'Plead on your behalf? You're crazier than I thought. You really think my word's going to save you from the punishment you deserve? You're guilty as Hitler.'

'Sure we're guilty, if by that you mean we done all the stuff they say we done, but that ain't the point, is it? Not these days. These days, no matter how guilty you are, you can still be innocent.'

He had lost them. They all stared at him, all except Scout, who had hold of one of her feet and was inspecting her toenails.

'For instance,' Wayne explained, 'like that spick chick who cut off the guy's pecker, right? She was guilty for sure, she never denied it. She cut off that ol' boy's manhood and threw it out of a car window. Do you see that bitch in prison, huh? Is she breaking rocks in the hot sun? No, I don't think so, because although she was guilty she was innocent too. In America you can be both.'

Scout looked up from her toenails. 'That's right, she done it, but she was innocent and I agree. That bastard beat up on her and he done raped her too. He got his, and I hope she used a rusty knife.'

Wayne winced. 'Now, Scout, you know that you and me disagree on this issue. Personally, I don't see as how no woman can get raped by her husband, on account of the fact that he is only taking what's his anyway. What's more, I think that any Mexican bitch who cuts the dick off an ex-United States Marine who has served his country should rot in a hole.'

'She was abused.'

'If you think a man's abusing you, honey, you leave him. You do not cut his dick off.'

'The court agreed with her.'

'The court was a bunch of lesbians and faggots.'

Scout made a sulky face and returned to her toe-nails.

'Yeah, well, whatever,' Wayne said, 'we're getting off the point here. What I'm saying is, right or wrong, the greaseball bitch walked free. She done it, she said she done it, she was glad she done it, but she walked. Guilty but innocent, you see. You can be both in the Land of the Free, always assuming, that is, that you got an excuse.'

'Are you suggesting' – Bruce tried to sound firm and intelligent – 'that there is any excuse for mass murder?'

'Bruce, there is an excuse for anything and everything in the USA! What about them cops who beat up on the nigger and started a damn riot? They was videoed! You see them doing time? No sir you do not. Remember O.J.? They said he killed his wife. Turned out they'd got the wrong victim. The dead chick wasn't the victim at all. No way, O.J. was the victim. He was the victim of a racist cop, who incidentally also walked. Nobody gets blamed for anything in this country, *nothing is anybody's fault*. So why the Hell should we take the rap for what we done, huh?'

In his mind's eye, Bruce suddenly saw again the beautiful idiot he had harangued at the Bosom Ball. When had that been? The previous evening? The previous lifetime, more like. Bruce heard once more his own voice rising above the banality and the hypocrisy he'd thought he heard around him: 'Nothing is anybody's fault.'

He'd said it himself.

Could Wayne actually be right? Could the bastard get away with it?

'Wayne, be serious. You have killed so many people – there can be no excuse for that.'

Wayne smiled, picked up the phone and began to dial. 'Bruce, you just won the "Best Director" Oscar. I ain't flattering you when I say that you are currently the most celebrated movie-maker in the world. It ain't no more than you deserve, mind. You worked hard and you have reaped the rewards . . . Excuse me.' He turned to the phone.

On the other end of the line Chiefs Cornell and Murray grabbed their respective receivers and began simultaneously to announce their credentials.

'Shut up and listen to me,' they heard Wayne say. 'We gonna make a statement, y'hear? We gon' announce our intentions and tell it like it is, OK? Now what we want is a small ENG crew in here, jus' as soon you can get it together.'

'Yes, yes, an electronic news-gathering crew, OK,' said the head of NBC, pleased to be able to answer the questioning look on the police chief's face.

'I know what ENG is, else I wouldna asked for it!' Wayne shouted down the line.

'Yes, I was just explaining it to—'

'Shut the fuck up! I am *talking* here. One more interruption and that's it, we do our talking with guns, OK? Now, this crew has to be hooked up to all the other stations, you understand? Cable too. We ain't giving no exclusive here, everybody gets the story. One more thing. The recordist must have a direct feed to the ratings computer. I want to know just how big a TV star I am, minute by minute. Now, if you do this, I give you my word as a freeborn American that, whoever else I decide to kill, the TV people get safe passage. I guarantee they will not be harmed, on account of you are observers, man, we are the action.'

With that Wayne put the phone down and turned to his hostages. 'Now we wait,' he said. 'How 'bout we all have us a drink?'

'You seem to know an awful lot about the workings of TV,' Bruce said, and for one insane moment it crossed his mind that perhaps in some weird way or other this whole thing was a hoax. Maybe Wayne and Scout were not what they seemed, not mass murderers at all, but journalists or students or something, out to prove a point. Was it all an illusion? Brooke had tricked him before. Maybe she hadn't really been shot. Maybe this whole thing was a set-up . . . ?

It was a sad, hopeless thought and it lasted about a quarter of a second. His agent's blood and tissue still clung to the glass-covered poster on to which they had been propelled by Wayne's bullet. Fresh gore was welling up inside Brooke's mouth, threatening to choke her before she bled to death. Bruce could smell the torn and jagged flesh. There was so much stark, horrifying reality in the room it was a wonder that there was still room for the furniture.

'How'd I know about TV?' Wayne explained. 'Hey, Bruce, everybody knows everything these days. Especially TV. Think about it. Home video shows, community cable channels – real life as it happens. Not a simulation, actual footage. We're all part of it, man. It's an electronic democracy. There ain't no "you" and "us" any more because "us" is in your face every day. Appearing on your game shows. Caught on video, robbing your banks.

Confessing our sins on *Oprah*, 'n' getting them forgiven on the Inspiration Channel. People *are* television, man, and you're asking me how I know how to use it? Well, it sure don't take a lot of finding out. You know, for a smart man you're real dumb. Excuse me, I have to speak with the cops.'

Down below, in the armoured police command vehicle, Chief Cornell was almost quivering with excitement. Wayne Hudson was playing right into his hands.

'Get me the equipment he wants,' the chief barked at Murray. 'That little ENG crew is going to be composed of armed operatives from Special Forces. We are sending in an undercover SWAT team. Two seconds after my men get in there, they will have neutralized that maniac, plus the fucking she-devil he hangs with.' The police chief was already preening himself for the press conference that would follow this heroic operation.

The phone rang again. Both men grabbed it.

'Now, I know what you're thinking, guys,' they heard Wayne's voice say. 'You're thinking 'bout putting a bunch of damn commandos on me, right? Well forget it. The crew you send me best be the smallest crew there is. I am talking one camera operator and one recordist. That is two people, OK? Two. T–W–O. What is more, they have to come barefoot and wearing only their underwear. Y'hear me? Underwear, that's all, and I ain't talkin' no baggy long-johns or old lady's bloomers here. I am talkin' 'bout the smallest, tiniest, skimpiest fuckin' bits of nothing a person can wear and still keep their modesty. I'm going to check every inch of the people you give me, plus their equipment, and if I get even the *idea* that there might be a piece, a stun grenade, even a fucking penknife, within about fifty

yards of those two motherfuckers, I'm gonna holler to
Scout to spray bullets into every hostage we got, and
you know she'll do it, on account of how she loves me
and she does what the fuck I tell her. So basically what
I'm saying here is that if you fuck with me, cop, four
more innocent people gonna get very dead real soon,
and it will be your fault, man, and every TV station in
America's gonna see it. Bye-bye, now.'

The phone went dead again.

This time it was the newsman's turn to quiver with
excitement. Disaster had been averted. Police Chief
Cornell, had, through his crass, macho zeal, been on
the verge of hijacking what was clearly a cathartic media
event and turning it into a police matter. Television
had nearly been prevented from taking up its rightful
position at the very centre of the drama, not just
covering the story but being part of it. This, the news
and current affairs chief felt, was what news and current
affairs had been invented for. To get cameras and, if
possible, personalities deep, deep inside events, moulding
them, shaping them, actually *being* the news; while the
old forces of authority – the cops, the politicians, the
civic leaders – could only watch impotently from the
sidelines.

He had so nearly lost it. For a moment there it had
looked like the cop was getting ready to grab all the glory.
Thanks, however, to the villain himself having a proper
sense of proportion and society's natural pecking order,
the media would be centre-stage where they belonged.

Chapter Twenty-Nine

B ruce's mind was no longer reeling. It was reeling, jigging, jitterbugging and doing the mashed potato.

'You are bringing a TV crew in here? Into *my home*?'

'That's right, Bruce, and you, me and Scout are going to make a statement.'

'I will not make a statement with you, you crazy bastard. You can shove your damn statement up your ass!'

Bruce scarcely knew what he was saying. Farrah and Velvet gasped at his audacity, but on this occasion Wayne did not seem to mind being cheeked.

'That's right, Bruce, get all that profanity out of your system. Don't want to go using no lewd words on TV, now, do we? It might affect the ratings.'

Scout was absolutely thrilled. 'Are we really going to be on the TV, honey?'

'Yes, we are, baby doll, and so's Bruce here, because if he doesn't I'll kill his darling little girl.'

'What kind of statement? What the hell do you want me to say?'

'Well, Bruce, let me tell you. You are going to announce to the whole of the USA – and believe me it will be the whole of the USA because between you and us we got more celebrity right here than Elvis making out with Oprah, using Roseanne for a mattress – you are going to announce to the whole of the USA that Scout 'n' me are your fault.'

Wayne smiled as if to say, 'Great plan, huh?' Bruce had known it was coming but it was still a blow.

'You are going to say that having met us and talked to us, quietly, person to person, one on one, you realize that we are just dumb, stupid, poor white trash and that you and your glamorous Hollywood pictures done corrupted our po' simple minds.' He took up the bag which had recently contained the severed head and pulled out a bundle of bloodstained magazines and newspapers. He quoted from one: 'You're going to say you understand that your "wicked, cynical exploitation and manipulation of the lowest, basest elements of the human psyche has so disturbed—"'

'No, I won't do it!' Bruce nearly gagged at the man's audacity.

Wayne's strolled across the room to where Velvet had gone to stand with her mother. 'Open your mouth, darling.'

Velvet burst into tears again. Unmoved, Wayne took his pistol and forced its barrel between Velvet's closed lips so that the metal pressed against her clenched teeth.

'I'll bet you've had a lot of expensive dental work over the years, huh, baby? Let me tell you now, a bullet going through all that is liable to do a powerful lot of damage.'

Having made his point, Wayne removed his gun

from Velvet's lips, turned back to Bruce and waved the bloodied magazines in his face.

'You, Bruce, are going to say that we are "products of a society that celebrates violence". You are going to say that we are weak-willed, simple-minded creatures who have been "seduced by images of sex and death", images *you* create, man, and for which you have just been honoured with an Oscar. You are going to say that your eyes have been opened and you are *ashamed*. In fact, I got an idea, man – oh yeah! You're going to return your Oscar. Live on TV, you're going to give it back out of respect for your victims. The people *you* killed through me and Scout.'

Bruce was not a callous man. He knew that other people had problems greater than his. He was aware that two people were already dead and that another was clearly dying. Nevertheless, at this point he could think only of the dreadful fate Wayne had prepared for him. To make the kind of statement Wayne was proposing that he make, and to make it to the entire nation, would be the most profoundly humiliating thing imaginable. Career suicide. Intellectual disgrace. The complete loss of every ounce of the credibility he currently enjoyed. The immediate end of his life as an artist. And for a *lie*.

He struggled to find an argument to sway Wayne from his terrible course. 'It won't work, Wayne. It can't. Whatever I say, it won't change the law. You're guilty and the law will get you.'

'That's bullshit, Bruce, and you know it. The law is whatever people want it to be. It ain't never the same thing twice. It's one thing to a white man, another to a black, one thing to the rich, another to the poor. The law is a piece of fuckin' Play Dough – no one knows what shape it's going to be in next. Man, after you've made your broadcast me and Scout here won't be no punk killers no more. We'll be a hundred things. We'll be heroes to some, victims to others, we'll be monsters, we'll be saints. We will be the defining fuckin' image of a national debate. A debate which will go to the very core of our society.'

Wayne's eyes shone with the glory of his idea. He assumed the deep, censorious tone of the typical TV news anchor: 'America will look at itself and ask itself the questions "Who are we? Where are we going? Did Wayne and Scout act alone? Is Bruce Delamitri to blame, or do we all share something of their guilt?"'

Scout just loved it when Wayne was on a roll. He was *so* classy. 'Defining image', 'core of society' – those were real ten-dollar sentences. She never knew how he picked all that stuff up. Like her, he'd left school at the first opportunity, which was about three years before he was legally entitled to do so. Since then all he'd done was hang out and watch TV like everyone else in the country.

Which was, of course, the point.

Wayne had been watching TV his entire life, and it had not all been sit coms and re-runs of *Star Trek*. Decades of surfing the remote had meant a million bites out of the Discovery Channel, CNN, *Oprah* and *Sixty Minutes*, a never-ending diet of 'information' and 'in-depth analysis'. With their inexhaustible supply of doctors, therapists, psychologists and 'experts' of every type, news and chat shows have introduced entire nations to the instant-coffee version of a vocabulary of words and ideas that traditionally take years of study to acquire.

An intelligent man is going to pick up an awful lot

of earnest bullshit and portentous psychobabble if he watches TV his entire life; and Wayne, as Bruce was discovering, was a very intelligent man.

Because Bruce knew that Wayne was right. Right, right, RIGHT. A villain could get turned into a hero inside a single soundbite. And, as in Bruce's case, a hero could end up a villain.

He attempted a defence of sorts. 'Oh yeah. Well, what happens when I go on the TV tomorrow and retract everything? When I tell the world you forced me into accepting responsibility?'

Scout didn't think Bruce was giving Wayne sufficient credit for his brilliant plan. 'You might be dead by then, Mr Big Shot,' she said. 'You might be dead any time.'

Wayne laughed. 'You tell him, baby. But frankly it don't matter what you say tomorrow, Bruce – always assuming you're alive to say it. By tomorrow our little story here will have a life of its own. Every talk show, every paper, will be asking the question "Who's guilty?" Whatever you say tomorrow won't wipe out today. *This* is the image, man. This is the defining moment, the one they'll all remember – bigger than the Rodney King video, bigger than O.J.'s committal, bigger than the Kennedy motorcade.'

'Hey, don't undersell yourself, Wayne,' said Bruce through gritted teeth.

'Come on, man! It doesn't get any better than this. The king of Hollywood, two mass murderers, a dying *Playboy* centrefold, a rinsed-out old hag of an ex-wife, a spoilt, sexy little weeping teen . . . blood, guns . . . we've got it all. Nobody will ever forget this. It'll be burnt into their minds for ever.'

Wayne walked up to Bruce and put his face right

up close. 'And every time anyone sees you, Bruce, they'll remember this image above all the others. They'll remember you with your arms round me and Scout, your daughter weeping, your girlfriend bleeding at your feet. And you saying, "America, wake up! We sow a wind and we reap a whirlwind. These two poor benighted sinners could be kin to anyone of us. They are my kin. My son and daughter. I begot them. My sins were visited upon them . . ."

'Now, how 'bout that drink?'

Chapter Thirty

O liver and Dale had been in their studio conference room, preparing to present that morning's edition of *Coffee Time*, when the call came.

'I need high-profile personalities central to the action,' the head of NBC News and Current Affairs had demanded, 'anchoring not from the studio, but from inside the story. The nation needs a friend in that house.'

Murray had already won the battle to be the station which would provide the crew for Wayne's broadcast. 'We were the company of contact and we should have priority,' he had pointed out rather pompously to the other networks, adding, 'What's more, if you don't let us do it I shan't tell you what their demands are, so the people you send in will get it all wrong and get killed.'

Having achieved the priority he desired, Murray had only to persuade Oliver and Dale, in whose celebrity the station had so much invested, that they should be the station's representatives at the centre of the drama. He didn't have much time. Wayne had demanded only a camera operator and a recordist, there had been no talk of presenters. Dale and Oliver would have to do the work of the technicians. They would need to be told how to use the equipment and the minutes were ticking away.

There was of course much to tempt the two slap covered hairspray heads into accepting the job . . . It was a tantalizing prospect, to be elevated in a moment from famous person who reads an autocue and interviews celebrities, to news hero of the decade.

On the other hand, the people inside the house *were* mass murderers.

'You're sure he guaranteed safe conduct?' Oliver asked. 'I'm only concerned for Dale, you understand.'

'Absolutely safe conduct,' the chief assured them, 'and I trust him. Why would he harm you? He needs you. The guy is feeding off the media. With our co-operation he's a star, a superstar. Without it he's just a nobody who's going to get the chair. He needs us as much as we need him.'

Dale and Oliver exchanged nervous glances. It occurred to them both that a person who craved fame could get quite a dollop of it by murdering the *Coffee Time* team on live TV. On the other hand, what an opportunity! They would be fearless seekers after truth, war correspondents, risking all to bring the number-one story of the decade into the nation's lounges.

Their boss pressed home his advantage. 'I'm telling you he's given us an unequivocal guarantee.' He lowered his voice. 'But listen, we don't have to tell the world you got that guarantee. We can let the world think you've gone in there with no guarantee of your safety at all, because that's how much the people's right to news and current affairs means to you.'

'Wow,' said Dale.

'"Wow" is right. They'll probably give you the medal of honour,' the chief added.

'And of course we do have a very real duty to the public,' said Oliver, who was ever conscious of his self-appointed status as one of the nation's premier moral guardians.

'So that's settled,' said the chief. 'The equipment is fairly simple. I'll get one of the guys to run through it with you, and after that all you've got to do is take your clothes off and we're cooking.'

He nearly got away with it. For a moment he thought he had.

He hadn't.

'Take our *clothes* off?' Dale stared, aghast.

'Yeah, yeah, yeah. It's no problem,' said Murray, trying to hustle them along.

'You mean *change* our clothes, surely,' said Oliver. 'You mean you want us to put on combat fatigues, no doubt.'

Like all news reporters, Oliver relished the idea of donning a flak-jacket and looking like a soldier.

But the Chief of News and Current Affairs did not mean change their clothes. 'I mean you'll have to take your clothes off. The guy's worried about concealed weaponry. What's the big deal?'

'Ahem,' said Oliver, clearing his throat nervously, 'I think the question is one of presentation.'

Dale and Oliver looked good and were proud of it. Their image was the classic template of the news anchor team, the standard by which all other news anchor teams were judged: he silver and dignified in his late fifties, she cute and feisty in her mid-thirties. In the studio, with their make-up, hairspray and designer power clothing they looked, quite simply, superb. The American dream behind a desk; like some splendid ambassador and his gorgeous second wife.

The problem was that underneath the story was rather different. As, indeed, it normally is.

He, for instance, wore a corset. She was midway through a cellulite-reduction programme. He had two massive and unpleasant hernia scars. She had an insane tattoo on her thigh, smudged by botched efforts to have it removed.

He suddenly remembered that his housemaid was sick and he was into the second day of his last, rattiest pair of jocks. It suddenly occurred to her that she was planning an après-show tryst with her new lover, the second assistant floor assistant. She had therefore come to work wearing a pair of lacy scarlet split-crotch panties with a heart-shaped hole cut out of the bottom.

'Hey, we can get you new underwear for Christ's sake,' Murray said. 'We can put make-up on your blemishes.'

'I don't think so, boss,' said the head make-up artist, who was hovering in the background. 'Oliver and Dale use quite a lot of foundation on their faces. If the same proportions are applied to their whole bodies, I don't think they'll actually be able to walk.'

'I really do think, Chief,' said Oliver, 'that the proper place for the nation's premier anchor team in a crisis like this is in the studio – controlling the operation from the centre, so to speak. After all, generals don't go into battle, do they?'

'I'll do it, but only with a body double,' said Dale, who had not really thought it through.

And so Oliver and Dale missed their chance at media

immortality but, much more importantly, they kept their nasty bits under cover. Considerably relieved, the two of them retreated to the studio, where their wonderful researchers had already lined up an exclusive interview for them with Dove, the actress whom Bruce had reduced to near tears at the Bosom Ball.

As it happened, Police Chief Cornell, already miffed at having his authority usurped by the news broad-casters, would not have allowed Oliver and Dale to do the job anyway. 'We've got to use an experienced news-gathering team,' he insisted, 'preferably one that's seen combat. If we send in someone who fumbles or fucks up, it could push this guy over. I want the best two journalist-technicians you've got.'

And so the call went out for an experienced operator and recordist who had steady nerves and acceptable bodies and were reasonably relaxed about the state of their underwear.

Chapter Thirty-One

The arrangements were made, and Wayne made his way down through the house once more, to await the camera crew.

Meanwhile Bruce paced about the lounge, desperately trying to think of a way out.

Scout was proud of how deeply Wayne's plan had affected him. 'Ain't Wayne smart, huh?' she said.

'I can't do it,' Bruce replied. 'I just can't.'

Velvet was with Brooke, attempting to re-dress her wound with torn cushion covers. She stared up at her father. 'Daddy, you have to. This woman needs a doctor and you heard what he said he'd do to me. He said he'd shoot me in the mouth.'

Velvet was fighting back her tears but none the less was showing a strength of character of which her parents had been completely unaware. Years of wandering round shopping malls with too much money to spend had never brought out the best in her.

'Yes, all right, Velvet. I'm sorry. I won't let that happen.

But I have to think. This is a very terrible thing for me. For us. Wayne's right, you see. Once I do this thing, my life as I know it will be over, no matter what I do, no matter what I achieve, this is all I will be remembered for.'

Brooke, whose life looked as if it was very nearly over already, tried to protest at this. Although it came out only as a gurgle, her meaning was clear: she felt her problem should be number one on the group agenda.

Bruce simply could not bring himself to agree. 'Brooke, I know you're seriously wounded, and, believe me, when I can do something about it I will, but right now I am powerless to help. And I have a problem too. Ten minutes from now the entire world is going to hear me confess to mass murder.'

'But you're being coerced. You can deny it afterwards,' said Farrah. It had begun to dawn on her just how seriously Bruce's defeat was going to affect her own fortunes.

'Oh sure, Farrah. Some plea in mitigation – a retrospective claim to be a pathetic victim, outplayed and manipulated by a piece of scum out of the lowest trailer in the Midwest.'

'You'd better watch your mouth.' Scout did not like to hear Wayne spoken of in that way.

Bruce was too scared to care. 'What? You want me to *like* the guy, Scout? Your boyfriend is a sadistic maniac, a heartless psychopath.'

'You don't know his nice side.'

Bruce actually laughed.

Now Farrah had something to say. She crossed over to the couch where Scout was sitting and sat down beside her. Scout covered her warily.

'If you're thinking of trying to make friends with her,'

said Bruce, 'don't bother. Brooke tried that, and got a busted lip.'

But Farrah had other things on her mind. She had been thinking a lot since Wayne announced his plan and now she had a favour to ask. 'Look . . . Miss . . . um, Scout? Speaking of nice sides, I would like it so much if you could do something for us. A favour.'

'What kind of favour?'

'Would it be all right if my husband made a call?'

'A call? Who's he going to call? The whole world's standing right outside on his lawn.'

'What's on your mind, Farrah?' said Bruce. 'Who do you want me to call?'

Farrah had to make her pitch. She knew it would not sound good, but she had no choice: everything she had was in danger of disappearing with the morning dew. Farrah was a woman who knew what it was like to have nothing, and as far as she was concerned it sucked.

'Bruce, think about it. This thing isn't just going to ruin you as an artist. It will completely destroy you financially as well. Once you claim responsibility for inciting murder, the family of every victim of violence in America is going to sue you, and not just Wayne and Scout's victims' families either, but everyone whose life has been touched by violence. We will be in litigation for ever. Velvet's grandchildren will still be paying. Do you understand? Overnight bankruptcy. What we have to do is transfer all your assets into my name, right now, before you make the broadcast – it won't wash afterwards. So if Miss Scout here will just let you send a little fax to our bank . . .'

It was an impressive display. Everyone was surprised.

'Mom!' Velvet protested. 'This is *so* tacky.'

'Lady, I am protecting your future here.'

Scout was laughing. 'You're something, ain't you?' she said.

'*I'm* something? I'm not the one breaking into people's homes and murdering them. I just don't particularly want some Milwaukee waitress whose husband got knifed in a bar getting hold of my daughter's money, that's all.'

'Well, no one's making any calls, and no one's sending no faxes either, so I guess you'll just have to start thinking 'bout being poor. So there!'

The room was silent for a moment.

'Besides which,' Scout added irritably, 'I reckon maybe that waitress in Milwaukee would have a point. Maybe the great Bruce "Mr Oscar" Delamitri shouldn't have gone making them films and all. Maybe all that stuff Wayne's going to make you say ain't so dumb.'

Bruce was angry now, angry enough to ignore his fear. 'I don't believe it! You are actually trying to convince yourself that you're not really to blame, aren't you? It's not just a trick, you seriously want to believe it. You actually want to dodge responsibility for what you've done. You cowardly little bitch!'

'Daddy, be quiet,' Velvet pleaded. 'She'll kill us!'.

Scout fondled her automatic weapon. 'I ain't going to kill no one, cutie, not 'less they don't do what we tell 'em. All I'm saying is that—'

'*You* are the sole perpetrators of your crimes,' Bruce shouted. 'Nobody pulled the trigger but you.'

'I know that, Mr Delamitri. I admit that. It was us done our crimes, I admit we're to blame.'

'Well, that's mighty big of you, I must say.'

'Daddy, please, be nice,' Velvet begged.

'It's just, well . . .' Scout continued, 'I don't think it

helps any that everything is so ugly all the time. That's all.' She seemed almost wistful.

'What's that supposed to mean?'

'Well, you know, songs and films and stuff. All that used to be an escape from being poor and living in fear. Now everything just seems to rub your face in it. I mean, your films are like, what's that word? . . . when someone's getting off looking at stuff that's none of their business . . .'

'Voyeuristic,' Velvet said helpfully, hoping to mitigate her father's aggression.

'That's right. They're voyeuristic. I mean, you live in a big old house in Hollywood with a pool and a security guy and all—'

'Until your boyfriend cut his head off,' Bruce said bitterly. 'Now I have a decapitated security guard.'

'I *told* you I know we done that stuff and we're to blame.' Scout was getting angry too. 'I'm just saying you got all this luxury, like a king or a president or something, and you pay for it by making films about ordinary, sad, dumb people, people who live in ghettos and projects and trailer parks, and making them look ugly and sick and violent—'

'You *are* ugly and sick and violent!'

'Yes, I guess I am, and I deserve whatever I get. It just seems to me that half of America lives in hell and the other half gets its rocks off watching.'

Scout didn't want to talk about it any more so she put on the TV. Bruce's house was still on the screen and approaching it, rather nervously, were two people in their underwear.

Chapter Thirty-Two

Wayne opened the front door carefully and let the near-naked camera operator and recordist into the house.

'I sincerely apologize for the undignified working conditions,' he said, somewhat taken aback to discover that one of the team, the sound recordist, was a woman, and wondering what Scout would make of that. 'But I'm sure you understand my position here.'

Across the lawn, behind the ring of armoured vehicles that the police had established, the forces of authority watched the scene.

'Well, yet another murdering bastard is about to get his fifteen minutes of fame,' Chief Cornell reflected. The chief had with him his number-one siege team, his top negotiator, his Commander of Special Weapons and Tactics, and his press and media publicist.

'And maybe when he takes a dump we can send someone in to wipe his ass,' said the SWAT boss, furious at the lack of direct action. 'I have Special Forces in position and

253 ◆

ready to move, sir. Let my men take this bastard. We can
be in and out again in forty-five seconds.'

The publicist was adamantly opposed to this. 'It's too
big a risk, sir,' he said. 'All the hostages are in one room,
and both targets are heavily armed. If the SWAT guys go
in, there could be a complete bloodbath, which I need
hardly remind you would be in full view of every TV
camera in Hollywood.'

'Yeah, and supposing we pull it off?' the SWAT man
replied. 'Stun grenade the bastards and bring 'em out in
chains? How about that for the cameras, huh?'

It was a tempting prospect. There is nothing quite
so glamorous as a siege broken and hostages saved,
especially if those hostages happen to include teenage girls.

'There is no way Wayne Hudson is going to let you
take him out of there alive,' the publicist argued.

'Dead then. Even better. As long as we save the
hostages.'

'As long as.'

In the end Cornell decided that, for the time being at
least, cautionary counsel must prevail. 'I think we have
to see if this media stuff works. Who knows, maybe once
he's had his say he might throw the towel in.'

The head of SWAT turned away in disgust. Chief
Cornell did not blame him; the decision stuck in his
craw too. Even before the Uni Bomber, criminals had
been showing a worrying predilection for blackmailing
their way on to the media. Deep down, everyone wants
to get on TV. A glance at any game show is enough
to show just how far people will go to achieve that
aim. Why should criminals be any different? More and
more, it seemed to Chief Cornell that he and his men

were becoming extras in a procession of lunatics' private movies.

'It's getting so we ought to turn ourselves into agents and start charging ten per fucking cent,' he reflected bitterly.

Of course the police were themselves partly to blame, and Cornell knew it. It is the police who supply the footage for police camera shows. It is the police who give never-ending press conferences and appear on public-involvement TV programmes, appealing for witnesses. Chief Cornell knew that he himself had staged many spectacular operations with the cameras and publicity principally in mind. If the cops wanted to be stars, why shouldn't the hoodlums?

Chief Cornell sighed. 'Just as long as the bastard doesn't throw a tantrum and keep us here all day while he sits in his trailer and sulks.'

Chapter Thirty-Three

Inside the house Wayne returned to the lounge with the little ENG crew.

Scout was still watching TV. 'Shhh,' she said.

'A camera operator and a recordist are now inside the siege mansion,' the studio anchorwoman was explaining, 'so we should be getting pictures soon. The recordist is trailing a two-hundred-metre cable feed to the control truck which is parked in the grounds . . . there you can see it there, that's the truck . . . That is the control truck isn't it, Larry?'

'I believe that is the control truck, Susan,' said her partner, 'but I can't be sure. Let's bring in Doctor Mark Raddinger, of the East LA Academy of Media Studies. Doctor Raddinger, is that the control truck we can see now?'

'Yes,' replied a bearded man in polo neck and corduroy jacket who was seated beside Larry, 'that is the control truck.'

'So you can confirm that?' asked Larry.

'Yes, I can confirm that,' replied Doctor Raddinger. 'That is the control truck.'

'Well, it's as we suspected, Susan,' said Larry, 'and we have a confirmation on that. The truck currently on our screens is, as you rightly predicted just moments ago, the control truck.'

'And we can confirm that?' Susan asked.

'Yes,' Larry replied. 'We do now have confirmation. It is the control truck. The truck to which the recordist, who is currently situated inside the siege mansion, is linked by a two-hundred-metre broadcast feed cable.'

'Thanks, Larry,' said Susan. 'And further to that, I can also confirm that the recordist is linked to the TV ratings computer.'

'The TV ratings computer?' Larry enquired. 'That would be the computer which analyses and delivers the TV ratings, right?'

'Yes, it would, Larry.'

'Let's bring in Doctor Mark Raddinger again, here. Mark, can you give us a little background detail on the TV ratings computer?'

'Yes, I can, Larry. The TV ratings computer is the computer which the TV companies use to analyse and deliver an accurate statistical analysis of the TV ratings via computer.'

'I see. Fascinating. And you can confirm that?'

'Yes, I can.'

'And the TV ratings would be how many people are watching?' Susan enquired.

'Statistically and demographically speaking, yes it would—'

Wayne turned the set off. It was giving him a head-ache.

'That's enough TV now, Scout. We got work to do,' he said. 'OK, everybody, listen up. This is Bill and Kirsten, and they are going to make us stars.' He ushered the crew into the room.

Bill and Kirsten entered rather gingerly. They were a tough pair, who had covered wars, famines and presidential elections, but their current circumstances were scarcely likely to put them at their ease. It wasn't so much the woman in the blood-soaked gown who lay gurgling on the floor near the drinks cabinet who bothered them. Nor was it really the two psychopathic maniacs who were pointing automatic weapons at them. It's just never easy to be the only people who turn up at a social gathering dressed only in your underwear.

They felt naked. Bill and Kirsten were a tough, lean young news team, and they liked to look the part. Bill missed his survival tunic with its numerous pockets, out of which he often claimed he could live and work for a month. Kirsten missed her sixteen-lace-hole combat boots, the mere pulling on of which always made her feel tougher and braver. Most of all, they both missed their trousers. There was, however, nothing either of them could do about it, so they applied themselves to the task in hand like the proud professionals they were.

'How do you want to stage this thing?' Bill asked.

Wayne looked at Bruce. 'Bruce, you're the director. Where should these people set up?'

But Bruce remained tight-lipped. He wasn't going to facilitate his own disgrace if he could avoid it.

Wayne shrugged. 'Well, I guess I can do this myself. Maybe I'll get an Oscar too, ha ha! OK, I reckon you guys should set up the camera right there in front of the fireplace.'

Bill and Kirsten did as they were bidden and began to arrange their equipment. Meanwhile, Wayne thought about his staging. 'I believe we should use this couch as kind of centre of the action, OK? 'Cos one thing I know is that whenever anybody's doing any talking on the TV there is just about always a couch somewhere. So if I push it round a little, then I guess you'll be able to include Brooke in the shot. Is that right, Bill?'

'Yes, I can see her,' Bill answered.

'Well that's good, because I think she looks just great lying on the floor like that. Like some kind of wounded swan or something.'

Scout loved it when Wayne talked like that. She firmly believed that, given an education, he could have been a poet. Bill would not have agreed. Seen through his viewfinder, Brooke did not look like a wounded swan at all. She looked like a wounded person, a badly wounded person. Bill had seen many such sights during his career as a war correspondent but he never got used to them and never found them anything but appalling.

'She's dying,' said Velvet, placing a coat over Brooke.

'We're all dying, darlin',' Wayne replied, 'from the very first day we're born. What I'm saying is that her pathetic condition kind of underlines the point I'm making here. A kind of livin', or maybe I should say dyin', example of what men like Bruce here exploit and promote. So get that coat off her, sugar. It ain't cold and that coat's spoiling my picture. Ain't nothing sexy 'bout a coat.'

Velvet did as she was bidden.

'OK, that's good.' Wayne nodded his approval. 'This thing's really coming together now. So how 'bout you?' He turned on Farrah. 'What can we do with you?'

'What do you mean?' Farrah was startled. She had

begun to imagine herself exempt from the action. She was sadly deluded.

'This is TV, honey. Good-lookin' woman like you's gonna be a big draw, particularly 'longside of your cute li'l daughter. Scout baby, take Mrs Delamitri and Miss Delamitri and cuff them to that lampstand behind the sofa . . . C'mon, c'mon, get over there, girls. We ain't making *Gone with the Wind* here, this is live action.'

Scout put her hand in Wayne's bag and produced a pair of handcuffs.

'Got these off a cop,' she explained, adding darkly, 'He don't need 'em no more.'

As Scout manacled Farrah and her daughter to the lampstand, with uncharacteristic humility Wayne asked if it would be OK to take a look through the camera lens.

'You're the director,' said Bill.

'Well, that's right, I guess I am.' Wayne dropped the humility and strutted over to the camera as if he was Cecil B. de Mille. Pressing his eye to the viewfinder, he surveyed the scene thoughtfully. He could see Bruce sitting on the couch. Behind him were Farrah and Velvet and to one side lay Brooke.

'OK now, Scout,' Wayne said, further composing his shot, 'get down there beside Bruce, 'cos that's where we gonna to be sat, OK? Right next to the man.'

But he was still not quite satisfied.

'It seems all right to me,' Kirsten commented nervously. 'I mean, it contains all the elements, doesn't it?' She wanted to get done and get out of there.

'The elements is just the basics of the shot,' Wayne replied. 'What we got to do here is make one compelling fuckin' image. I mean *compelling*. Because if we ain't good, pretty soon the networks are going to go back to their regular schedules and all we'll be left with is CNN. What are we up against, honey? What's the opposition? I guess you know more about daytime TV than any woman of your size and weight in the whole USA.'

'*Star Trek: The Next Generation, Family Ties, Cosby* and *Oprah* repeats,' Scout recited proudly. 'I don't know all the cable stuff.'

Kirsten looked up from her equipment. 'Wayne, when this goes out live, every station in the country will pick up on it. You'll be the only thing showing nationwide.'

'Y'hear that, Bruce? I'm making you bigger than you was already. Now, you sure you're going to be able to get all this in, Bill? What's your edge of frame?'

'Edge of frame'. Scout nearly cried, she was so proud of Wayne.

'We have plenty of width,' Bill said. 'I'll just lock it off and take the whole thing in a static five shot. Have another look.'

Wayne did so and then, with a thoughtful frown on his face, crossed to the two handcuffed women. He studied them for a moment and then ripped open Velvet's smart little pink jacket, causing the buttons to fly off.

Scout was not at all happy with this development. Nor, of course, was Velvet, but she was in no position to protest.

'Wayne, take your hands off that girl right now!' Scout shouted.

'You want the ratings, honey? Huh? You want people to watch this thing? Sex is important on TV, sex sells.' Wayne tore open Velvet's blouse and pulled it down off her shoulders, revealing her brassière. 'Cute, huh?' he said. 'Can't show too much. There's strict rules. Just enough for the couch potatoes out there in TV land to get themselves off on . . . OK, I guess we're just about ready. Bruce, in just a moment or two you're going to sit here on this couch 'tween me and Scout and tell America what I said to tell them.'

'Look, Wayne, this is—'

'And if you don't, I'll kill sweet little Velvet here, and Mrs Delamitri – not that you give a flying fuck in a thunderstorm 'bout her. Also of course, I'll kill you. I think you're going to do what I tell you. Ain't you, Bruce?'

Chapter Thirty-Four

O utside they were waiting for pictures. The media, the police and, increasingly, the nation were all waiting for pictures, because the siege was now the number-one news story US-wide.

'So is this asshole going to make his statement or not?' said Chief Cornell, pacing about outside his command truck. 'How long do we wait before we hit him?'

Already the police chief could sense his splendid day getting away from him. He wasn't the only one, either. His subordinates were getting increasingly frustrated and were putting Cornell under enormous pressure to take control of the situation. Sieges, in their opinion, were a matter for the police, not the media, and a lot of cops felt pretty bad about being usurped and upstaged in this manner. Particularly the SWAT boss.

'We're being blackmailed,' he said. 'This killer has bought his piece of immortality by murdering people, and now we've brought every TV station in the country to his door. The guy is making us kiss his ass, when what

265 ♦

we need to do is *kick* his ass. We should pull the damn plug, get in there and show that motherfucker, and every motherfucker watching, that you do not mess with the LAPD.'

That was easy for the SWAT man to say. His wasn't the uneasy head that wore the crown. Chief Cornell was the cop with whom the buck would stop, and he knew that if he crashed in now and deprived the media of its prize they would finish him. If even one hostage got killed, which in all truth would almost certainly happen, he and his force would be pilloried as gung-ho, macho assholes, Neanderthals who couldn't wait and talk like responsible adults but had to barge in like the over-excited thugs they were.

Besides which, as the police publicist pointed out, there was another way of looking at it. 'With respect, we have no right to go in now. By any standards at all, a televised confrontation between the country's top action film-maker and the country's top criminal is an astonishing event. It's genuine and important news, no matter how it may have been brought about. The police have to allow the media to do its job. It's our responsibility to defend, and if necessary facilitate, an open and democratic society.'

The SWAT commander had never heard so much pansy bullshit in his entire life. 'It's our responsibility,' he barked, 'to fuck all over these scum until we have made damn sure that they never fuck with us again. Besides which, you know damn well that if someone gets killed while we're hanging around and holding the media's hand, the media will turn right round and blame us for *not* intervening. They can't lose and we can't win, so we should ignore the fuckin' parasites and get on with our damn job.'

Ignore the media? The police publicist nearly fainted.

Even Chief Cornell knew it was a stupid thing to say. 'You might as well say ignore the traffic, ignore the buildings, ignore the public,' he said. 'TV isn't an observer any more. It isn't two hours of news and entertainment in the corner of people's lounges, in the corner of people's *lives*. It's in the middle, right alongside of food. There's two results to every event, what actually happened and what people think happened. That's a fact, pal, and if you believe you can ignore it, then you don't have no election to face come the spring.'

If Brad Murray had heard Chief Cornell speak, he would have nodded sagely. Like it or not, the chief was right. It had long been accepted that TV shaped events, that things happened because the cameras were there, that what the cameras saw was what the event became. Now, however, TV was the event. Before, events didn't get seen without television; increasingly events no longer *existed* without television.

'We wait,' said Chief Cornell. 'Let the guy have his air time.'

'It's our duty as democrats,' said the police publicist.

'Bull-double-shit,' said the SWAT commander.

Chapter Thirty-Five

Inside the house Bruce found himself sitting on the couch between Scout and Wayne. The camera was directly in front of him and he was staring down the barrel. He knew he was about to enter the national consciousness as a patsy, a pathetic loser, coerced and abused into making a snivelling, never-to-be-forgotten, cowardly confession on live TV.

He would be like those combat pilots who are shot down by foreign dictators and then trotted out the next day, drugged and bleary, to renounce the US and profess allegiance to their adopted country. Everybody knows those guys have no choice, that they have been coerced, but somehow people never feel quite the same way about them afterwards. You can't just forget it when your hero suddenly and publicly denies every principle he has ever held dear. There is a secret feeling that he should have fallen on his sword. Unfair and unreasonable, of course, but none the less there.

Bruce struggled to master his panic and anguish.

'Wayne, this isn't going to work,' he pleaded. 'You're both hated murderers and one single statement from me, made under duress, won't change that. All it'll do is screw up my life for ever.'

'Well that's a shame, Bruce, because it's the best shot I've got and we're going to try it. Bill? Kirsten? Everything ready?'

'Yes it is, boss,' said Bill, who had deduced rightly that Wayne would enjoy being called 'boss'.

Bruce decided the time had come to make a desperate pitch, one he had been considering ever since the camera crew had arrived. He turned and tried to look Wayne in the eye – not an easy thing to do when you're sitting next to someone on a deep, soft couch.

'Debate me,' he said.

'Say what?'

'Debate me.'

Wayne frowned; he didn't understand. Bruce hurried to establish his idea.

'Listen, Wayne. You're not stupid, and neither is Scout. You know that the best you have here is a long shot. You know, deep down, that me sitting here with a gun at my head, claiming reponsibility for your actions, is not necessarily going to cut a lot of ice.'

'Like I say, it's all we got,' Wayne said. 'OK, Bill let's—'

Bruce pushed on. 'It isn't. It isn't all you've got. You could take a risk. Debate me, prove your point without coercion. Establish your case live on TV.'

'You be careful, Wayne.' Scout was uneasy. 'You got a plan, you stick to it.'

'Come on, Scout.' Bruce twisted round on the couch to face her. 'Think what you were saying earlier – all that stuff about me exploiting the ugly and the downtrodden, how I get rich leeching off the suffering of the poor. That's a better argument than just using me as some kind of puppet. Put your case. Establish my guilt and let me deny it. Think what extraordinary television it would make . . . You guys could be *real* stars, not just blackmailing hoodlums but proper participants. Stars.'

'Stars?' said Scout. That had got her.

'Of course stars. It's obvious. The public loves a fighter.'

Bruce had to win them round. He knew this was his chance to snatch victory from the jaws of defeat, to turn himself from a victim into a hero, to be the man who stood by his principles even when the very forces of darkness and reaction had invaded his own home. To be the man who gave America its wake-up call establishing for once and for all that 'We are all responsible for our own actions' – particularly violent criminals.

'Think about it, Wayne,' Bruce said. 'I represent the cultural élite of this country. You represent the dispossessed, the underclass, the lowest group in society. What a confrontation, what an image!'

'Yeah, and what's in it for you, mister?' Scout was no pushover. She had already demonstrated in her terrifying defeat of Brooke that she was not to be taken in.

'I get my chance to refute your allegations. I get a chance to present you as the independently minded, personally responsible murdering maniacs that I believe you to be.'

'Daddy, be nice,' Velvet pleaded, but Bruce did not even hear her.

'That's the risk you take,' he continued. 'Put your case, see if you can beat mine. If you win, you *really* win: the nation will never forget you or forgive me. If you lose, I honestly don't think you're any worse off.'

'Don't do it, hon. Your plan's better. Just make him say the stuff.'

But Wayne was intrigued. 'Well, I don't know, babe. I mean, I think we've got a pretty good argument here. Let's face it, half the Republican Party plus just 'bout every preacher in the country reckons Bruce here's the devil incarnate . . .'

For the umpteenth time that terrible night, Bruce allowed himself a moment of hope. 'Think of your image, Scout,' he said. 'What do you want that camera to see? A couple of sullen thugs on a couch, or good-looking, articulate anti-heroes? If you survive all this and avoid the chair, you'll be on every teen T-shirt in the country. You'll be able to name your price.'

This was the right button to press for Scout.

'You really think we'll be stars?'

'Of course you will. This is national TV. Win or lose, half the country's going to fall in love with you. In actual fact you can't lose.'

'You want to be a star, baby doll?'

'Of course I do, honey, but . . . Oh, I don't know . . .'

Meanwhile the outside world was getting impatient, and poor Kirsten, the recordist, crouching in her underwear in front of Bruce's fireplace, was getting the sharp end of their anger.

'What the hell is going on, Kirsten?' The producer's voice screamed along the cable link and into her headset radio receiver. 'When are we going to see some pictures?'

The producer completely ignored the delicate nature of Kirsten's situation, demanding, as TV producers often do, that everyone be told to jump to the command of the cameras. In some ways it was not his fault. He had a whole line of senior producers, editors, section chiefs and channel-controllers crushed into his ENG truck, not to mention the chief of the LAPD, accompanied by an angry man in a flak-jacket who kept muttering, 'Bullshit. Bull-double-shit.' Outside the truck there were countless more police and media operatives milling around, and all of them, inside and out, were demanding that the producer punch up some visuals pronto.

'What's going on, Kirsten? Talk to me,' he shouted into Kirsten's headset. 'We have over two hundred stations nationwide requesting footage, and all the majors have crashed into their schedules. We can't broadcast pictures of the outside of his house for ever. The studio anchors are running out of crap . . .'

The studio anchors were indeed getting a little desperate.

'Our cameras are still located outside the Delamitri mansion,' Larry and Susan were able to confirm for the millionth time. 'And we have with us an expert on the exteriors of celebrity homes. Doctor Ranulph Tofu, of the New Age Academy of Astral Learning, will be able to give us a reading on Bruce Delamitri's state of mind, based principally on the colour of his garage doors.'

In the control truck they were tearing out their hair.

'What are we waiting for, Kirsten?'

The producer got no reply. Kirsten heard him but said nothing, so he kept on shouting, turning up the volume until Kirsten's head shook.

'How long does this jerk think we can tie up the networks on his behalf? Ask the asshole what he thinks he's doing.'

In his desire to make TV, the producer was forgetting that Kirsten was ten feet away from a mass murderer. She rightly felt that to ask the asshole what he thought he was doing was not tactically the right way to go about things. But she had to say something, if only because, after ten minutes of her producer's voice screaming directly into her brain, a bullet in the head was beginning to look like a reasonable option.

'Excuse me,' she said, trying to appear as detached an observer as possible, 'the people in vision control are asking what kind of timescale we're looking at here. Just so they can give you the very best coverage they can. They don't want to lose the audience we've built up.'

Wayne looked at Bruce and made a decision. 'You want to debate me, Bruce? Let's do it.'

'And will you let Farrah and Velvet go afterwards? Will you let Brooke get to a doctor?'

'Maybe. I never know what I'm gonna do, Bruce. It's my job: I'm a maniac.'

Kirsten finally spoke into her talkback. 'Stand by in the truck.' She turned to Wayne. 'OK, Mr Hudson, they're ready whenever.' She was desperate to get out of that room and into some clothes.

'You ready, Scout?' Wayne enquired. 'Ready to be a TV star?'

Suddenly Scout realized the enormity of what they were about to do. She hadn't checked her hair, her make-up, her clothes . . . 'Oh Wayne, I look a sight. Can they send in someone to do make-up?'

'You look gorgeous, honey. Brooke did your hair just peachy. Are you ready, Bruce?'

'Yes I am, Wayne.'

'Can I give control a picture?' Kirsten asked.

Wayne said she could, and Bill turned his camera on.

'Speed,' said Bill. Kirsten flicked a switch. In the control van ten screens jumped into life and the assembled opinion-formers finally got what they wanted.

Chapter Thirty-Six

'Jesus!' The producers and cops whistled as they caught their first glimpse of the little tableau Wayne had created.

'Stand by to broadcast,' Brad Murray shouted, forgetting for a moment in his excitement that, within the control truck, etiquette dictated that he should relay his commands via the producer.

Outside, in the grounds of Bruce's mansion, a hundred hairsprayed anchors alerted the viewing public to the imminence of developments.

'I believe we should be getting pictures from inside of the Delamitri abode any moment now. It appears there's going to be some kind of joint statement from the multimillionaire director and his captor, mass-killing Mall Murderer Wayne Hudson.'

In the studios, the anchors hurried to explain the situation yet one more time. 'The ratings computer is fed by a representative sample of the nation as a whole, whose televisions are connected to a central monitor.

This monitor can then give an instant picture of what people are watching. Wayne Hudson will be aware, quite literally second by second, how many people have tuned in.'

'We know that!' the viewers of America shouted as one. 'You told us a million times. Get on with it.'

Inside the besieged house, Kirsten informed Wayne that control had a picture. 'We can go live to air any time.'

'OK, let's do it,' said Wayne.

'Let's do it,' said the Chief of NBC News and Current Affairs.

'Yes, let's do it,' his opposite numbers at the other networks and major cable stations agreed.

'Stand ready, you guys, in case we have to pick up the pieces,' the chief of police said loudly to his senior officers, attempting to remind the media types that there were people around who didn't work in television.

'We're live!' the producer screamed into Kirsten's ear.

'We're live, Mr Hudson,' Kirsten said calmly, 'live across America.'

It hardly seemed real, sitting there as they were in Bruce's lounge. Wayne grabbed Bruce's remote control and flipped on the TV. Sure enough, there they all were on the screen, the framing exactly as Wayne had wanted it. He tried another couple of channels. There they were again, and again. Scout screamed in embarrassment, and buried her head in her hands. Wayne turned the sound down on the TV but left the vision on: he wasn't taking any chances that the bargain would be broken.

'OK, Bruce,' said Wayne, trying to look calm and collected, 'you're the professional. Why don't you just explain to people what's going on?'

Scarcely able to believe it was real, Bruce addressed Bill's camera.

'Um . . . Hullo, everybody. I'm sorry that your morning's viewing has been disrupted but I guess you all know what's going on here. I'm Bruce Delamitri, the film-maker. The two women you see manacled behind me are Farrah, my wife, and our daughter, Velvet. The wounded woman on the floor to my right is Brooke Daniels, the model—'

Brooke, whose condition had stabilized somewhat with Velvet's help, croaked in protest.

'—I'm sorry, Brooke Daniels, the actress. Anyway, we are all prisoners of Wayne Hudson and his partner, Scout, whom you see sitting beside me.'

'Hey,' said Wayne, with nervous bravado.

'Hello, America,' Scout mumbled, her head still buried in her hands.

'So, introductions over. Let's come to the point.' Incredibly, Bruce was beginning to enjoy himself. Here was his chance, the chance he had dodged the night before, the chance to take on the censors and reactionaries. And oh, such a chance. The Oscars podium paled in comparison to his current platform. What an opportunity! To face down two vicious, heavily armed murderers on live TV and bring them to some understanding of their personal responsibility for their actions. Bruce glowed with excitement. This would be a genuine moment in the social history of the United States, and he was to be the mouthpiece. He must be careful, he must concentrate. There must be no 'legs of fire' this time.

'I make films in which actors and stunt artists pretend to kill people,' he said. 'Wayne and Scout actually kill people. Not long ago, they decapitated my security guard, and they shot my agent, Karl Brezner, dead in this very room – his corpse lies in my kitchen. They have also seriously wounded Ms Daniels here. They are, of course, the notorious Mall Murderers and have over the last few weeks slaughtered numerous other innocents. Is that a fair summary, Wayne?'

Wayne thought for a moment. 'Well, Bruce, my sweet momma brought me up a Christian, so I guess I know that none of us is truly innocent, because even tiny babies are born with the original sin upon them, passed down to us all from Adam.'

'Is that why you shoot people? Because they're sinners?' Bruce enquired, a sense of huge intellectual superiority welling up inside him.

'To tell you the truth, I don't know why I shoot people. Partly, I guess, because it's so easy.'

'Well, innocent or not, I think we can all at least agree that Wayne and Scout have made something of a habit of shooting people they don't know.'

'That is the case,' Wayne admitted. 'We sure do that.'

'So what has all this to do with me?' Bruce continued, sounding more like a schoolmaster every minute. 'Well, Wayne and Scout have broken into my house and attacked my friends because they claim that I am in part responsible for their actions. They contend that in some way my work "inspired" them to do what they do. Now, I of course utterly refute this puerile concept—'

'We never said you'd inspired us, Mr Delamitri.' Scout's head finally emerged from her hands. 'Now don't you go putting words into our mouths.'

'Forgive me, I thought that was what this whole debate was about,' Bruce replied.

'Daddy, don't be so patronizing,' Velvet cried out from the lampstand.

Wayne considered Bruce's answer. 'No, Bruce, Scout's right. "Inspired" is the wrong word altogether. I mean, it ain't like we saw a guy and a girl shooting people in your movie and said, "Hey, I never thought of that. That's what we should be doing."'

'So my work does not inspire you? Then I'm confused. I cannot imagine what other point you make when you seek to equate me with your crimes.'

Wayne knew when he was being talked down to. 'It ain't a direct thing, Bruce,' he answered sharply. 'We ain't morons. We didn't walk straight out of *Ordinary Americans* and shoot the popcorn seller—'

Scout had been brought up to be honest. She couldn't let this go by. 'Actually, Wayne, we did.'

'Once,' Wayne conceded. 'We did that once, that's all. I must have seen *Ordinary Americans* fifty times, and only one time did I walk out and shoot the popcorn seller. What is more, that wasn't because of no movie, it was because the stupid bastard in question was a popcorn seller who would not sell us any popcorn.'

In the control truck the producer nearly gave birth in horror. 'For Christ's sake!' he screamed into Kirsten's ear. 'Can't you tell that dumb fucker to watch his dirty fucking mouth? It is ten thirty in the fucking morning!'

'Excuse me, Mr Hudson,' Kirsten interrupted nervously, 'could you possibly moderate your language? We're picking up a massive audience share but adult dialogue is going to cause problems. The children's channel has already gone back to *Sesame Street.*'

'Yes, Wayne,' Scout scolded, 'you watch your mouth, now.'

'Well, I'm sorry, honey, and I 'pologize to you good people out there, specially if you're watching with young people. But you know, what I'm describing here was a very aggravating situation.'

'Yes, honey, it was.' Scout turned to the camera as if she was speaking to a girl friend. 'We'd just come on out of the movie and I said to Wayne to get me some popcorn and Wayne said, "Sure, honey pie. If that's what you want I'll get you a big bucket." But the popcorn seller said he only sold popcorn before the movie, and it was after the movie so I couldn't have none.'

'He was there, man.' Wayne appealed to the camera. 'With the popcorn and the buckets and a scoop and a hat on and all that stuff, but he would not sell me none.'

'So you shot him?' Bruce enquired.

'Yes, sir. Yes I did. I shot that boy, because it ain't as if the world's short of assholes, now is it? The world is not going to miss one asshole more or less. Pardon me for my language.' He addressed this last to the camera.

In the control truck, there was furious debate about whether they could continue to broadcast such an intensely unpredictable situation live. Murder and mayhem were one thing, bad language was quite another.

Eventually it was decided that they could not censor the news while it was happening, that they had a duty to broadcast. They would, however, try to bleep out the strongest bits of Wayne's language.

On the numerous screens in the truck and the many millions around the nation, Bruce was still trying to get to the core of Wayne's argument. 'So you shot the popcorn seller because he was an asshole? Not, and this is an important point, because you'd just seen a movie full of death and destruction?'

Wayne sounded almost weary. 'Bruce, like I say, you are taking all this far too literally. Does anybody shoot a popcorn seller in *Ordinary Americans*?'

'I don't believe so.'

'You don't believe damn right. Fifty-seven people get shot in *Ordinary Americans*, did you know that?'

'I knew it was a lot.'

'Wayne counted them,' Scout said proudly.

'Well, of course I counted them, honey pie, or how would I know? They don't put it up on the titles do they? Like, um, that damn film you liked, *Marrying and Dying* or something – there was some faggot in a kilt who should have died a whole lot earlier as far as I'm concerned, like before the damn film started.'

'*Four Weddings and a Funeral*.'

'That's right. Well, Bruce here did not call his movie *Fifty-Seven Murders, Plus People Taking Drugs and Screwing Each Other*, did he?'

'I guess not, honey.'

'Then don't talk dumb in front of the American people. I counted who got shot in your movie, Bruce. Cops got shot, drug dealers got shot, pregnant teenage girls got shot, an old lady got one straight through the colostomy bag – man, that was a great scene, Bruce. How do you think up that stuff?' Wayne turned to the camera to explain his enthusiasm. 'There's a shoot-out, right? And this sweet little old lady takes a stray and guess what, man? It goes through her colostomy bag, and do you know what she says? She says, "Shit." That's all, just "Shit." I mean, man, is that a good line or what? Everyone in the movie house just cracks up. Pardon my language but it was in the movie and Bruce here did get an Oscar for it, so I guess it's art.'

'I'm glad you liked it,' Bruce said woodenly.

'I sure did, but what I'm saying is, no popcorn seller got shot.'

Bruce was getting irritated. 'So what's your point? I thought you were claiming diminished responsibility on account of my influence over you. Isn't that what all this is about?'

'Who was the guy who rang the bell and the dogs dribbled? Pancake or whatever. I saw a thing about him on *Timewatch*.'

'I think you mean Pavlov,' said Bruce.

'That's right, Pavlov. Well, you ain't no Pavlov, Bruce, and we ain't no dribbling dogs. There ain't nothing specific here. I am talking generally. I'm saying that you make killing cool.'

Bruce leapt at the point. So far his heroic battle had not been going quite as splendidly as he'd hoped. He had allowed himself to be sidetracked. He had to regain the initiative.

'No, Wayne. I make going to the movies cool. Let me put it plainly. You are sick.' He addressed the camera directly. 'These two people are sick. They have erred from the acceptable norm. They have diseased and unbalanced minds. Did I unbalance them? Certainly not. Did society? I doubt it. No, they are simply sick. There have always been murderers and sadists. Long before there was TV and movies, people got killed and raped. Now—'

Bruce was on a roll, winding up to utterly discredit these sad nobodies with the massive force of his intellectual power. Unfortunately, Wayne interrupted him.

'Tell me something, Bruce. I've always wanted to know, do you get a hard-on when you make that stuff?' He said this with a wink at the camera. 'I'll bet you do, boy, 'cos I admit it just thrills me. What's more, I look round the movie theatre and I can see all the other guys and they're just loving it too. Every one of them is just itching to haul out a gun and blast away. Of course, they don't do it, but I can see them licking their lips and wishing, just the same.'

'That's the point, Wayne, nobody *does* anything.' Bruce was slightly shaken. He wanted to keep the debate on what Wayne did, not on what he himself did. 'It's just a story.'

'It ain't no story,' Scout protested. 'First time I saw *Ordinary Americans*, I said to Wayne to tell me when the blood and gore happened so I could close my eyes. I guess I had my eyes closed just about the whole picture.'

'That's right,' Wayne agreed. 'Ain't no room for a story in your pictures, Bruce. A story is like . . . um . . . so the dude kills the dude because of, like, this reason and that reason, and afterwards he goes away and does some other stuff. A story is, well a *story* – stuff happens. Showing the dude killing the dude, in slow mo', now, that's a fantasy.'

Bruce knew this was madness, nonsense. He made movies. These two killed people. There was no connection, and yet somehow he could not nail the debate down. It was slipping away.

'To sane people, it's a diversion,' Bruce said. 'It's an entertainment, perhaps not a very edifying one, but an entertainment none the less. It's only a fantasy to people who are sick in the head like you and your girlfriend here.'

'So we're sick, are we?'

Wayne shifted his gun on his lap but Bruce was determined to press the point. 'You're sicker than a rabid dog.'

From behind the couch in the back of Bill's picture Velvet cried out in anguish. 'Daddy, be careful. Don't make him angry.'

In the control truck they cheered. They loved it when the cute little girl chipped in. Now that was television.

'Sneak a close-up on the daughter,' the producer whispered into his microphone, but Bill ignored him. As far as Bill was concerned, Wayne was producing the show by the authority of the gun he had on his lap.

Bruce attempted to reassure his daughter. 'He isn't going to kill you, honey. We're on live TV. He's pleading for his life.'

'If I'm sick, Bruce, and you said I was,' Wayne said, 'what does that make you?'

'Excuse me?'

'Well, don't your movies exploit my sickness? Don't you use the terrible, sick, mental condition that afflicts psychopaths like me, just to give people a thrill? You never saw no Aids or cancer movie where the sick people were the bad guys, did you? But that's the way it is in your movies. You want to know what I am, Bruce? I am the exploitably ill.'

Things were beginning to go horribly wrong. The question seemed to be getting more complex. Bruce had set out to shoot down gloriously a fatuous contention, but his target was moving, putting up smokescreens.

'Perhaps you're suggesting that you committed your crimes as a protest against my treatment of psychotics as a class?'

It was a weak response. Bruce knew that this was not what Wayne had suggested at all. He was trying to buy time with smart comments, in order to collect his thoughts.

'I don't know what I'm suggesting,' Wayne replied, 'except I'm suggesting that it ain't only the criminals who create a culture of violence.'

'It's only the criminals who commit the crimes. Violent people create a violent society.' This was the point Bruce wanted to make. He needed to stick with that and not allow himself to be diverted. 'It is violent people who create a violent society,' he repeated, firmly and loudly.

'Are you sure?' Scout suddenly shouted. 'Are you absolutely sure about that? Are you one hundred per cent absolutely sure that no matter how many times you show a sexy murder to a rock and roll soundtrack you have no effect on the people who watch? Because if there's even one shred of doubt in your mind, then what right have you to make your movies?'

'I am an artist. I can not ask myself that question.' Bruce regretted it the moment he'd said it. It was true, but that wasn't the point. He knew that claims of intellectual immunity would be unlikely to impress in the heartlands.

'Why? Why can't you? If you won't take responsibility for your actions, why should we take responsibility for ours?'

Damnation, where did this bitch suddenly learn to talk?

'Because my actions are peaceable and within the law.'

It was weak. Bruce knew it, she knew it.

'A real man answers to his conscience, not to the law.'

'And I am perfectly happy to do that. Is your conscience clear?'

Wayne laughed. 'Of course, it's not clear, man. We kill people we've never met.'

'Yes, like every king and president there ever was,' Scout added.

Bruce felt his bowels almost move with tension. This woman was pulling out red herrings like a demented fishmonger. Christ, if they were going to spread the debate that wide, he was finished. To Bruce's intense relief, Wayne himself headed this one off. 'Now I've told you before I don't want to hear that kind of Communistic bull Scout. I do not respect much in this world but I do respect the American way. And in my opinion things'd be a whole lot better if the president was to shoot a few more people, 'specially them damn A-rab towel heads who keep burnin' Ol' Glory.'

'Excuse me,' Kirsten said nervously, looking up from her equipment. 'Um, this is all very interesting, of course, and the producers are delighted, they're *very* happy in control . . . it's just that the ratings are beginning to drop – see here, it's all displayed on my monitor. The chief wants to know if it would be OK to record this and then edit it for the evening news?'

'No need for that, Kirsten. I have an idea. Hey, America!' Wayne shouted at the camera. 'Listen, phone your friends, tell them all to tune in, because in ninety seconds I'm going to shoot Farrah Delamitri. In one minute and one half, the wife of the guy who just got the Oscar gets shot dead live!'

Chapter Thirty-Seven

Farrah screamed. Velvet screamed. Even Kirsten thought about protesting, but then she remembered the sacred duty of the news-gatherer: never intervene, not even if the news is being created for your benefit.

'Please, Wayne, don't,' Bruce said.

'She's my Mom!' Velvet sobbed.

Outside, in the command truck, Chief Cornell was in agony. Should he send his SWAT teams in now? If he did, there would certainly be bloodshed. If he didn't, likewise.

Oh, how he wished that somebody else would take responsibility.

Inside the mansion, Wayne had got up and was studying the ratings on Kirsten's computer screen.

'They're climbing, aren't they?'

'Yes they are,' Kirsten replied, 'but none the less my producer is saying please don't kill the woman.'

Farrah sobbed, pulling pathetically at her manacled hand.

In the control truck a lively debate was in progress.

'We have to terminate the broadcast,' some were saying. 'He's feeding off it. It's creating his crimes.'

'He killed plenty of people before there were any cameras to play to,' others contended. 'We can't turn off. We don't choose the news. We don't have a right to censor national events just because they're unattractive.'

'But if he's creating the news for *us*?

'We can't take responsibility for his actions.'

'Can we take responsibility for our own?'

The cameras stayed on, as no one had doubted for a moment that they would, and the ratings continued to climb.

Inside the lounge Wayne showed off his guns to the camera. 'Hurry up now, y'all,' he said. 'You don't want to miss it, do ya?'

When the ninety seconds ran out Wayne shot Farrah dead.

Chapter Thirty-Eight

'OK, hit it,' said Chief Cornell, and silently, through the doors, the windows and even the roof, the SWAT teams began to enter Bruce's house.

In the siege room the shot still resonated.

'You bastard! When will this end!' Bruce had rushed over and was holding Velvet, who sobbed hysterically, still handcuffed to the lampstand beside her dead mother.

'You saw the ratings, man. They went up. Blame the couch potatoes.'

'You hypocritical swine!' Bruce shouted '*You* killed her – no one else did! What is it you're saying? That the media, the public, is responsible for the fact that you're a murdering lunatic?'

'I'm just saying I wouldn'ta shot her if people hadn't switched to *The Simpsons*.'

'You are responsible!'

'Yes. I'm responsible for me, but you are responsible for you and they are responsible for them. I don't see anyone doing much about that. I've got an excuse, I'm a psycho. What's your get-out?'

Kirsten received a message from the producer. She turned to Bill. 'Get down! There's a SWAT team coming in!'

'No!' Wayne shouted into the camera.

Above them they could hear the sound of the roof being breached. Wayne grabbed Scout by the hand, and addressed the camera. 'Wait! Hold it. I'll give myself up, Scout too, I swear. Stop the attack. Keep the cameras rolling. We'll give up.'

Outside, Chief Cornell signalled that his forces should pause. Was it possible that they could get out of this nightmare without further bloodshed?

Wayne continued to shout at the camera. 'But we give ourselves up to the people. The people are responsible. They decide our fate, the fate of everybody in this room.' He had hold of the ratings computer now. 'It's up to you, the people out there . . . the lives of us all are in your hands. Here's how it is. When I've finished talking, if everybody watching switches off their TV, I swear me and Scout will walk out of here with our hands up . . . But if you keep on watching, I will kill every last mutha in this room, including myself and Scout. Not a bad show, huh? Exciting, right? And to see it, all you have to do is stay tuned for another few seconds. Well, you're responsible. Are you gonna turn off your TV?'

Chapter Thirty-Nine

INTERIOR. THE LOUNGE. DAY.

Wide shot. The room eerily still. Wayne stands with Scout before the television camera. In one hand he carries his weapon, in the other the ratings computer.
Close-up on Wayne from the TV camera's point of view. Grainy, video-style quality to the picture.

> WAYNE
> (Snarling into camera)
> I said, are you gonna turn off your TVs?

Whip pan down from Wayne's distorted face to the ratings computer. Picture turns to sudden hard focus. We see what is clearly some kind of graph climbing.
Wide shot of room. Wayne hurls the computer to the ground.

> WAYNE
> (Shouting)
> No you ain't!

Cut to : . .

INTERIOR. THE TV CONTROL TRUCK. DAY.

Chief Cornell and the others are watching Wayne on the screens. Fast, jagged, staccato zoom on to Wayne's image on one of the screens. Mid two shot of Cornell and the SWAT commander.

CHIEF CORNELL

Take him.

EXTERIOR. THE ROOF OF THE MANSION. DAY.

SWAT officers blast their way through.

Jump cut to ...

EXTERIOR. A WINDOW OF THE MANSION. DAY.

SWAT officers swing through windows on abseiling ropes, smashing glass.

Jump cut to ...

INTERIOR. OUTSIDE THE LOUNGE DOOR AT THE TOP OF THE STAIRWAY INSIDE THE MANSION. DAY.

SWAT officers smash door down.

Jump cut to ...

INTERIOR. THE LOUNGE. DAY

Extreme wide shot. Wayne and Scout at centre.
Mute sound. Slow motion.

SWAT officers burst through the windows and doors. Wayne and Scout open fire.

A little later the room was filled with strange green figures. Green jump suits, green rubber boots and gloves, green face masks. The green figures were tracing the outlines of the dead. One of them tried to draw a line around Wayne. The chalk made little impression on the sticky swamp of congealing blood in which his body lay. The green man tried using some white tape but nothing much sticks to blood soaked shag pile.

The whole room was alive with flashing light, the effect was almost stroboscopic. Hundreds and hundreds of photographs were being taken for further analysis. The contorted features of the corpses flickered in brief moments of glorious illumination. Their grotesquely twisted limbs seemed almost to twitch in the jaggedly pulsating light.

Hundreds of bullets and cartridge cases were being tweezered from the floor, more prized from the walls. Hairs were plucked from clothing, bloodied thumb prints carefully preserved. The green men and women missed nothing. A pair of pink Doc Martens, freckled with a few spots of blood, were photographed where they lay then placed in a plastic bag marked LAPD. Lab. Likewise a can of hair mousse, a pair of panty hose, a tiny glass, miraculously still upright and containing a splash of *crème de menthe*.

There was little point in this forensic zeal. Everyone knew who'd killed whom, who had died and who had survived. The whole thing had been captured on television and would shortly be available on video in all good stores.

There is however a process and the green figures had a job to do. A full inquiry into the events of that terrible Oscar night had already been promised. The authorities were anxious to show that, despite everything, they remained in control.

Outside Bruce's house the survivors were carried away in screaming ambulances. Other ambulances waited for the dead.

Epilogue

B ruce survived Wayne and Scout's bloody confrontation with the officers of the law but his career never recovered from the terrible events for which many felt he was partly responsible. He now makes tired, cynical movies in France. He has written a book about the night Wayne and Scout entered his life, called *Who Is Responsible?*. In it he divides the blame equally between Wayne and Scout, the media, the police and the millions of people who did not turn off their TVs.

Brooke died of her wounds. Her parents subsequently claimed that by pursuing a selfish debate, rather than making the simple statement Wayne had asked him to make, Bruce denied Brooke proper medical care for the vital period in which she could have been saved. They hold him responsible and are in the process of suing him.

Bill and Kirsten both died in the police assault. Their

families now claim that as they were both employees of the television companies there was a duty of care and that the companies are therefore responsible for their deaths. Both families are currently suing the networks. They are also suing the police, whom they hold responsible for not intervening earlier. In a separate claim they are again suing the police, whom they also hold responsible for intervening when they did.

Velvet was also killed in the crossfire. During a memorial service at her school, her principal reminded the congregation that society had a responsibility to protect young people like Velvet and had failed to do so. Her grandparents are investigating the possibility of suing the estates of Wayne and Scout. In the largest single claim in history, they are also suing the millions of people who did not turn off their TVs, who they feel are also responsible.

Many of the people who did not turn off their TVs have formed themselves into action groups, claiming that they have experienced anxiety, stress and mental torment as a result of the terrible moral dilemma that the TV companies allowed them to be put in. They hold the TV companies responsible and are pursuing claims for damages.

The TV companies are currently lobbying for more specific guidelines on how to act under similar circumstances. They claim that, in the final analysis, only government can be responsible for how public amenities operate. They have announced that they will attempt to offset losses resulting from claims made against them by taking action against Congress and Capitol Hill.

*   *   *

Police Chief Cornell and News and Current Affairs Chief Murray both lost their jobs as a result of the débâcle and hold each other responsible. Murray claims that Cornell should have taken charge of the situation and ended the siege sooner. Cornell claims that Murray should have denied the killers the oxygen of publicity which precipitated the final drama. In private lawsuits they are suing each other for loss of earnings.

Wayne Hudson's family are currently pursuing the Department of Welfare. They claim that it was early neglect of Wayne's problems by social workers that was responsible for turning him bad. They assert that it was clear that they were bringing Wayne up inadequately, and feel he should have been taken into care. They are suing.

Scout's family are also suing the Department of Welfare. They claim that constant intervention by social workers when Scout was younger left her insecure and easily influenced. They claim she should not have been taken into care and are suing.

On Capitol Hill, in the aftermath of the bloodbath, the Republicans claimed that the liberal values perpetrated by the Democrats were responsible.

The Democrats blamed Republican opposition to gun control.

Scout survived the gunfight and was eventually sent to a secure mental hospital, where she has discovered religion. She feels that the Almighty does all things for a purpose, and that in the long run God is responsible.

So far no one has claimed responsibility.